# Marcus could hear Rachel singing in the shower.

She sang in the shower every morning—and it was driving him crazy. Not that she didn't have a sweet voice. She did. The part that drove him crazy was the image he had of her, her long hair dripping on her shoulders, her pale body soaped and slippery....

He groaned and rolled onto his back just as the shower stopped running. Now she'd be climbing out, grabbing one of her mother's fluffy white towels to pat her body dry. Then she'd be putting on one of those silky robes she was so fond of. And it would cling just a little to her slightly damp skin. He knew exactly how it would cling. He'd run into her on Sunday morning—and he'd vowed he'd never put himself through that again.

In fact, he'd been so shaken by the sight of her— and so seduced by the smell of country ham frying and the breeze drifting in with the scent of the crystal lake across the street—that he'd borrowed a car and driven to the city, looking for action. He hadn't found any. Or maybe he just hadn't really wanted any. But this woman singing in the shower, this house, this town—this couldn't be what he really wanted, either—

Could it?

## ABOUT THE AUTHOR

One of the things Nikki Rivers loves about writing romance novels is creating irresistible men. "It comes naturally to me. After all, I'm married to one. How else could I explain putting up with him for thirty years!" Another thing Nikki enjoys is creating strong, determined women—women who win despite the odds. "I started writing fiction when my own life was going through some tough changes. Creating women who beat the odds helped me to beat the odds in my own personal struggle."

Nikki's 1997 Harlequin American Romance, *Romancing Annie*, won the Wisconsin Romance Writers of America Write Touch Readers' Award in short contemporary romantic fiction.

Nikki lives in Milwaukee with her fascinating, unpredictable husband.

## Books by Nikki Rivers

**HARLEQUIN AMERICAN ROMANCE**
550—SEDUCING SPENCER
592—DADDY'S LITTLE MATCHMAKER
664—ROMANCING ANNIE
723—HER PRINCE CHARMING

# For Better, For Bachelor

## NIKKI RIVERS

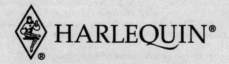

### HARLEQUIN®

TORONTO • NEW YORK • LONDON
AMSTERDAM • PARIS • SYDNEY • HAMBURG
STOCKHOLM • ATHENS • TOKYO • MILAN • MADRID
PRAGUE • WARSAW • BUDAPEST • AUCKLAND

To my good friend Rasma Pulvermacher
for helping to save my sanity by introducing me to
romance novels, and a very special thank you to
Kathy Zdanowski for sharing her experiences working on
a small-town newspaper.

ISBN 0-373-16764-4

FOR BETTER, FOR BACHELOR

Copyright © 1999 by Sharon Edwin

# Chapter One

"Please don't let it be daylight," Rachel Gale murmured under her breath. Something had dragged her from sleep—she wasn't sure what—all she knew was it hadn't been the alarm clock. Reluctantly she opened her eyes, saying a silent prayer that the world would still be dark and she could roll over and go back to sleep.

The room was in a hazy half darkness, the gray sky outside the open window not yet streaked with dawn. Rachel let out a sigh. She'd get a few more hours in, at least. And she needed it. The night before she'd practically put the paper to bed by herself while her boss Grant Phillips had been carousing thirty-five miles away in Milwaukee with an old newspaper buddy whose identity he'd been very mysterious about. It'd been late when she'd finally crawled between the sheets. Another two hours snuggled between them sounded like heaven.

Rachel stretched and rolled over—and ended up nose-to-nose with a man!

She froze, scarcely daring to breathe, moving nothing but her eyes as she took in the strange man sleeping perilously close to her.

She frowned and peered closer. Well, maybe he wasn't all that strange, after all. He looked remarkably like that newsman—the one on TV. What did they call him? Oh,

yes—the Helicopter Hunk; famous for dropping by helicopter into international hellholes to report for one of the
major networks.

She squinted, focusing more clearly in the darkened
room. My goodness, it *did* certainly look like him! The
thick, straight dark hair in need of a cut, the scruffy stubble
on his face shadowing his lean cheeks and square chin,
the high cheekbones and thick lashes. It was Marcus Slade,
all right.

But what was he doing in her bed?

"Well, nonsense," she murmured. "He *isn't* in your
bed, Rachel." She was dreaming, that was the only expla-
nation. Dreaming, or having some kind of vapors—the
kind spinsters always had in gothic novels. With the practicality that had gotten her through life thus far, Rachel
turned away from the apparition and closed her eyes.

In the morning the ghost of Marcus Slade would be gone
from her dreams—and her bed.

BIRDSONG FINALLY WOKE HER. But she wasn't ready to
open her eyes—not yet. She burrowed deeper into the mattress, breathing in the scent of budding spring wafting in
through the windows along with some other, spicier
scent—pleasant but new. She felt cozy, peaceful, surprisingly rested considering her late night. "Mmm," she
moaned, stretching and arching her back, running her hand
languidly over the smooth, warm bed. She felt, in fact,
delicious.

And then the bed sighed and moved!

Her eyes flew open and she found herself staring at a
smooth, tanned expanse of male chest. Was that *her* hand
practically cupping that muscled male breast, the fingers
so near the flat, dark nipple?

Slowly her gaze worked its way up that chest, over a
tawny, corded neck, until she found a face. And it was

staring down at her, a rakish grin on its lips, a shimmering light in its cool green eyes.

"Good morning," it said.

Rachel gasped and sat up, dragging the hair back from her face.

"My God," she gasped, "it really *is* you!"

"Who did you think it was?" he said in a much sexier voice than he used on the news.

"Well…well, I don't know. Last night, I thought I was dreaming.…"

"No dream, sweetheart. You've managed to sneak your way into the bed of Marcus Slade. Now," he said, his green gaze sliding over her face, down to her breasts, "as tempted as I am to find you almost naked in my arms, I'd like you to sneak out the same way you came in."

His gaze was still on her breasts and Rachel looked down. *Oh, my Lord!* Her arms flew around herself, trying to cover what the skimpy ivory lace teddy was revealing. She never, ever wore anything sexy to bed. But she did have a penchant for wearing beautiful lingerie under her plain, everyday clothes. Last night she'd been far too tired to even look for one of her voluminous cotton gowns and had crawled into bed in the lace teddy she'd been wearing under her skirt and blouse.

"A little late for modesty, don't you think?" Marcus Slade drawled.

Her gaze flew to his. "What?"

"You didn't seem to consider modesty when you managed to sneak into my room last night, take your clothes off and crawl into my bed."

For an instant Rachel's mouth dropped open. "What are you talking about? This is *my* room—*my* bed!"

He drew himself up on one elbow, the sheet that covered him slipping down to his waist, his rakish grin deepening, the glitter in his eyes going dangerous. "I have to hand it to you, sweetheart—that's not an approach I've heard before. *I* wandered into *your* bed, huh?''

Her gaze had gone to where the sheet had slid to just below his flat, firm waist. She couldn't seem to get her eyes off the edge of that sheet, until his fingers brushed her arm and she looked in time to see his finger hook around her teddy strap where it had fallen and drag it back to her shoulder. She shivered, watching his long, tanned fingers skim over her pale skin.

''Very nice,'' he drawled, his fingers running lightly over the edge of lace that barely covered her breasts, ''but you'll have to go peddle it elsewhere. I'm just not interested.''

She gasped again and grabbed a piece of the rosebud-sprigged sheet to cover herself. Too late she realized it was the same piece that covered him. Or *had* covered him.

Not only was there a man in Rachel Gale's bed—there was a naked man in it.

A spectacularly naked man.

Tanned.

Tanned in places she thought the sun could never reach.

Well, how could she help but stare?

''Are you finished?''

''Finished?'' she croaked, her eyes still fascinated by one particular spot just below—

''Finished *looking,* sweetheart. Because that's all you're going to get the chance to do—look.''

She tore her gaze away from his fabulous flesh and looked into that unshaven, rugged face again. ''What are you suggesting?'' she asked, drawing herself up, trying to sound as haughty as Miss Huffington at the Birch Beach Public Library did whenever anyone spoke above a whisper. Rachel had to acknowledge that it certainly lost some of its effectiveness when the speaker was wearing a selection from the Victoria's Secret catalogue.

Marcus Slade's laugh was even more unsettling than the

body he didn't even bother to try to cover. "You're good, I'll give you that."

"Good?" she asked in confusion. At what? At the moment about all she felt good at was gasping and staring. And holding the sheet even closer against her as that green gaze raked over her again.

"I'm tempted, sweetheart, but this is an old, old game and I prefer to find my own bed partners. So if you don't mind…"

*"Bed partners!"* Rachel sputtered. "You think that I—?"

"I *know* that *you*," he answered, in that same deep voice that she'd heard a thousand times on the ten-o'clock news. "Why else would you be here?"

"Well of all the conceited, of all the *absolutely* conceited…"

Suddenly his eyes went hard, his mouth thinned. "Save it, will you, sweetheart. Just get your luscious pale body out of my bed—and out of my room."

Mouth open, she stared at him.

He gave an impatient movement of his head. "Look, I'm in no mood for this. I had a late night last night and I prefer to be alone."

"Well, so would *I*. So I suggest that you take your…your—" What could she say? Take your virile, tanned, fabulous body out of my bed?

"Okay, I've had just about enough of this."

She gasped again as he jumped out of bed. But she had only a moment to appreciate what the morning sun streaming in through her bedroom window was doing to his impressive flesh. For he came around to her side of the bed, ripped the covers from her hands, swept her up into his arms and strode to the door.

"Put me down, you…you—"

"Oh, I fully intend to put you down."

With that, he opened the door, set her none too gently on her feet in the hallway and slammed the door in her face.

MARCUS LEANED against the door and laughed softly, shaking his head. Maybe he'd been too rough on her. But, damn it, he was sick to death of women finding their way into his hotel rooms. He was forever finding lustful females hiding in closets, under beds or lurking on balconies. One enterprising lady had even scaled a very narrow window ledge from the hotel room next to his—in the middle of a driving rainstorm, no less! He was a newsman, for heaven's sakes. A respected television journalist. Not some sex symbol. Not that he didn't like women—lots of women. He just preferred not to find them like a morsel of wedding cake left under his pillow when he woke up in the morning.

Even if this particular morsel had been especially engaging. She'd actually managed to pull off the shy act quite effectively. Marcus had almost believed her wounded and flustered look, when he'd reached out and touched her. Then she'd managed to drag the sheet off his body to get a better look at him, and he knew she was just like all the rest. After one thing. A piece of Marcus Slade.

"MOTHER! Where are you?"

Rachel ran from the empty kitchen back up the stairs. But when she threw open her mother's bedroom door, the room was empty. She tried the bathroom next, pounding and calling until she recognized the voice singing in the shower as Timmy's, the seven-year-old foster child who lived with them. She threw open the door to the first guest bedroom. Empty. But when she turned to the second one, she found her mother standing in the doorway.

"What are you shouting the house down for? I'm right here."

"Mother," Rachel began, "there's a man in my bed.

And he wouldn't believe me when I said it was *my* bed. And he just picked me up and threw me out, slamming the door in my face!''

Her mother grinned. ''Oh, so that's where he went. Must have taken a right instead of a left.'' She glanced back into the guest room behind her. ''I wondered why his bed hadn't been slept in.''

''It hasn't been slept in because he's been in *mine* all night!''

Her mother's eyes twinkled. ''Hmm, if that's the case, then I wonder why you aren't in a better mood this morning.''

''Mother!''

Frances Gale chuckled. ''Oh for heaven's sakes, Rachel. If I'd known you were going to act like a Victorian old maid, I never would have named you after my great-great-aunt Rachel Biggers.''

''I am *not* acting like an old maid! How would you feel waking up with Marcus Slade in your bed—naked!''

Frances chuckled again. ''Oh, I imagine I'd be feeling a damn sight better than you obviously are.''

''Very funny!'' Rachel said, tossing her hair over her shoulder. ''The man accused me of sneaking into his room last night to have my way with him and then refused to believe me when I told him it's *my* room. And then he threw me out bodily—and you think I should be grinning from ear to ear!''

Laughing, Frances shook her head and went back into the guest room to open the window. ''So what you're really mad about is the fact that he kicked you *out* of bed?''

''Mother—honestly!'' Rachel huffed. ''What's he doing here, anyway?''

''Well, this *is* a guest house, honey.''

''I mean, what is a man like Marcus Slade doing in Birch Beach?''

''Oh, he's a friend of Grant's.''

Rachel looked at her closed bedroom door across the hall. "You're kidding? *That's* who he was out carousing with last night?"

"Yup. Got in pretty late, too, I expect. And he must have been in some condition—"

Rachel frowned. "You mean to not notice that he'd turned right instead of left?"

"No, to not notice that you were in bed beside him all night in that skimpy little getup."

Rachel, who'd forgotten that she was standing there practically naked, looked down at herself. "Oh—"

"Yes, oh. And I think the shower just stopped. Timmy will be out of the bathroom any minute. Better scoot into my room and borrow a robe."

"Right," Rachel said, turning toward her mother's room. "But what are we going to do about Marcus Slade?" she threw over her shoulder.

Frances chuckled again. "We're going to fix him breakfast."

By the time Rachel finished in the shower, the door to her bedroom was open, her bed blissfully empty. Cautiously she went into her room. No stray hunks seemed to be lurking about. With a sigh of relief, she sank down onto the bed, only to jump to her feet again. Unconsciously she'd sat in exactly the same place Marcus Slade had spent the night. She touched the indentation of the rose-patterned sheets his naked body had made. It was still warm from his skin.

Her hands flew to her cheeks. They were hot. She put a hand to her chest. Her heart pounded unsteadily. "Goodness, Rachel," she murmured to herself, "you'd think you'd never seen a naked man before."

Well, she had—but a very precious few times.

And she had never before seen the naked body of a man that thousands of women fantasized about every night.

She turned briskly away from the bed, firmly shut her

bedroom door and went to her closet to find something to wear.

One thing she knew, she told herself as she rummaged through her clothes, she was glad that she wasn't the type to fantasize about him. Okay, so maybe she'd watched the ten o'clock news a couple of times and wondered how that chiseled mouth would feel. Or how that ragged black hair might—well, never mind that. The point was, she was never going to wonder again. The man was much too conceited and sure of himself. To think that she was just another Slade groupie come to try to have her way with him! The idea!

Oh, true, he was definitely the stuff from which fantasies were made. They hadn't labeled him the Helicopter Hunk for nothing. But she wanted nothing from a man who thought that every female with a beating heart was out to get him.

She paused, a white blouse dangling from her hands. Well, he wanted nothing from her, either, she supposed. After all, he had kicked her out of her own bedroom!

"Oh, so what, Rachel," she muttered, stripping a pink skirt from its hanger. "You've been kicked out of men's beds before." Well, kicked out of a man's life, to put it more accurately. She'd never actually been in Eric Ludington's bed. For which, the way things had turned out, she was definitely not sorry.

"Rachel!" her mother called from below. "Breakfast is almost ready!"

"Coming!" she called back as she threw her mother's old robe on the bed and started to dress, purposefully brushing Eric Ludington from mind. "One spoiled, outrageous man at a time," she muttered. The thought of Marcus Slade served for breakfast with the biscuits wasn't exactly giving her an appetite.

"SO YOU'RE THAT GUY from TV, huh?"

"Yup, that's me," Marcus said to the boy on the other

end of the table.

"Yeah, I seen you on the news," the kid said.

"You *saw* him on the news," Frances corrected.

Timmy wiggled his nose. "Yup, that's what I said, Aunt Frannie."

Frances Gale's eyes danced, and Marcus thought back to how Grant had spoken about the woman who ran the only guest house in town. Grant was smitten and Marcus could see why. She was short, bouncy, with an easy, ready laugh, dark curly hair and a smile that didn't quit.

A buzzer sounded from the kitchen. "That'll be the biscuits. Be right back."

"So you ride in helicopters, huh?" Timmy asked.

"Sometimes," Marcus answered. "When that's the only way to get where I need to go."

"I'd like to ride in a helicopter someday," Timmy said, nodding his head with certainty.

"You'd like it," Marcus answered. The kid was unbelievable. Carrot red hair, freckles to match, wide innocent blue eyes. He looked like something out of a Norman Rockwell painting. And so did this house. The dining room was big, comfortable, the table long enough to seat a number of guests, lace curtains blowing in the breeze from windows open and overlooking the tree-lined, quiet street. No bombs would be exploding out there. Well, none but the one that had exploded in Rachel Gale's bedroom that morning.

When Marcus turned his gaze from the open windows, she was just walking into the dining room. He almost looked away again, thinking that this was an inhabitant of the house he'd yet to meet. But his gaze returned to her and lingered. Her hair was no longer lying in disarray about pale, smooth shoulders, but there was no mistaking the color. Brown streaked with a lighter color that put him in mind of champagne. She had it pulled tightly back from her face in a thick braid that fell over her shoulder. He would have liked to see it down again, but the braid brought out the champagne streaks even more than letting it loose had. Yup, he thought, it was Rachel, all right. But surely not the same Rachel he'd found lying in his arms when he'd opened his eyes that morning?

When she caught him watching her, she paused in the doorway, then lowered her eyes and quietly came into the room, taking the seat across from him.

Marcus stifled a grin as he watched her. This was the same woman who had tempted him in ivory silk that morning? When he'd opened his eyes to find her cuddled up to him, ivory lace barely covering the breast brushing his chest, he'd almost broken his rule about making love with groupies. When she'd stirred enough for him to see her mouth—wide, pale, and soft looking—he'd come closer to breaking that rule than ever before. But when she'd opened her eyes, all innocent and drowsy looking with what he'd assumed was feigned sleep, his mind had gone hard enough to rival the hard swell of his body. He'd thought she was about as innocent as he was. Which wasn't anywhere near innocent at all.

But he'd been wrong. Because as soon as he'd come downstairs, Frances had told him, amid much laughter, that he had, indeed, been in the wrong bedroom. He supposed he owed Rachel an apology.

"About time you got down, Rachel," Frances said as she breezed in from the kitchen with a platter of steaming scrambled eggs and bacon and a basket of hot biscuits.

Marcus smiled at Rachel and said, "Rachel apparently had a busy night last night."

"That why you're late for breakfast, Rachel?" asked Timmy as he reached for a piece of bacon.

Rachel glared across the table at him, and Marcus tried not to laugh.

"I am late, Timmy," she said pointedly, her gaze still

on him, "because Grant was out with one of his old drinking buddies last night and I had to put the paper to bed all by myself."

"Must be why you decided not to put yourself to bed all by yourself, hmm, Rachel?" Marcus asked. God he was awful…he should be apologizing, but he couldn't resist teasing her. Light, fresh pink rose into her cheeks, but the sparkle in her eyes was anger, not embarrassment.

"I did put myself to bed by myself—I just didn't wake up that way," she told him huffily.

Timmy munched bacon, looking back and forth between them. "Aunt Frannie? What are they talkin' about?"

"Nothing you need to know about," Frances answered. "Now you eat some eggs then get out of here. You'll be late for school."

Timmy wolfed down two huge forkfuls when footsteps sounded loudly on the front porch. "Hey, Timmy!" someone called.

"Oops, gotta go, Aunt Frannie."

"Well, guess you better before that Stewie does damage to my front porch."

Timmy laughed, grabbed another strip of bacon and took off on a run.

"And don't slam the door!" Frances yelled, then laughed when the door banged shut. "That boy," she muttered, shaking her head. "And that friend of his, Stewie, has the biggest feet I've ever seen on a seven-year-old."

"Your nephew lives with you?" Marcus asked.

"Oh, he's not really my nephew. Timmy's my foster child. He's from Milwaukee."

"My mother is fond of taking in strays, Mr. Slade," Rachel said pointedly.

Marcus raised a brow. "Is she? Well, I guess that's lucky for me, because I'm going to be staying awhile."

Rachel almost choked on her orange juice. "What?" she sputtered.

"I've decided to stick around awhile. Haven't seen Grant in much too long. I've got some time off between assignments. What better place to spend it?"

Marcus couldn't believe what he'd just said. *What better place to spend it?* Any place would be a better place than Birch Beach! Having grown up in one, Marcus was allergic to small towns. When he wasn't slogging through mud, riding in a rickety jeep across a desert, dodging bullets and scud missiles, or jumping from a low-flying helicopter, he preferred the bright lights of a big city—and the easy, sophisticated women he found in them.

When Grant had asked him to come for a visit, he'd planned on one night only. One night of drinking and shooting the bull in a dark, whisky-smelling tavern. And then he'd be off to Chicago where he had a mind to look up a certain redhead he'd spent some time with at a snowed-in airport. Lord, what that woman could do in the stall of a washroom—

So why on earth had he just said he was going to stick around awhile?

He looked across the table. To bait Rachel, why else? With her high-necked white cotton shirt, a thin pink ribbon tied under the rounded collar, and her modest pink skirt, she looked like a little school marm sitting at a boarding-house table. His gaze scanned the shirt, wondering what she was wearing underneath it. Spinsterish Rachel obviously had a taste for fine, silky things next to her skin.

"Well, we aren't scheduled for any visitors until Memorial Day so the room's yours as long as you want it," Frances said.

Again he couldn't resist. "Maybe we better ask Rachel first. She may not be in the mood to share."

Rachel's eyes flew to his, her face grew pinker—with obvious anger this time. "This is my mother's house, Mr. Slade, so I can't keep you from staying. But in the future, you'll stay across the hall where you belong!"

There was an angry scrape as she pushed back her chair.

"Oh, Rachel—for heaven's sake," Frances began.

"I'm going to work," she said, throwing down her napkin and flouncing out of the room.

Frances chuckled and shook her head. "You're a bad boy, Marcus, you know that?"

Marcus grinned. "Can't seem to help myself. Your daughter apparently brings out the worst in me."

"She's a little uptight," Frances said as she stood to start clearing the table.

Rachel obviously didn't take after her mother. Frances Gale wore short white shorts over a curvy little figure, a bright red shirt tucked into them and sexy little sandals on her feet, toes painted to match the shirt.

"Doesn't follow in her mother's footsteps, huh?"

Frances gave him a smile. "Don't go getting ideas, young man."

"Ahh, but, Frances if I were just five years younger—"

Frances hooted. "You mean if *I* were *ten* years younger!"

Laughing, he stood, picked up a platter, and followed Frances into the kitchen.

"Oh, no, you don't," Frances said, taking the platter from him. "You're getting a bill, Marcus. Don't think you're going to work any part of it off by doing dishes. Go on, it's a beautiful day—get out and enjoy it."

"And how would you suggest I spend this beautiful day in Birch Beach?"

"Well," suggested Frances with a twinkle in her eye, "you could start by walking my daughter to work."

THE IDEA WAS CRAZY, the last thing he wanted to do, but somehow he found himself wandering out to the wide front porch, his hands in the pockets of his shabby jeans, and just casually gazing around. White clapboard houses lined one side of the street, shaded by huge oaks. Across the street a park sloped down to Birch Lake where a small band shell stood next to the water, rows of benches facing the stage. Marcus didn't have any trouble visualizing a band playing there on a summer's evening, ladies in filmy dresses and hats, men in suspenders milling about, chatting with neighbors and sipping lemonade.

He shook his head as if to clear the image, as if to bring himself back to the present. Maybe finding Rachel and walking her to work wasn't such a bad idea, after all. If he stood gazing out at the bucolic scene before him much longer, he was afraid he might enter another dimension and wake up days later with a straw boater on his head and some white bucks on his feet.

He leaned farther out and scanned the street again. She hadn't gotten far. There she was, the sun causing the champagne of her hair to sparkle while she talked to a little old lady in an enormous gardening hat just two doors down.

He sauntered down the steps and started that way.

"Miss Finch, I've never seen your lilacs look prettier," he heard Rachel say as he got nearer.

"My, yes. You must take some, Rachel, dear, to put on your desk at the paper." The tiny old woman held a stem of purple flowers to her nose. "Mmmm," she sighed, breathing in, "the scent is heavenly."

"Yes, Rachel, you *must* take some," Marcus said. "I'll help you carry them."

Rachel swung around and almost bumped into him. "Wha-what are you doing here?"

"Your mother suggested I walk you to work."

"Oh, she did, did she?" Rachel answered, thinking all the while of ways she could possibly kill her mother— slowly, painfully.

"Why, Rachel," Molly Finch said, "who's your young man?"

Rachel gritted her teeth and threw Marcus a look, daring

him to say anything. "He's not my young man, Miss Finch."

Marcus shouldered her aside. "I'm Marcus Slade, Miss Finch. I'll be staying at the Gales' for a while."

"Oh—" Miss Finch looked a little flustered. "Oh, my yes. How do you do?"

She held out a withered hand to Marcus, and he took it in his, raised it to his mouth and brushed it with his lips.

"Oh, brother," muttered Rachel.

"Oh, my," breathed Miss Finch. "My, my," she said again, patting the spit curls of gray hair peeking from under her gardening hat.

"So pleased to meet you, Miss Finch. Perhaps if you'd just lend me your garden shears there, I could cut Rachel some lilacs."

"Oh—" Miss Finch fluttered and held up her gardening shears, looking at them like they were an object from outer space, not the very shears she pruned and trimmed and cut with every day as soon as the ground thawed in the spring.

Marcus took them from her hand and whistled his way over to the lilac bush.

"My dear," Miss Finch confided, "such a handsome fellow. And so rakish with that five o'clock shadow." Miss Finch turned to watch him for a moment. "You know," she said, tapping her thin, dry lips, "he looks very familiar."

"He should. He's been on television almost every night since the Gulf War."

"Really?" Miss Finch breathed, then turned to stare at him again.

Rachel couldn't help but stare, either. Marcus Slade was reaching up to the highest branch, his white T-shirt taut against the outline of the muscles in his back, his biceps bulging from under the short, misshapen sleeves. Rachel tried to keep her mind—and gaze—above the waist, but she couldn't make either of them behave. His jeans weren't all that tight, but they were so worn that the faded and frayed denim clung to his rear and thighs, fitting him like they'd been shaped to his body by years of wear.

And they probably had been. Even on camera, Marcus Slade wore jeans, torn T-shirts, worn army field jackets— forever needing a shave, forever needing a haircut.

"Well," said Miss Finch, "he's certainly handsome enough to be an actor."

"He's not an actor," Rachel began.

Just then Marcus Slade turned, his arms full of lilacs, and Miss Finch gave a little ladylike squeal.

"It's the Helicopter Hunk!"

"At your service, ma'am," Marcus said with a little bow and a brandishing of the shears.

"Oh, my! What brings you to Birch Beach, Mr. Hunk…uh, I mean, Mr. Slade?"

"An old friend, Miss Finch. Grant Phillips at the *Birch Bark* was city editor at the paper where I got my first job after college."

"Was he? Why Grant is the sweetest…"

Rachel had heard enough. Besides it was time she got to work. Sweet Grant Phillips no doubt had a hangover and was going to be as useless today as he had been last night.

Miss Finch looked occupied, if not enthralled, so Rachel slipped out the garden gate and started down the sidewalk, walking as fast as she could.

Not fast enough, apparently. Seconds later she heard running footsteps behind her and Miss Finch calling, "But I want an autograph—"

"Looks like you've got a fan, Mr. Slade."

"Call me Marcus, sweetheart. After all, we *have* slept together."

She gave him a sideways look. "You're insufferable, you know that?"

"I've always preferred the word *incorrigible*."

"No doubt. And don't you ever shave?"

"Is that an invitation to join you in the bathroom as you shower? I'm surprised at you, Rachel."

"Oh, shut up and get lost, will you?"

"Can't. I promised Miss Finch that I'd carry these lilacs to your office myself. And you know how small towns are. If I don't she'll surely find out before lunchtime. In fact, I'm sure she's on the phone right now, spreading the word that I'm staying at the Gale Guest House."

She gave him a sideways glance. "You sound like you don't really care for small towns, Mr. Slade."

"I don't. People knowing your business, putting labels on you that stick for the rest of your life like a tenacious leech."

His voice had lost its mocking tone. He sounded surly with just a hint of disgust. "Sometimes, Mr. Slade, having people know your business can be a comfort."

He snorted. "Yeah, right."

She opened her mouth to tell him about the time five years ago when many in the town had rallied round her. But that would entail telling Marcus Slade that he wasn't the first man to kick her out of his bed. And that, she had absolutely no intention of doing.

She kept quiet as they walked along Elm then turned onto Main. In front of Cheevers' Market, Mr. Cheevers was sweeping the sidewalk as he always did just before the store opened. He tipped his cap and said good day as they passed.

"Wonderful day, Mr. Cheevers," she agreed.

Farther along the street, the Buzzing Bee Diner was already open for business, the usual regulars sitting at the counter, hunched over their coffee cups, Olive giving anyone who ordered an omelette a hard time. There was a short line of baby strollers lined up outside, and Rachel knew that this was the morning that some of the young mothers in town got together for breakfast at the Bee and then walked on to the park to sit on a bench and talk about how Billy was teething, how Susie was allergic to milk. Routine. And Rachel relished it. She found these people, these places, comforting. Things didn't change in Birch Beach—not much, anyway. It was the one thing you could count on.

But, of course, the man at her side wouldn't understand that. He obviously thrived on change. Never stayed in one place long. Probably never stayed with one woman long.

Rachel only hoped he wouldn't be staying in Birch Beach long, either.

## Chapter Two

The newspaper office was only six blocks from where Rachel lived. It seemed farther that morning. And was it her imagination, or were there more people on their front stoops and porches? She felt like she was in a parade, everybody waving brightly at her as she passed.

Lord, maybe Miss Finch really had gone right to the phone.

"Hmm," Marcus Slade said, when Mitzi Taylor came running out of the Drug and Beauty Emporium across the street to shout hello to Rachel.

"Hmm, what?" Rachel asked, knowing she'd be better off if she hadn't.

"Whole town seems to have turned out."

There was no mistaking the cynicism in his voice. Rachel decided to ignore it. "A town like this wakes up early. Especially in the spring."

"Right."

She stopped walking. "*Right?* What's that supposed to mean?"

Two steps later he stopped and turned toward her, his green eyes dancing. "I believe it's the opposite of wrong."

"But said with your particular tone of voice, right means wrong—and you know it!"

His sculpted lips frowned, but those green eyes still

laughed. "I think this morning's little escapade has unhinged you a little." His gaze left her and became suddenly, deeply interested in the leaves of a tree overhead. "I've heard excitement sometimes takes a spinster that way."

"Spinster? I'll have you know that in today's market, thirty-five is not considered a spinster!"

"Really?" He turned his attention back to her, scrutinizing her face the same way he'd scrutinized the maple leaves. "According to Miss Finch you are. Let's see—how did she put it? 'Rachel Gale is such a sweet thing. Pity she's remained a spinster.'"

"I don't believe you."

Marcus put his hand over his heart. "A direct quote, sweetheart. I swear."

She *hmphed* and walked on, hoping to leave him contemplating the leaves again. Hell, he could contemplate the garbage in the gutter for all she cared. Except, Birch Beach never had any garbage in its gutters.

"I told you, didn't I? Small towns are poison. People in each other's business—making judgments—old maids gossiping across garden gates."

"Then I suggest you get out while you can, Mr. Slade, before someone starts gossiping about *you* across a garden gate. Apparently you find war a lot easier to deal with than people. I suggest you go find one so you'll feel safer."

The statement stopped him in his tracks. She'd hit it on the head, all right. He was more comfortable dodging bullets than dodging the slings and arrows of people's sharp judgments. As a foreign correspondent, he often worked alone, only himself to rely on. And he liked it that way. The big shots at the network were thousands of miles away. If they got on his back too much, he just made himself scarce—blamed it on bad communications or a roadblock. He'd done it his way—all the way.

Rachel was right about something else, he thought as he

watched her walking ahead of him, the sun dappling her hair, the breeze swishing her pale pink dirndl skirt against her legs. He should get out while he could. Now.

He slouched down onto one of the garden benches lining Main Street and wondered why he didn't.

"Morning, Boss," Rachel called as she entered the newspaper office, shutting the door behind her.

Grant Phillips groaned. "Do you have to bang the door like that?"

Rachel smiled. Grant was leaning back as far as his old-fashioned desk chair would allow, his thick wavy, gray hair falling away from his face, his eyes closed, an ice bag on his head.

"Rough night, Boss?" she asked innocently.

"Can't keep up with that boy anymore," he mumbled. "Should have known better."

"That's no boy," Rachel said.

Grant chuckled and lowered the ice bag. "I take it you've met, then."

Oh, brother, had they, thought Rachel. But she wasn't about to let Grant in on the circumstances of their first, auspicious meeting. Instead she asked, "Why didn't you tell me it was Marcus Slade you were going out with last night?"

"The guy asked me not to mention that he was in town." Grant's bloodshot eyes suddenly cleared enough to twinkle and dance at Rachel. "Seems he sometimes has trouble keeping the females in his vicinity at bay." He shook his head. "You should hear the stories. Why, once…"

"Spare me," Rachel cut in. "I've already been treated to a dose of Marcus Slade's insufferable ego."

"Oh-oh." Grant looked at her, his bushy gray brows lowered over his slate-colored eyes. "You two didn't hit it off?"

Rachel gave him a rueful look before picking up a copy of the *New York Times* from Grant's desk and scanning the headlines. "What do you think?"

Grant shrugged and swung his feet off his scarred oak desk. "Guess I should have known. You two are too much alike."

Her head shot up. "Are you kidding? We're nothing alike!"

"Oh, yes you are," her boss said mildly. "Both headstrong, stubborn, passionate. And both good journalists."

"Utter nonsense," she muttered, throwing the paper back on his desk and heading over to her own desk, not ten feet away. Grant liked the informality of being out in the main office where the action was. The smaller of the two inner offices was allocated to the advertising department, which consisted of Daisy Mae Watkins who was assisted part-time by her mother, Lucille. The larger inner office held the layout department, manned by Daisy's husband, Luke, and a part-timer who was a journalism student at the high school. The office was a family, as comfortable to Rachel as the rest of the town.

At her desk, she leafed through a small stack of messages, pausing at one that caught her eye. "What's this about Miss Huffington being upset about something?" she asked her boss.

"Oh...yeah. Telephoned as soon as I walked in the door." He pressed his fist to his head. "The sound almost killed me. And then to pick up the phone and find Ariel Huffington's voice in my ear." Grant gave a dramatic shiver. "Gave me the willies."

Rachel laughed. "But what did she want?"

"Some gibberish about the five-and-dime. Couldn't make it out. The woman was incoherent."

"She was incoherent or you were muddled?" Rachel asked dryly.

He gave her a look. "Hard-nosed journalists don't get

muddled. Now, why don't you get down to the library and see what she wants?''

"As soon as I call the capital about—'' Rachel stopped midsentence. A shadow had passed over the glass half of the front door. She turned around. Marcus Slade. About to enter. The library and Miss Huffington suddenly looked a lot more pleasant than they had a moment ago.

"Yeah, you're right,'' she said. "I'll get right on it.''

She grabbed a legal pad, stuck a few pencils in her skirt pocket, and went out the door as Marcus Slade came in it.

"Something I said?'' he called after her.

Grant chuckled. "See you've riled my best reporter already—and you haven't even been here twenty-four hours.''

Marcus grinned and shut the door. "Your best reporter? Isn't she your only reporter?'' he asked in amusement.

"True, but that doesn't change the fact that the lady is good. She gets wind of something, she sticks with it. Exposed a scandal at the county dump last year. The services picked up part of her story.''

"Scandal, huh?'' Marcus asked as he strolled around the office, the floorboards creaking with every step. "Someone dump an old sofa in the wrong pile of burning trash?''

"Arrogant as ever, I see,'' mumbled Grant.

Marcus stopped at the bulletin board across from Rachel's desk. "It's what got me where I am today,'' he said as he scanned a line of clippings thumbtacked to the cork board.

"And where is that, Marcus?''

Marcus had been squinting at a story that involved a complaint about someone's tree branches getting in the way of someone else's clothesline when Grant asked his question. He turned around to face his old mentor.

"What kind of question is that, old man? I'm on the top of the world, that's where I am.''

"Really?" Grant stood and went to a coffeemaker on a table in the corner of the room. He picked up the pot, and the smell of coffee grew stronger as he filled two mugs. "Then what are you doing here?" he asked.

"What do you mean? I'm here because you asked me here."

Grant held a steaming mug out to him. "I've asked you here before. You never showed."

After a moment's hesitation, Marcus took the coffee and tried to take a swallow, but it was too hot. That left him with trying to answer Grant's question.

He lifted a shoulder. "Maybe I needed a change. Maybe I needed to see you. Hell, maybe I just needed a vacation," he finished impatiently.

Grant chuckled again as he plopped himself back into his desk chair. "And Birch Beach is the vacation capital of the world."

"Okay, old man," Marcus said, sitting on the edge of Grant's desk. "You answer me a question. Why did you ask me here?"

Grant took his time sipping his coffee, then setting the mug carefully down. "Maybe I just wanted to see you."

"Uh-huh," Marcus answered.

"Maybe I'm feeling like the old man you call me and I just needed to see someone from my younger, sweeter past."

Marcus stared at him for a moment before saying, "That doesn't sound like you, Grant. What's going on?"

Marcus didn't care at all for the look in the older man's eyes. It held a little bit too much fear. Not the kind of fear Marcus was used to seeing on the faces of people in a war-torn country. But the kind that spoke of changes, things left behind, things uncertain ahead.

"See, hotshot," Grant finally said, "it's like this..."

Before he could go on, the door burst open and Rachel

came marching in, her longish pink skirt swirling out from her legs, her long braid hanging over one shoulder.

"We've got a story on our hands, Boss. Might be a big one."

Grant grunted. "Get a good tip from old lady Huffington?"

"The five-and-dime is closing its doors. Miss Huffington got it from Mabel Harper—and you know Mabel. She might be the biggest gossip in town, but she's almost never wrong."

"Five-and-dime, huh? What next? Better get down there and see what's what."

"I intend to. Just came back for my tape recorder."

Marcus laughed.

"What's so funny?"

"*This* is the big story? A dime store closing? What do you need the recorder for...quotes?"

She gave him a look, then pulled open a desk drawer. "Exactly. And it *is* big stuff. We lost our JCPenney last year, and the year before that..."

Marcus couldn't stop laughing. She was taking it all so seriously. If it had been anyone but Rachel, he would have thought it was a joke. But he didn't think the lady had that kind of sense of humor.

"Look, Mr. Slade, there may not be any body bags or bombed-out buildings to report on, but this will change the lives of a lot of people in this town. It may not be your cup of tea, but it *is* news."

She was an astonishing woman, this Rachel Gale. She stood there in her demure schoolgirl blouse, her full skirt falling nearly to her ankles, her hair severely pulled back from her face. But there was fire in her eyes, passion blushing color into her pale mouth and turning her cheeks the color of her skirt. She looked almost as beautiful as she had that morning, the ivory lace sliding off her shoulder.

And just as angry.

He was aware of Grant looking from one to the other of them. "Why don't you go with her, hotshot?" Grant suggested. "Maybe you'll learn something."

"No way!" Rachel blurted out. "Absolutely not!"

If she hadn't said it, if she hadn't been so damn adamant about it, the last thing he would have wanted to do with his day was tag along to cover the demise of some dusty old five-and-dime that probably should have closed years ago. But baiting Rachel Gale seemed to be the best entertainment in town.

He grinned. "You know, old man, I think you've got a point. I think I will tag along."

"That's what you think," Rachel mumbled, pulling her tape recorder out of the drawer and checking the batteries.

"That's what I know," he said.

Her gaze shot up to him. "If you think…"

"Yes, I *do* think," he answered, before she could even finish.

"Over my dead body," she ground out through a clenched jaw.

Marcus couldn't help it, there was a bad boy lurking just beneath the surface, and Rachel Gale knew exactly how to make him come out and play. He let his eyes travel over her body, from the tiny pink bow at her throat, down past the rise and fall of her breasts, and on to her ankles, then back up again.

"I think I might find better uses for your body, sweetheart," he drawled. "In fact, if you pull a stunt tonight like you did last night," he added, taking a couple of steps closer to her so she had to draw back her head to look up at him, "it might have a different ending altogether," he finished as he lifted a hand and tucked a wisp of hair behind her ear.

He'd started out just to tease her, to push her—she was such an easy mark. But the look she was giving him, the wide innocence of those eyes, the slightly parted flushed lips, the rapid movement of her breasts against the fresh, white cotton—he looked at it all and knew that she wasn't the only one being teased. He was teasing the hell out of himself, too. And his body was liking it just fine.

She opened her mouth wider, he took a step closer, she put up a hand—and shoved him with all her might so that he almost landed on his backside across the room.

"I didn't pull any stunt last night, and you know it! You're the one who was in the wrong room—not me. And if you think I have any desire to repeat any part of that distasteful episode—"

A shrill whistle interrupted Rachel's tirade, and both Marcus and she turned to look at Grant.

"If you two don't mind, I'm running a newspaper here. You've got a story to cover, Gale—and Slade here is going with you."

"But, Boss…"

"That's right. I'm still your *boss*, you know. And *I'm* giving the orders—something I don't do often enough apparently. Now, go—get the scoop on the five-and-dime. And take Slade here with you."

Rachel glared at both of them, then headed for the door. Grinning, Marcus gave Grant a mock salute, then followed that floating pink skirt right out the door.

KNICKERSON'S Five-and-Dime was empty. The little bell over the doorway announcing their arrival and the whir of the old, wooden-bladed ceiling fan were the only sounds from within. Rachel took a deep breath of the cool air: wood polish from the gleaming, but uneven floor; the sweet smell of chocolates rising from the glass-fronted cases where you could still point and choose which ones you wanted—just like Rachel had when she'd been a child. The scent of dusting powder and plastic and the potted geraniums that were going for one dollar apiece. Rachel loved it all. And she hoped for once that Miss Huffington down at the library had it all wrong.

"Agnes?" she called out.

Curtains covering a narrow door at the back of the first aisle opened and Agnes bustled out. "Rachel! How nice! I was just going to have a pop. Want one?"

"No thanks, Agnes," Rachel answered.

"A pop?" Marcus asked.

"Soda pop," Agnes answered. "Don't tell me ya never had it? You from outer space, boy?"

"No, he's from the city, Agnes, where they call it soda."

Agnes looked him up and down, sticking her handkerchief down the front of her wildly floral shirt, in the cleft of her enormous bosom, letting the yellow lace peek out. The shirt was a stunning array of shades of turquoise and pink to match her turquoise pedal pushers. "Look a might familiar," she said, throwing back her head and taking a gulp of the orange crush right from the bottle, her well-lacquered French twist not moving a hair.

Apparently Miss Finch hadn't spread the news this far yet, Rachel thought, before remembering that Molly Finch and Agnes Summers hadn't talked in five years.

"This is Marcus Slade, Agnes. He's an old friend of Grant's. Came to visit."

Agnes narrowed her eyes on Marcus's unshaven face. "Holy cow!" she cried, her eyes popping wide behind her thick glasses. "It's the Helicopter Hunk!"

From the look on Marcus's face, Rachel could tell he wasn't all that happy with the title. Which suited her just fine.

"Yes," she said, beaming at Agnes, "Mr. Hunk, himself. He's tagging along with me to see if he can learn anything about real reporting."

"Well," Agnes said, apparently taking the remark seriously, "you couldn't find a better one to learn from than

Rachel, here. Why I remember when she won that contest back in—let me see now,'' Agnes pondered, taking another swig of orange crush.

''Never mind,'' Rachel interrupted. ''I'm sure Mr. Hunk here wouldn't be interested.''

''Oh, but Mr. Hunk would,'' Marcus said. ''Definitely. Agnes, tell me. What was the prize for?''

Agnes snapped her fingers. ''I remember! It was an essay to protest putting gum ball machines on the corners of Main Street. Said it'd be an eyesore. Regular little crusade she started.''

Rachel thought it might be a good idea if the uneven floor of Knickerson's Five-and-Dime would suddenly open and suck her in, leaving not a trace.

''Gum balls?'' Marcus asked, arching a dark brow.

Agnes nodded emphatically. ''Yup. The issue divided the town. But once Rachel's essay came out and she won, the town council voted it right down.''

''The end of gum balls as we know them, eh?'' Marcus asked, his voice far more serious than his eyes.

''Well, in Birch Beach at least,'' Agnes answered just as seriously.

Marcus started to open his mouth again, but Rachel shouldered him aside, took a pencil out of her pocket and turned to a clean sheet on her legal pad. ''What we're here for, Agnes, is to find out if it's true. Is the five-and-dime closing its doors?''

Agnes, bottle of orange crush halfway to her mouth, froze and stared at them. Suddenly her eyes filled with tears.

''Oh, Rachel, honey! What are we going to do without Knickerson's? What am *I* going to do?''

HALF AN HOUR LATER they were back on the street, Marcus munching from a white paper bag of burned peanuts.

"The town's going to be in an uproar over this," Rachel stated.

"Over losing that little place? You're joking."

She gave him a sharp look. "No, I'm not! Every time Birch Beach loses a place like that, the town dies a little more. That five-and-dime has been there since before World War II. It means something in this town."

"Yeah," Marcus said, shaking peanuts from the bag into his mouth. "It means that you can get all the plastic doilies you want for ninety-nine cents apiece."

"You're heartless, you know that? No wonder you can stand in front of death and destruction without blinking an eye. If there's blood in your veins, it must be cold as ice."

"Don't be too sure of that."

Something in his tone made her whip her head around to look at him. His eyes were hard, the green deeper, cloudier. He seemed to have lost interest in his peanuts, wading up the bag and shoving it into his pocket.

"Don't tell me I hit a nerve."

He ignored that, just kept walking. After another block he said, "Milwaukee isn't that far. The people in this town can drive there if they need darning needles or hair ribbons."

He was clearly getting the subject off himself again.

She easily rose to the bait.

"Miss Huffington doesn't drive. Where will she buy her dusting powder? Old man Crawford from the bakery had his license taken away because he can't see well enough anymore. Where is he going to go buy his shoelaces?"

He shook his head. "Rachel, you are one bleeding heart of a woman."

"And Agnes. What is she going to do for a job?"

He shrugged. "She'll get another job."

"Where?" she demanded. "She's fifty-nine years old and she's never worked anywhere else! If she wasn't the

Knickersons' niece she probably wouldn't have that job, either.''

Marcus stopped walking and put his hand out to halt her. ''You're serious about this, aren't you? You really care about these people.''

She looked up into his green eyes, clear again, incredulous again. The feel of his hand on her bare arm evoked something that seemed to meld with the smell of spring on the air, the sunlight that dappled the planes of his face. He was even better looking than he appeared on the nightly news. More visceral, more dangerous. Surely more dangerous, because her heart was reacting like she was running for her life.

She tugged her arm away. ''I wouldn't expect a man like you to understand.''

''And what would you expect from a man like me?'' he asked with a dangerously soft voice.

''Nothing,'' she answered. ''Absolutely nothing.''

She left him there, walking down the street as fast as she could. For once, he didn't follow.

HE HAD DECIDED to go for a run. Long and hard. He stopped at the guest house to trade his jeans for running shorts and his boots for athletic shoes then headed out.

His feet slapped the pavement as he ran; his breath tore through his lungs; his calves felt tight. He was reaching his maximum heart rate, the point at which everything left him but the sensation of motion. A sensation he'd craved since he'd been a boy growing up in a town as small and narrow as Birch Beach.

He waited for his mind to go blank. He waited for his body to become one with the pavement. He waited for the thought of Rachel Gale and her champagne-streaked hair to get the hell out of his brain.

None of it happened.

He ran on, up a hill, toward a white church steeple soaring into the blue sky. Around another bend, and the lake the town was named for became visible again, spreading out before him, sun glittering on the deep blue water. He slowed and turned toward the narrow strip of sand at the water's edge. He ran straight for it, never stopping, until the water was deep enough to dive in, his chest nearly scraping the bottom when he did.

"Damn!" he shouted when he surfaced. The water was cold, ice. It was just what he needed. He set out at a steady pace, churning the water with his legs, parting it with his arms. The cold seeped in and numbed his body, but his mind was as alive as ever.

And Rachel Gale and her disapproval were right there in front of him despite the fact that he was a mile from shore.

"YOU LOOK BETTER," Grant growled.

"A cold swim, a hot shower and a shave."

Grant grunted. "Did you eat?"

"No, and I don't want to."

"Frannie puts on a damn fine dinner. Let's see—it's Thursday so it must be spaghetti and meatballs."

The corner of Marcus's mouth lifted. "Sounds like you'd like some of that—and maybe some of Frannie. Why don't you go on over?"

Grant looked at him. "Don't miss much, do you?"

"You taught me that. 'See what isn't visible' you used to say."

Grant gave a bark of laughter. "Yeah, hotshot, you followed my advice, and look where it got you."

Marcus didn't want to go down that particular road. Not tonight. Because for the first time, he wasn't sure what it had gotten him.

"Go get some spaghetti, old man."

Grant shook his head. "Naw, there's something I gotta do first."

"What's that?" Marcus asked.

Grant reached down, pulled open his bottom desk drawer and came up with a nearly full bottle of Jim Beam. "Gotta get drunk."

"Now you're talking," Marcus said. "Got any glasses?"

MARCUS HALF DRAGGED Grant up the flight of stairs to the apartment he lived in above the newspaper office. He kicked open the door, threw his old mentor onto the bed, and started to get him out of his shoes. The man sure couldn't drink like he used to.

"Hey, hotshot!"

Grant sat up and Marcus pushed him back down. "Hey, old man—get some sleep. You're gonna feel lousy in the morning."

"But I gotta tell ya—"

"Tell me tomorrow, old man. I'm whacked."

Grant sprang up again. "No, waited long enough—"

Marcus pushed him down again. "Then it'll wait till morning. Go to sleep, Grant."

Marcus waited until he heard the man on the bed start to snore, then he left the apartment, locking the door behind him.

The streets were deserted, the sidewalks all but rolled up. He shoved his hands into his jeans pockets and hunched his shoulders against the night chill. God, it was quiet. Quiet enough to hear the rustling of the leaves on the trees that lined Main. And if you looked up, the night sky was laden with enough stars to make it look like a wide, white sweep. The Milky Way. He'd been in places where the stars were just as bright. Where neon lights didn't live. Where streetlights were shot out. Oh, he'd experienced that kind of dark sky before, the kind that let you see every star that ever lived.

But none of those places were as peaceful as Birch

Beach. If there was quiet, it was only the calm before the next grenade or the next scud attack. It was a waiting sort of quiet. A nervous sort of quiet.

This was different. This was peace.

"And you are drunk, boy," he murmured to himself. But he wasn't—not really. He'd mostly sipped while Grant had gulped. Sipped and listened to the old man while he reminisced about other times, other places, while he got misty-eyed over Frannie Gale. While he tried to work up the courage to tell Marcus whatever he'd asked him there to tell. No, Marcus was far from drunk. But maybe just mellow enough to forget for a moment that this place was poison. Just like all small towns. And the sooner he left it the better.

He turned onto Elm and walked the two blocks to Frannie Gale's Guest House, turned up the front walk and sauntered up the steps. The porch swing creaked in the breeze, a small intrusion on the quiet. He let himself in, leaving the light off, his vision accustomed to doing without light many years ago.

He started up the steps, then stopped, one foot on the bottom step, head cocked. He'd heard something. What was it?

His ears picked up the sound again. It came from the kitchen. A lilting, soft sound. Like a woman's hum.

Quietly he went through the dining room to the kitchen door and pushed it open. Rachel was there. Another Rachel yet again. For this one wore a long, white cotton gown. The neck was a modest scoop. The skirt fell down to her toes. Her hair was still in a braid, but trying to escape, tendrils and strands of it gleaming in the light from the ceiling like a halo around her head. She could have been a little girl in her nightgown, freshly scrubbed, ready for bed, sneaking down to the kitchen for a midnight snack.

But she wasn't a little girl. How well Marcus knew. And he knew what was under that pristine, white gown. And his body, reckless with the faint mellowness of whisky and the peace of the night, full of a yearning he couldn't explain, wanted it.

"Rachel," he whispered.

## Chapter Three

Rachel spun around, almost dropping the wooden spoon she held.

"Marcus," she said, the name catching slightly in her throat.

He was standing in the doorway, his shaggy hair tousled, his faded chambray shirt unbuttoned and hanging out of his jeans. His smooth chest gleamed in the ceiling light overhead. He'd shaved and it should have made him look less dangerous, but the glint in his green eyes made up for it.

"I startled you," he said.

"I...I wasn't expecting you. It's late. I thought you and Grant had gone into the city again."

He took a step into the room, the corner of his mouth lifting slightly. "So you did think of me."

She shook her head emphatically. "Nonsense," she said shortly, not at all sure which one of them the word was supposed to convince.

"Is that why you're still up, sweetheart? Couldn't get to sleep in that big, soft bed all by yourself? Maybe you liked having the company last night."

"If you must know," she answered primly, "I couldn't sleep because of thinking about the closing of Knickerson's."

His gaze went to the spoon she held. "So you decided to bake a chocolate cake?"

"Brownies," she corrected, turning back to the sink to rinse the spoon.

"Wait!"

She swung around to find him coming toward her, that lethal glint still in his eye. No wonder he did so well in third-world countries, thought Rachel. All he'd have to do is glare and he wouldn't have to speak the language to get what he wanted. He held out his hand just as he reached her.

She raised her chin. "What?" she asked, hating the defensiveness in her voice.

"Aren't you going to let me lick the spoon?" he asked, his voice a teasing rumble.

She could smell the whisky on his breath. She knew she should hate it, but, mixed with the dangerous glint in his eyes, and the glimpse of hard, bare chest, it was faintly arousing.

Faintly, hell. *Be honest with yourself, Rachel.* Well, she had to be, didn't she? Her nipples had gone hard against the smooth white cotton of her gown. Quickly she handed him the spoon and turned back to the sink, hoping, praying that he was too drunk to notice.

"So why is it closing?" he asked.

"What?"

"The five-and-dime," he said between licks on the spoon. "Why is it closing?"

"Oh. Looks like the town council is going to approve building one of those Big Bill's Bargain Palaces outside of town."

"So they're just going to close their doors?"

She shrugged and shut off the water. "They've already lost some of their business to the Big Bill's that went up over near Pine Village. Once one goes up just outside of town they'll lose even more."

"Can't halt progress."

She shook her head. "Yeah, if you can call neon-lit warehouse aisles progress. Personally I'd rather buy my plastic doilies from a place that doesn't smell like chemicals."

"And from a woman who stuffs her handkerchief in her cleavage."

She turned angrily around to face him. "Yes," she replied emphatically. "I'd much rather take Agnes Summers's advice on which bug spray works the best than rely on some national warehouse chain that just happened to buy up a load of cut-rate stuff at cut-rate prices."

"But obviously, not everyone in this town feels the same way or Knickerson's wouldn't be in danger from Big Bill's."

"There's not a lot of money in this town, Slade. If people can save a few dollars by driving a mile, they will. And who can blame them? It was different when they had to go all the way to Pine Village. But with a Big Bill's just outside of town…" She let the words trail off.

"So why don't they fight it?"

"The Knickersons?"

"Yeah. Why don't they go to the town council and protest?"

"Because, Slade, the Ludingtons own the land that Big Bill's is going to lease. And the Ludingtons *are* the town council. Always have been. Eric Ludington—just like his father before him—has enough power and money to sway the rest of the council to his way of thinking. Not many in this town can afford to go against them."

Marcus snorted.

"Got something to say, Slade?"

"Just this—small towns, small people. Narrow, scared little minds. The spoils going to the exalted few and the rest can go to hell."

His anger was a potent presence. But as she looked into

that hard face, it was already changing, softening. Her gaze went to his mouth, and she knew that it would be far more dangerous all soft and sexy than it was hard and brutal.

"And what makes you such an expert on small towns, Slade?" she flung at him, hoping to incite him into another tirade. Hoping for anger that would keep him hard and distant.

She didn't get the anger. What she got was a lopsided grin. "I like it better when you call me Marcus," he murmured.

She managed to turn a shiver into a shrug. "Sorry, but you know how narrow-minded everyone in this town is."

He laughed and turned from her, throwing himself sideways into a kitchen chair, leaning his head against the wall at his back and closing his eyes. "Point for you, Rachel. But the fact is, I am an expert on small towns because I grew up in one. Worse, yet, I grew up in one on the wrong side of the tracks. They put their label on me when I was four and swiped a Hershey bar from the drugstore."

"My guess would be that that wasn't the last thing you swiped."

He opened his eyes. "Damn straight it wasn't! Why be any better than they let you? When I was two my old man stole money from the cash register where he worked, hot-wired someone's car and headed out. My Ma took money from men to keep food on the table. Men from the right side of the tracks. They crossed over any damn time they pleased. But it wasn't a two-way street. They came but we could never leave."

His eyes were slits watching her.

"So what are you thinking now, Rachel?"

"I'm thinking you had it rough," she answered softly. "I'm thinking that you must have had a lot of guts and determination to finally cross over those tracks. And," she added more softly, "I'm wishing that I'd known that little

four-year-old boy, because I would have bought him that
Hershey bar.''

His head came up, his eyes opened wider. The only
sound in the room was the night breeze brushing the
branch of the birch tree in the backyard against the kitchen
window, and the faint ticking of the clock on the wall.

''Don't look at me that way, Rachel,'' he whispered
gruffly.

She swallowed and took a breath. ''What way?''

''The way that makes me want to hold you and sink
into you—the way that tells me that you want it, too.''

The words stunned her. It was as if she stopped all
breath for a long, painful second, then life slammed back
into her with a fierce longing that shook her.

''You're mistaken,'' she said evenly, carefully. ''Just
like you were mistaken this morning.''

She turned back to the sink, hoping he'd give her one
of his sarcastic replies and leave.

She heard him get up from the chair. Heard him move
over the floor.

And then she felt him. Felt him as he came up behind
her and slid his hands around her waist and down to let
them rest on her belly. Her breath drew in, her breasts
leaped to painful, urgent life.

''I don't think I'm wrong, Rachel,'' he whispered
against her neck. And then his lips were there, running
down to the dip of her shoulder and back up again. She
was helpless. She arched her neck, wanting that touch,
wanting the breath of him on her skin. His hands moved
back and forth across her belly, and her insides quickened
along with her breathing.

''What do you want, Rachel?'' he whispered. ''Tell me
what you want.''

Oh, goodness—she couldn't stand it. She'd never felt
anything like it in her entire life. Before she could think
of what she was doing—and just how crazy it was—she

spun in his arms, shoved her fingers into his hair, and brought his mouth down to hers.

And she took. Took with her lips, took with her tongue. He tasted of whisky and freedom, sensuality and greed. No—she was the greedy one, moaning into his mouth, fingers raking that thick dark hair.

"Rachel," he said against her mouth, and then his hands skimmed up her hips, up her rib cage and settled on her breasts.

She gasped and pulled away, one hand flying to her mouth, the other pushing at his chest.

He grinned down at her, the rakish devil she'd watched every night on the news, and said, "Don't stop now, you're wonderful."

"Oh," she said, the sound gushing out of her on a high note. "Oh—oh—oh—"

And then she pushed away from him and ran.

"Damn," Marcus muttered, collapsing back against the counter, shoving his hands into his hair. "Man, oh, man— the lady's got a volcano inside of her." He snorted. "Yeah, hotshot, and you're about to explode yourself," he muttered.

Had he ever wanted a woman as much as he wanted Rachel at that moment? If he had, he couldn't remember it. "Man, oh, man," he muttered again, his hand going to the back of his neck to work at the kinks of frustration knotted there.

A buzzer sounded and he nearly jumped, his muscles tensing, his hand automatically going for the gun in his pocket—the gun that wasn't there.

"Cool it, hotshot," he told himself. "You're not at war anymore."

*Oh really?* he thought to himself, a rueful smile forming on his lips. If he stayed in this town any longer, he'd have a constant war on his hands. Because if he stayed, he'd have to have her. He'd have to win Rachel—and that would be the war to end all wars.

A buzzer sounded again, and he looked at the oven, saw the red light blinking there. The brownies.

He opened the oven door, grabbed a dish towel and took the pan out, turning off the oven and taking the pan over to the table. He found a sharp knife in a drawer and threw himself back into the chair.

He needed something to assuage this craving, some sort of instant gratification. Chocolate would have to do—for now.

BY MORNING he'd decided that a nice war in Eastern Europe would be easier to handle than one in Birch Beach, Wisconsin. Damn good thing he hadn't unpacked much, he thought as he threw his shaving gear into a knapsack. He was getting out of the Frances Gale Guest House and Home for Sexy, Scared Spinsters. And he was getting out that morning.

"Marcus!" Frannie called from downstairs. "You coming down for breakfast? The biscuits are just out of the oven."

Marcus paused in fastening his knapsack. It wasn't like he was hungry—not after devouring half a pan of Rachel's brownies at midnight last night. Never mind that what he'd really wanted to devour was Rachel herself. But damned if she didn't make the best brownies he'd ever tasted. Still they were no substitute for the taste of the lady's lips.

"Marcus?" Frannie called again.

"Oh, hell," he muttered. Those biscuits did smell good. One more meal under the same roof with her wasn't going keep him from going. It would just keep him from going until after breakfast.

SHE WOULDN'T LOOK AT HIM. There she sat, right across from him, demure and cool as ever in a white cotton dress with a scooped neck, her braid tickling her collarbone, licking melted butter off her fingers.

If she kept it up, he wasn't going to be able to stand until everyone else had left the room.

"Timmy, stop kicking the table leg," Frannie said. "Your shoes will wear out fast enough as it is."

"Sorry," Timmy said. "Can I have another biscuit?"

"Of course. What about you, Marcus? Another biscuit?"

"Uh—" He should just tell them he was leaving and go. Hell, he could take the damn biscuit with him! Instead, he took the basket that Frannie held out to him, selected a biscuit, buttered it and reached for the jar of honey— and ended up with his hand on top of Rachel's who'd reached for it at the same time.

Instead of jerking his hand back right away, he tightened it around hers. Damn it! She was going to look at him once before he left. Look at him and prove to him that it was the whisky last night. Look at him so that he would feel nothing and know that Marcus Slade, who was used to real danger, was in no danger from a sassy spinster who made great brownies.

Her eyes met his.

"Do you mind?" she said heavily.

Her brown eyes bored into him, angry, a little haughty, and danger hit him like a scud missile to his gut.

He snatched his hand back. "Ladies first."

"Thank you."

He watched her spread honey, bring the biscuit to her mouth. Watched her bite off a piece and start to chew. His mouth went dry as he watched her lips moving.

Hell, how could this be happening to him? He'd had women try to turn him on in every way imaginable. But chewing a biscuit?

Damn good thing he was leaving after breakfast.

"Anybody home?"

"Grant? That you?" Frannie yelled. "Come on in, screen door's open!"

"Those your biscuits I smell, Frannie?"

"Isn't that why you're here, Grant?" Frannie asked him with a wink.

"Well, that and those great little legs of yours, Frannie. I was hoping it was warm enough for shorts today."

Frannie laughed while Rachel rolled her eyes.

"Sit yourself down, Grant. I'll get you a cup of coffee."

Grant watched her walk into the kitchen. "Woman's got a fine pair of legs on her."

Rachel threw down her napkin and pushed back her chair. "I think I'll skip the seduction of my mother over breakfast, Boss. See you at the office."

"Wait!"

Marcus watched her freeze. Damn he hadn't intended to even speak to her. He figured he'd just be gone by the time she got out of work. Then he wouldn't have to watch relief on her face when he told her. That was the plan.

"I'm leaving this morning, Rachel. Just wanted to say goodbye." So much for plans.

He watched her face, but it was Timmy who reacted. "Aww, yer leaving? Nuts, I thought you could take me on a helicopter ride."

Marcus looked at the kid. He knew it was tough having no father. He knew a kid Timmy's age would crave male attention—he'd been there himself. "Hey, sorry, soldier. How about we take that kite I saw in the front hall for a flight before I go?"

Timmy sprang out of his chair. "*All right!* I'll go check the string. I think it's maybe a little tangled," he added sheepishly before dashing out of the dining room.

Marcus turned back to Rachel. Her face was blank. "You're leaving?" she asked.

"Yup—" he grinned at her "—and I'd appreciate it if you didn't start the celebration until I'm long gone."

"Leaving," she repeated. "This morning."

"That's right." What was going on with her? He couldn't read her face as the emotion came back into it. But he could have sworn that it wasn't relief.

"Well, then," she said, holding out her hand to him across the table. "Goodbye."

The devil was in him. It certainly was. He was leaving, so what the hell? He scraped back his chair and stood, moving too fast around the table toward her for her to guess what he was up to. He reached for her, snaking an arm around her waist and pulling her to him.

"You can do better than a handshake, can't you, sweetheart?" he said, and then he took her mouth with his own. She was warm, soft—the white cotton dress she wore smooth under his hands. For one sweet, heady moment she kissed him back. Then all hell broke loose.

She twisted her mouth away from his. "You rat! Just when I was almost sorry to see you go! How dare you? How could you? By all means *leave,* Mr. Slade—and don't let the door hit you on the backside!"

He chuckled as she flounced out of the room.

"You must be losing your touch, hotshot," Grant said.

"Don't you believe it, old man. If I were sticking around, Rachel Gale would fall just like the rest of them."

"Which," Grant said, taking a bite of biscuit, "is why you're not sticking around."

Marcus twisted his lips and shook his head. "See what isn't visible, huh, old man?"

"Oh, it's visible enough, hotshot."

"Then I guess I really am slipping."

Grant snorted. "Pity you're leaving. Wanted to talk to you about something before you went."

Marcus raised his brows. "Oh? Now's as good a time as any."

Grant looked toward the kitchen. "Kind of private. Maybe we better take it outside."

Marcus frowned. He didn't like the tone this was taking. "Anything you say, Grant. Come on—let's go give that porch swing some action. I haven't been on one in years."

Frannie came out of the kitchen with Grant's coffee just as they were headed for the door. "Your coffee, Grant. You're not leaving?"

"No, honey, just gonna sit on your swing and talk to the hotshot here for a minute."

"Well, take your coffee with you, then."

Grant shook his head. "Naw, I'm trying to cut down. Got any herbal tea?"

"Herbal tea?" Marcus and Frannie said in unison.

"A man's never too old to change."

"Sure, sweetie, herbal tea it is," Frannie said, shooting a questioning glance at Marcus before heading back for the kitchen.

When the two men had set the swing to moving gently, Marcus asked, "What's this all about, old man?"

Grant snorted. "Heck, you been calling me that since I was your age, you know that? And now it's finally happened. I'm old."

"What are you talking about?" Marcus scoffed. "You'll never really be old—"

"Tell my body that," Grant muttered.

Marcus didn't want to hear this. He wanted to be far away somewhere where all the people who died were strangers. "What are you telling me, Grant? What's wrong?"

Grant sighed heavily. "Doc says I've got to retire. It's the ticker. Had a mild heart attack this past winter." He glanced at the front door. "Nobody here knows about it, hotshot. And for now I prefer to keep it that way."

"Damn," Marcus muttered. "But, last night, the drinking—"

"My swan song, hotshot. That bottle of Jim Beam you helped me polish off last night was my last. Heart trouble runs in the family. If I want to get any older, I gotta start living healthier. Need to sell the paper, move to a warmer climate.'' He paused and nodded at Marcus. ''That's where you come in, hotshot.''

Marcus's brows lifted in surprise. ''Me?''

''Yeah, you.''

Marcus frowned. ''Well, what? How?''

Grant snorted. ''Ever since I knew I had to go, I've had one dream. For you to buy the *Birch Bark,* settle down here and run it.''

Marcus shot to his feet. ''What?''

Grant looked up at him through narrowed eyes. ''You heard me, hotshot. Time for you to come in from the cold, too.''

''Are you crazy? You know how I feel about small towns. I'd suffocate here!''

Grant looked at him shrewdly. ''Sure you're not suffocating out there?''

Before he could answer, the screen door opened and Frannie came out, a steaming cup of tea in her hands.

''Here you go, Grant,'' Frannie said, handing it to him and sliding in next to him on the swing.

Grant held the cup in his large hands, looking into the liquid for a moment before raising his gaze to Marcus again. ''Think about it, hotshot. Just stick around for a day or two more and think about it before you go.''

''Go?'' Frannie asked. ''You're leaving us already, Marcus?''

Marcus shoved his hands into the pockets of his jeans and moved over to the porch railing, leaning out to glance down the street.

''Yoo-hoo, Mr. Hunk!'' Molly Finch called out as she leaned over her front fence. ''Don't forget about that autograph!''

Marcus waved at her, then shook his head. ''Lord, Grant, you know what you're asking?''

"You know what I'm *offering?*" Grant asked back.

Marcus turned around. Frannie was snuggled in next to his old mentor, a puzzled look on her face. "Are you leaving, Marcus?" she repeated.

"No," he said after a moment's hesitation. "Not yet."

RACHEL HAD ALWAYS LOVED Saturday afternoons at the newspaper office. The paper was out for the week, things were slow. Only Daisy was present, manning the telephones behind the advertising department door. Rachel would usually spend the quiet afternoon making notes for new articles, going over the wire services or covering some social event. Weddings were not her favorite things to cover. But today there were no weddings in Birch Beach. So she should be happy with the quiet—happy to work on a feature article or just sit and read the papers that Grant subscribed to from all over the country.

Instead she lolled dispiritedly in her desk chair, barely noticing the warm, fragrant breeze drifting in through the open doorway.

Marcus Slade was leaving.

Already.

Well, hadn't she wanted him to?

Of course she'd wanted him to. Especially after last night. Lord, she'd all but mauled the man. Acting, no doubt, exactly like the kind of female he detested. The kind of female who was after him. Goodness, he might have even thought she'd staged the whole thing! Lurked about the kitchen in her nightgown hoping to entice him with her brownies!

"Oh, Lord..." she moaned, putting her hands to her cheeks. "Thank goodness he *is* leaving."

Yes. So why wasn't she happier about it?

A shadow fell across her desk, and she shot up straighter in her chair.

"Rachel," the man standing in front of her said with a nod of his blond head.

Great, she thought, just what I need. "Eric. What brings you into the *Bark* on a Saturday afternoon?"

"I think you know the answer to that, Rachel," Eric Ludington said testily.

She looked away from his milky blue eyes and started to shuffle papers on her desk. "Afraid I don't." She looked up at him again, smiling sweetly. "Why don't you tell me?"

He leaned forward, putting both his hands flat on her desk, so close that she was caught by the glitter of the heavy gold chain he wore in the open throat of his Arnold Palmer golf shirt. Her gaze went down to the white belt at the waist of his blue-and-white seersucker pants, surprised to see it there. White belt meant white shoes. And it wasn't even Memorial Day yet. Pretty reckless for one of the Ludingtons, Birch Beach's first family.

He totally mistook the reason for the slight smile on her face as she stared at his belt.

"You still want me, Rachel, don't you?" he said in a voice that tried to be sexy, ended up sounding like Mr. Rogers making an obscene phone call.

She fell back into her chair and started to laugh. "Oh, Eric! Really!"

He straightened and shot her an affronted look. "If you're not still in love with me, then what is the reason for this vendetta against me and my family?"

She bit her lower lip to stop the laughter. "What vendetta is that, Eric?"

He slapped a paper down in front of her. It was yesterday's.

"Ahh," she said, "I see you've still got a subscription."

"But not for long if this shoddy excuse for journalism keeps up."

"Something you object to in yesterday's paper, Eric?" she asked him innocently.

"You know darn well there is, Rachel. That opinion piece on my daddy's rental properties was inexcusable. How could you, Rachel? Doesn't it mean anything to you that you were almost my wife?"

Rachel stood up. "Yes, Eric, it does. It means that every year when June rolls around I thank my lucky stars that you jilted me and married someone else."

He glared at her. Or at least she would have considered it a glare if she hadn't been so recently treated to one by a real man. Oh, dear, she thought, now was not the time to start thinking about Marcus Slade. He'd dropped into her life for one quick moment, just long enough to turn her body restless, and then he was gone again. And with any luck, Eric Ludington would be out of her office even quicker.

"Rather mean of you, Rachel. You never used to be mean."

"And I'm still not, Eric. Just stating the facts like any other good reporter would do."

He had the temerity to actually give her what she supposed he thought was a knowing smile. "I hate to see you so bitter, my dear. If it's any consolation to you, I think of you often, too."

She sighed. "Eric, the only time I think of you is when I get to write a scathing editorial on one of your family's dubious business practices."

"Aha!" he blurted out like a bad actor in a bad movie. "Then you *did* write it?"

"Yes, Eric, I *did* write it."

"Then you can write the retraction, too."

She firmed her lips and shook her head. "Nothing doing, buddy. Every word in that piece," she said, pointing her finger at the paper, "was the truth. You want some good press? Clean up those rental properties. Do the repairs the tenants have been complaining about. Give them a decent place to live for the more-than-adequate rent you charge them.''

"Rachel, you're turning into a bitter old maid. It's a shame.'' He shook his head. "Damn shame. I could fix that, you know.''

She sighed heavily. "What are you talking about?''

He started to move around the desk, a mottled flush climbing up his neck. "We could meet, Rachel, in the city. There's a motel on the highway that doesn't ask questions.''

"What are you talking about?''

"You need it, Rachel. You need to feel like a woman so you can stop this foolish vendetta.''

She thought she was going to throw up when he started to reach for her. But before she knew what was happening, someone's arms were around her—and they weren't Eric's.

"Sweetheart! Where did you go in such a hurry this morning? I missed you,'' he said and then his mouth came down on hers.

She was too dumbfounded to even struggle.

When the kiss was over, Marcus Slade put his arm around her shoulders and drew her close in to his side. "Oh,'' he said, as if he'd just noticed Eric at that moment, "you've got business. Sorry, didn't mean to interrupt.''

Rachel tried to clear her throat and almost choked. "Uh—Marcus Slade, this is Eric—uh—Eric—''

"Ludington,'' Eric supplied with a rather surly look at Rachel. He turned a much pleasanter facade to Marcus. But then all the Ludingtons were capable of changing color faster than a lizard. Which wasn't surprising, considering that all the Ludington men tended to have cold, clammy hands.

"Marcus Slade, the newsman?''

"Right,'' Marcus said, ignoring Eric's offered hand.

"What brings you to town?"

"Why, Rachel, of course," he answered, as if there could be no other reason in the world.

He kissed her temple and hugged her closer while Eric's pale eyes moved from Rachel to Marcus.

"If you don't mind, buddy, we'd like to be alone," Marcus said.

"Oh—oh, yes, of course," Eric sputtered, and Rachel tried to keep from laughing. "Good day—so nice to meet you. Maybe we could get together while you're in town."

Marcus ignored him and bent to kiss Rachel again. When they came up for air, Eric was gone.

"Really!" she exclaimed, pushing out of his arms. "What on earth was that for?"

"Hey, you should be thanking me, not pulling that haughty spinster act on me."

"Thanking you? For what?"

"Coming to your rescue."

"I didn't need any rescuing!"

"The hell you didn't! The man was suggesting a sexual liaison as payment for services rendered. And from the look of things, he was ready to begin delivering."

"Just how long were you eavesdropping?"

"Long enough, baby."

"I'm not your baby!"

"Oh, so maybe you wanted to shack up in some cheap motel room with lover boy, huh?"

"Give me more credit than that!" she snapped.

"I'd like to give you more than credit," he drawled, starting to reach for her again.

"Oh, please." She batted his hand away. "That line is worse than Eric's. What are you doing here, anyway? I thought you were taking Timmy kite flying and then getting the hell out of Dodge."

"He's at the dime store picking out a new kite. His was

a mess. As to leaving—I've changed my mind," he said. "Damn good thing for you that I did."

"Oh, yeah, just what I needed," she said, slumping against the edge of her desk. "For you to come in here and give Eric Ludington the wrong impression. He'll tell everyone in town that we're—that we're—" She couldn't say it, not with those glistening green eyes on her.

"Sleeping together?" he finished for her, a mocking lift to his brow.

"Yes! You know how small towns are!"

He laughed at that and started toward her again. "Exactly, sweetheart. And I know you can't beat down a rumor. So," he said, putting a hand either side of her on the desk, leaning so close that her back almost touched the desk as she tried to avoid him; "we may as well do it."

"Do—do what?" she sputtered.

"We may as well sleep together, Rachel. By nightfall, the whole town is going to think we are, anyway."

## Chapter Four

She had never seen such green eyes. They caught her, filled her vision, while she leaned precariously back—as far back as she could without risking being impaled on her mug of sharpened pencils. There was nowhere else to go—but into his arms.

"Come on, Rachel," he said, his voice a rough whisper, his deep green gaze fastened on her mouth. "Let's give 'em something to talk about."

Rachel groaned inwardly. At least she hoped it was inwardly, and that that sound of need hadn't really escaped her lips. And need it was. A wave of need rolling through her like nothing she'd ever known. When his mouth skimmed her chin on its way to her throat, she didn't even try to jerk farther away.

"Come on, Rachel," he murmured, his mouth moving against her neck. "We might as well get hung for the real thing as the rumor. Lot more fun that way."

This time she knew the sound had escaped her lips. The moan seemed to fill the room. And she wasn't the only one surprised by it. Marcus jerked his head back, his gaze going to hers, his face suddenly changing into something more sober, something even more dangerous.

His hands left the desk and cupped her face, drawing her toward him, while his glittering green eyes moved to her mouth, to her eyes, then back again. "Rachel," he whispered, and she felt his body stir against hers, felt the breath coming harder in his chest. "Rachel," he said again and she knew suddenly that this was no longer a game. The need was in him, too. And when her need met his, there would be no stopping it.

Her lips parted—

"Hey, Marcus!"

He jumped back so far he nearly ended up on the floor. "Timmy," he said, trying to still his pounding heart. "What's up, soldier?"

"I can't decide! Come on and help me pick one out, will ya?"

Marcus raked his hand through his hair, his gaze still on Rachel where she leaned against the desk. "Huh?" he managed.

"Help me pick out a new kite, will ya? I can't decide. They've got this red one that looks like…"

Dimly he heard Timmy rattle on while he stared at Rachel. He'd been with more sophisticated women; he'd been with women who'd worked hard to get him where they wanted him; he'd been with women who knew all about the mysteries of pleasing a man. But he had never seen such undisguised desire in their eyes. Such naked need as he'd just seen in the eyes of Rachel Gale.

Damn good thing Timmy had come in when he had. Because Marcus knew that he'd have gotten lost in that need, been only too happy to slake it, to take all that had been offered in her eyes and then some. But the price would have been high. Because the price would have been the noose of this town pulling a little tighter around his neck. Rachel, unlike all the other women who'd wanted him, would not be easy to walk away from. And he had no intention of staying. Best to leave her—and himself— untouched.

With the same will that'd gotten him out of a war zone

alive, he turned to Timmy. "Okay, soldier. Let's you and me go pick out a kite."

"Cool!"

Avoiding looking again at Rachel, he put his arm around Timmy's shoulders and started for the door. And he almost made it to the threshold, almost made his escape from the threat that was Rachel Gale. Almost—

"Hey, Marcus?" Timmy piped up, excited and eager. "Can Rachel come along?"

HE SHOULD HAVE SAID NO. The look of bright expectancy on Timmy's face wouldn't let him. So he'd hoped Rachel would say no. Apparently she couldn't resist that eager little freckled face, either. Because here the three of them stood, in Knickerson's Five-and-Dime, listening to Agnes Summers chatter to the old codger from the grocery store while they waited for Timmy to decide on a kite.

"Damn shame," Mr. Cheevers muttered while he shook his head. "Don't know why Big Bill's gotta have one store so close to the other, anyway."

Marcus didn't hear what Agnes replied to that, he was too busy wondering the same thing himself.

"Rachel?" he asked.

She turned from the kite Timmy was examining. "Yes?"

"How far is Pine Village from here?"

"Maybe ten miles. Why?"

He shook his head shortly, as if to clear it of a pesky fly. Only this was a pesky thought. Or half thought. Something about the conversation between Agnes and Cheevers was vibrating his reporter's radar. He just didn't know what.

"Just thinking," he muttered in answer to Rachel's question before brushing the pesky thought aside. "Timmy the sun will be down if you don't hurry up."

"Well," Timmy drawled. "I like this blue one that looks like a jet, but—"

Marcus tried to stifle the grin twitching at the corners of his mouth. "But that red one, the dragon one is really something, isn't it, soldier?"

Timmy's face lit up enough to flash his freckles like neon. "Yeah! Look at the tail! It looks like a real dragon's tail—all spiky and long."

"That the one you like best, soldier?"

"Yeah!" Timmy shouted, then immediately sobered. "But the blue one is okay, too, Marcus. I'll take the blue one," he added with a solemn resolve.

Marcus laughed softly and grabbed the dragon kite off the shelf. "No you won't, soldier. You'll take the dragon one."

And there was that neon again, lighting up as Timmy swung his head to look at Marcus. "Really?"

"Really," Marcus answered as he headed for the check-out.

"But...but, Marcus," Timmy called after him. "That one costs the most."

"I know, Timmy. The best one always does. Now, come on. We're wasting time."

Timmy jumped two feet off the ground and gave a whoop. "Cool!"

Back out on the sidewalk, Timmy running ahead, his small sneakers slapping the pavement, Rachel said, "You just won his devotion for life."

"It was only a couple bucks more."

"Timmy hasn't been used to getting what he wants. It means a lot to him. And it was very sweet of you to know that."

"Been there," he answered shortly. "How long has Timmy been with you?" he asked.

"Only a couple of months."

"His parents?"

"He never knew his father. His mother died last fall."

Marcus shook his head. "Rough. Any relatives?"

"None. At least none that ever came around or cared. He was close to his mom, I think, and she had to have been a good mother. Timmy's a good kid."

Marcus almost added that he was a lucky kid, but the incongruity of the statement coming out of his mouth stopped him.

They walked on, people passing, ladies ruffling Timmy's hair, stopping to chat for a moment with Rachel. Saturday afternoon in small-town America and he should have been feeling stifled as hell. But he wasn't. Instead he was breathing in the smell of new bread coming from the bakery they were passing. Instead he was watching how Rachel's simple white dress blew against her legs in the breeze. Instead he was chuckling at the sudden sound of Timmy whooping as they reached the park across from the Gale Guest House, with its small white band shell and Birch Lake glistening in the sun alongside of it.

He grabbed Rachel's hand and ran with her across the green grass, beneath the trees, and down onto the sandy beach.

They were both laughing by the time they reached the water's edge. She pulled him to a stop just as a gentle wave broke on the sand, and he swung her around, grabbing her other hand and gazing into her laughing face.

"You gonna kiss her?"

Startled, he looked down to find Timmy staring up at them. "What?"

"You gonna kiss Rachel, Marcus? 'Cause you both look like that gushy movie Aunt Frannie was watchin' the other night. Just before the guy kissed that lady with the blond hair."

Marcus laughed. "Well, I don't know, soldier. *Am* I gonna kiss her?"

Rachel twisted her hands out of his. "No, you're not!

Come on, Timmy, let's get that kite put together and see if we can make that dragon fly.''

"Saved by the voice of a child once again," Marcus muttered to himself as he watched Rachel and Timmy plop to the sand to start laying out the kite. Yeah, he'd have kissed her, all right. And she would have kissed him back. Luckily, Timmy had interrupted them. Because Marcus shouldn't be thinking about kissing Rachel. Not after what he'd seen on her face back at the newspaper office. Not knowing that she was a small-town girl, and he was allergic to small towns. Yeah, lucky Timmy was along to chaperon.

Only thing was, as he watched her head bent over the kite, the sun warming the champagne streaks, the breeze blowing her skirt around her knees, he wasn't feeling lucky at all.

And he was feeling even less lucky a half hour later as he watched her run with Timmy along the sand, dress blowing out behind her, wind tugging her hair out of its braid. Timmy fell suddenly, and he could hear the mixture of Rachel's laugh with Timmy's carried to him on the breeze. It did something to him, deep inside. But he didn't think he wanted to examine what that something was. Instead, he shouted and ran down the beach after them.

"Marcus! Look! The dragon can almost reach the clouds!''

"Timmy, you are one heck of a kite man."

Timmy chortled. "Think so? It's the dragon, Marcus. He can do anything.'' Timmy turned his sun-kissed, freckled face up to Marcus and it was impossible not to see the admiration in his blue eyes. "Thanks for gettin' him for me.''

Marcus ruffled his hair. "You're welcome, Timmy,'' he said around the sudden lump in his throat.

"You old softy,'' Rachel murmured.

Marcus carefully kept his eyes on Timmy running farther down the beach. "What?"

"You know what. He'll remember this day all his life."

Marcus tried to shrug off the feeling. "Big deal. I bought him a kite."

"You bought him the kite he wanted. And you helped him fly it. Big stuff for a boy who comes from poverty and never knew his father."

How well Marcus knew. But Rachel was already a danger to him. He wasn't opening up anymore to her. Not if he could help it.

He shrugged. "No big deal."

"You know better—" she began.

"Rachel!" someone yelled, and they turned to see Frannie running across the grass toward them.

"Grant needs you! Pile-up out on the Old Farm Road!"

Rachel immediately turned to Marcus. "Can you take Timmy home?"

"Sure—no problem. Get out of here."

"Thanks."

He watched her running beneath the trees, the leaves dappling her white dress with sunlight, tendrils of hair wildly answering the call of the wind.

He stood there and watched her until she'd disappeared. He'd recognized the war of expressions on her face. There was fear there, and excitement. Fear of what she might find, excitement to be in on the discovery, in on the chase. He knew the feeling well, he'd had it often enough himself. And suddenly he wondered if maybe Grant was right about Rachel—maybe she really was a hell of a newspaperwoman. And suddenly he was just itching to find out for himself.

He was about to run after her when he remembered Timmy. He turned to squint up the beach where the boy was running close to the gently lapping waves.

"Go ahead," said Frannie from his side. Surprised, he swung his gaze back to her.

"I've seen that look before. Go ahead, Marcus. Catch up to her. I'll stay with Timmy."

Marcus grinned. "No wonder Grant is in love with you."

Frannie shoved him with the flat of her hand on his chest. "Go on, get out of here. Take my car. The keys are on the table in the hallway."

RACHEL WAS STILL breathing heavily when she turned her car onto the highway. She'd run all the way back to the house, grabbed her purse and car keys, jumped in the vehicle and headed out, swearing all the while at the lack of real power in the engine. All the way out to Old Farm Road she felt like she was crawling and was amazed when she checked the speedometer that she was going sixty-five.

Less than five miles out of town, she came upon it. Red lights flashing obscenely in the morning sun, cars slowing to a crawl to gape at the convulsive line of twisted metal.

She swore under her breath as she counted six cars.

She pulled up to the other side of the road and parked on the shoulder. The ambulance was there, the attendants tucking a blanket around someone on a stretcher. She got out of the car and started across the highway.

There was no mistaking the plump form of Mrs. Cheevers under the blanket.

"Adelaide," she said when she'd gotten close enough. Adelaide Cheevers grabbed her hand.

"Rachel. Tell the mister I'm okay. Tell him not to worry. You know his blood pressure."

Rachel took her hand and squeezed it. "Don't worry, Adelaide. I'll bring him to visit you at the hospital myself," she managed to call out as the attendants took the older woman away.

A couple she didn't recognize kneeled next to a little

girl who was crying softly. Luther Ross's pickup looked sickly twisted, Luther still slumped in the front seat, a blood-stained cloth held to his forehead while a paramedic took his blood pressure. She recognized the small, sporty red car as belonging to Olive's teenage daughter, who stood hysterical alongside of it while Tommy Cole from the sheriff's department tried to question her.

But the car at the head of the grim procession was what really caught Rachel's eye. It was poised, nose pointed out, just on the edge of the ditch that separated the two-lane highway, like it had spun around, deciding at the last minute that it was going the wrong way. Rachel recognized the car. But what was really interesting was that Eric Ludington, the owner, was nowhere in sight.

A paramedic had taken over with Olive's daughter, trying to calm her, so Rachel waylaid Tommy on his way to his patrol car.

"Anybody bad?" she asked him, hurrying to keep up with his long strides.

"Don't know, Rachel. My guess is the little girl's got a broken arm. Adelaide Cheevers is on her way to the hospital. And Olive's oldest girl needs a good slap across the face. But it ain't gonna be me they accuse of police brutality."

"And Eric?

Tommy glanced at her. "Eric?"

"Come on, Tommy. That's Eric Ludington's BMW that decided it was going the wrong way over there. Where is he?"

Tommy shook his head. "You don't miss much, do you?"

Some compliment, thought Rachel. Eric's black BMW was the only one in town. And if that wasn't enough to recognize it right off, the vanity plates reading Eric 1 would have done the trick.

"Where is he?" she asked.

"Sheriff took him into town."

"He under arrest?"

That finally stopped Tommy. He swung around to look at her. "Why'd you ask that? You hopin', Rachel, honey?" he said with a short bark of laughter.

"Just doing my job, Tommy."

"Naw…he ain't under arrest. Just an accident is all. Skidded on oil or somethin'. But he was bellowin' as only a Ludington can about wantin' to see his own doctor. Sheriff obliged him. Probably at Doc Vanders's right now."

"Was he injured badly, Tommy?"

"Not far as I could see. He was walkin' under his own steam, hollerin' his head off."

"Thanks, Tommy," she called as she turned back toward the line of wrecked cars, hoping to find out who the couple with the little girl was. The *Bark* was only a weekly and this story would be old news by next Friday. Time to concentrate on the human aspect of the whole thing. Who were the couple? Where were they headed? And how did they feel about their pretty little girl lying out on the pitted surface of Old Farm Road, crying softly in the sun?

RACHEL BACKED AWAY as the paramedics loaded the little girl into the ambulance, watching as her parents climbed in after her. They were a nice family, who'd been heading off on their first vacation in years.

"What do you think?" she asked a paramedic as she hurried alongside of him on his way to the front of the ambulance.

"Broken arm—maybe a concussion," he said before he climbed in.

"Internal injuries?" she yelled up at him through the window of the ambulance.

He just had time to shake his head before the siren started up.

Well, that was a relief anyway, she thought, scribbling notes on a pad as she walked toward her car.

When she looked up, Marcus Slade was leaning against it.

"Couldn't stay away, huh?"

He shrugged. "Thought I'd catch a look at how you work."

"Right," she answered briskly as she walked past him. But the words had given her a little shiver. Marcus Slade, international television journalist watching her work. She wondered what he'd thought as she got into her car, intending to head over to the hospital.

Marcus knocked on the window.

She rolled it down. "What?"

"You heading for the hospital?"

"Right. Adelaide Cheevers was taken in. That's her and Sam's blue Chevy over there. Gonna see how she's doing. Check out information on the little girl. See if I can get a bead on why Eric Ludington cleared out of here so fast."

"Cheevers—that the old guy from the grocery store?"

"Yup. I told Adelaide I'd take him to the hospital myself but I need to clear up a few things first before I head over there."

She started the engine, and Marcus stepped back as she swung the car back into the road.

ADELAIDE CHEEVERS'S eyes finally fluttered closed, and Rachel gently pried the older woman's fingers from her own and laid them on the hospital bed.

"She going to be all right?" Marcus whispered from where he leaned in the doorway.

Rachel swung around.

"How long have you been there?" she whispered back.

"Long enough to know you could use a cup of coffee," he answered, holding out a foam cup to her.

"Thanks." She looked one last time at Adelaide Cheevers, running her fingers lightly over the woman's fore-head, then turned away from the bed and gladly took the cup from Marcus's outstretched hand.

"What are you doing here, anyway?" she asked him as they walked out into the hall.

Marcus shrugged. "Thought I better pick Sam up and bring him over. Good thing, too. The town wags had already gotten the news to him and he was pretty shook. I found him just standing out in front of the store, gazing blankly up and down the street like he was waiting for a ride."

"And so you gave him one?"

"Yeah. They waylaid him down at the front desk and forced some forms on him. Thought I'd come on up and check out the situation before he escapes the insurance department. I'd hate to see him walk into something he isn't prepared for."

Marcus wasn't sure he cared for the slight upturning of her mouth as he spoke or the amusement glittering in her eyes.

"So you can be a nice guy, huh, Slade?"

"Just interested in the story, Rachel, same as you," he said offhandedly.

"Uh-huh," she muttered as she started down the hall.

He started after her.

"What does that mean?"

She laughed softly, and the sound shot through him like quicksilver.

"It's not good, Slade, for a reporter to get paranoid. It colors everything."

That stopped him for an instant—long enough for her to get a few yards ahead of him. He hurried to catch up again.

"Oh, that's rich, *you* giving *me* advice on what makes a reporter."

That laugh again. "Isn't it, though."

''Look, if you think—'' A nurse in soft-soled shoes stuck her head out the door to give him a dirty look and purse her lips. He started over, lower this time. ''If you think that I'm going to stand here and take that from you—''

She kept walking, but the smile she gave him got to him on more than one level—one of them quite low indeed. In a place where his jeans felt suddenly too tight.

''No, actually, you're not standing anywhere and taking it. You're fighting to keep up with me.''

He opened his mouth, but he hadn't a clue as to what he was going to answer to that. Luckily he didn't have to answer anything, because just then the elevator doors to their right opened and Sam Cheevers stood there, looking lost, hands shaking as he asked the whereabouts of his wife.

THEY LEFT a much calmer Sam at Adelaide's bedside, Frannie's car keys in his pocket so he'd have a way home.

Rachel pulled her car out of the hospital parking lot and headed away from town.

''Where you going?'' Marcus asked.

''You know darn well where I'm going. The same place you would be if this was your story.''

Marcus knew. She was headed back out to the highway to check out the site of the accident again.

''So you feel it, too?''

She spared him a look before turning her attention back to the road. ''What do you think?''

He should have known. Grant Phillips was no fool. If he thought that Rachel was a hell of a newspaperwoman, then she probably was. Enough of one to know that something about this accident didn't ring true. Six cars don't pile up on a highway in the daylight where the speed limit is fifty miles an hour for no reason at all.

The last of the vehicles was being towed by the time

they got there, and Tommy Cole was about to move the sawhorses that cordoned off the area.

Rachel bounded out of the car and headed right for him. Marcus got out of the car and leaned against it, watching her go to work on him, finally getting him to agree to give her a few minutes before he opened the lane to traffic.

By the time Marcus sauntered over, she was on her knees on the asphalt, running her fingers over skid marks.

"What do you think?" he asked her.

"I think I smell a rat."

"The same rat I met in your office this morning?"

"The very one." She squinted up at him. "You see any oil slick on this road?"

He hunkered down next to her. "Nope."

She lifted her head, scanning the area. "Any injured or dead animals—or any sign of 'em?"

"Nope."

"No testimony of another car, shooting out of nowhere, or a kid on a bike, or a jogger from the city who didn't know enough to stay off this narrow road."

"Who'd you talk to?" he asked her as he watched her get to her feet.

"Adelaide, for one. Hers was the second car. All she saw was Eric Ludington's BMW head for the ditch then whip around suddenly and go straight for her."

"Think she was too scared and surprised to notice something?"

"Adelaide? No way. That woman delivered her first grandchild all by herself during an ice storm. She had the presence of mind to pour a bottle of olive oil on the floor behind a robber as he held a gun on Sam. The guy turned to run with his sack full of money and skidded right into a rack of cupcakes. Adelaide grabbed the gun, called the police and calmed Sam all at the same time."

Marcus laughed. "Yeah, I guess Adelaide would have noticed."

"You bet she would have."

Marcus stood. "So, what do you think?"

"I think I'm going to find out what Eric Ludington was doing just before he hit this highway."

AGAIN, MARCUS STOOD BACK and watched Rachel work. This time she charmed the bartender at the Shady Tree Pub into a nice long chat—and out of a couple of ice-cold beers. She brought them over to the table where Marcus was gazing out the window at a creek that flowed behind the pub, watching a tire swing shift in the breeze.

"He was here, all right," she said as she placed a tapper in front of him.

"You used to come here with him?" he asked, wondering if Rachel had ever swung on that tire swing—and if Eric Ludington had been the one pushing her?

"No," she answered shortly, offering no other information.

Marcus picked up the ice-cold glass and took a swallow. "So how did you know?"

She shrugged. "Only place out here a man like Eric Ludington would consider going—that is if he didn't want to be seen at the country club."

"A woman?"

"A redhead, according to the bartender."

"So after putting the make on you in your office this morning, he picked up a redhead and downed a few cold ones?"

Her head swung toward him, a genuinely surprised look on her face. "He wasn't putting the make on me."

He gave her a hard stare. "Could have fooled me."

She laughed and shook her head. "Every so often Eric likes to flex his muscles at the newspaper office."

"Yeah, and I know just which muscle he was flexing this morning."

Damned if he didn't sound just like some jealous guy,

he thought. Some guy who didn't want his woman messed with. Some guy who didn't like the idea of his woman caring enough to track down a man's movements—even if she was on the trail of a story.

Only Rachel Gale wasn't his woman. And if he kept his head about him, she never would be.

Rachel turned to look at him again. What was he digging at? Because he *was* digging. How much had he heard between her and Eric that morning? Enough for him to suspect that Eric Ludington had all but left her at the altar? She didn't want him to know that. For more reasons than one.

First, she couldn't bear the thought of a man like Marcus Slade knowing that she'd been rejected by a slimy piece of work like Eric Ludington. The other reason was a little more complicated—and far more dangerous to her peace of mind.

She didn't want Marcus Slade to know about her involvement with Eric because she didn't want him wondering if she was on the trail of this story as some sort of personal vendetta—a delayed evening-up of the score. That scared her. Because she knew that there was more to this accident than met the eye. She knew there was a reason the sheriff had gotten Eric out of there so fast. And the reason had to do with money and power and favors received. And wanting to find that reason had nothing at all to do with being jilted by Eric Ludington. And she couldn't bear the thought that Marcus, or anyone else in Birch Beach, might think so.

# Chapter Five

"What do you mean wait in the car? What do you think I am, some kind of kid?" Marcus almost squirmed when he said it, because that's what he was beginning to feel like—a kid. He'd stood back and let Rachel run with this story at the site, at the hospital, at the Shady Tree Pub, and lastly, at Doc Vanders's place, where all she'd managed to find out was that Eric had left already and wasn't badly injured. Marcus wasn't used to taking a back seat to anyone—let alone the star reporter from a small-town weekly. And he certainly wasn't used to being ordered to wait in the car!

He looked up at the massive Tudor-style house—all stone and mullioned windows—and said firmly, "I'm coming in with you."

"No, you're not," she answered just as firmly.

"Give me one good reason."

"Because I don't want you to."

He snorted. "Oh, really great reason, Rachel."

She thrust her chin up. "You said a good one—not a great one."

He watched her open the car door and climb out, waiting until she'd shut the door again before he followed, sliding silently out of the car and carefully letting the door rest without closing it.

She didn't even turn around to look at him. "You take one more step and you're dead, Slade."

"The woman has eyes in the back of her head," he muttered.

She did turn to look at him then, giving him a grin that stopped him in his tracks more effectively than any words she'd spoken.

"Doesn't every good reporter?" she asked, raising her brows in a good imitation of innocence.

He laughed, shook his head and leaned against the car, letting her think she was getting her own way for now. He'd think of a way to get even with her later. Right now he was having enough trouble resisting her.

THE LAST TIME Rachel had climbed these massive stone steps, she had been on her way to her own engagement party. It gave her the shivers just to think about it. Pushing a renegade strand of hair behind her ear, she lifted the knocker on the intricately carved dark wood door and let it fall. The sound seemed to echo, displacing the sound of birds and insects and the wind in the trees. Sort of like one of those horror movies where the forest goes still before something horrible strikes, thought Rachel.

It turned out the something horrible was Imogene Ludington, who—surprise, surprise—had answered her own front door.

"Yes?" she asked, a sweetly vague look on her face as she fingered the single strand of pearls around her chubby, pink neck.

Imogene Ludington wasn't really horrible—just weirdly out of it. A woman who had never even made it into the sixties, never mind the nineties.

"Mrs. Ludington," Rachel said, giving the woman who'd almost become her mother-in-law a kind smile, "I wonder if I might have a word with Eric?"

It seemed to suddenly dawn on Imogene just who was

standing at her door, for her plump cheeks dimpled and her pale blue eyes seemed to become more focused.

"Why, Rachel, my dear, how nice it is to see you." Her pudgy little hands fluttered like a couple of well-fed birds hovering about the feeder. "Why come in, dear, come in."

Rachel couldn't bring herself to step over the threshold. Imogene, scatter-brained on the best of days, had obviously forgotten that Rachel was a reporter for the *Bark* and wasn't here to sip tea, eat cucumber sandwiches and talk over the latest in gardening.

"I'm a little rushed for time, Mrs. Ludington," she said. "If I could just speak to Eric for a moment."

"But of course you can, my dear. In fact, it might be just the thing he needs," she confided with a girlish little smile. "He's been cooped up in his room since he got home and Lion has been grumbling and cursing. You could always deal with them better than I could, Rachel. Heaven knows, neither of them ever listen to me. I told Lion when he bought sonny that car that it was too fast, that one day sonny would have a little too much—"

"What is *she* doing here?"

At the sound of Lionel Ludington's words from behind her, Imogene suddenly seemed to lose all focus, her plump hand jerking up to the champagne-colored helmet that she regularly went in to Milwaukee to have relacquered, that vague look veiling her pale eyes again.

"Is there some problem?" Lion asked imperiously, pausing importantly at the first landing on the dark, dreary staircase.

"Why, no, dear. Rachel just wants to talk to sonny."

Lionel came down the rest of the stairs, a sure, steady stride, and Rachel was struck anew at just how handsome Eric's father was. Strange, given that their features and coloring were so much alike. But Eric always came across as a caricature of his more-commanding father.

"That would be impossible," Lion intoned in a voice carved out of granite.

"Well, I don't see why, dear. He's just been napping in his room all afternoon, and Cynthia is off in Chicago again." She turned to Rachel. "Our daughter-in-law just loves to shop. New York, Chicago—she's always off somewhere."

"I'm sure Rachel isn't interested in the habits of Eric's wife, Imogene."

Imogene nervously fingered the strand of matched pearls at her neck. "Why, no...of course not...I mean—"

Lion sighed heavily. "I'll take care of this, Imogene," he said, firmly placing his hands on his wife's shoulders and steering her away from the doorway. "You go get Alice to fix some tea."

"Oh, that would be nice, wouldn't it? We seldom get visitors anymore." Imogene bustled away toward the kitchen, where Alice, the amazon of a housekeeper, reigned, leaving Rachel alone with Lionel Ludington's piercingly blue gaze.

That deep, cold gaze had always given her a shiver in the past. She struggled against the same reaction now.

"Mr. Ludington, I'm here to get a statement from Eric about the accident that occurred at—"

"I'm well aware of when and where the accident occurred, young lady."

"Then, we'll skip the preliminaries, Mr. Ludington," she said, giving him a level gaze. "Now, if I may see Eric."

"Impossible."

"Why?"

"Eric has had a shock and he's resting. Perhaps you can try phoning him later."

Lionel started to shut the door, but Rachel stepped neatly into the opening. "Perhaps," she said in imitation of his own formal manner, "you would just tell Eric that

I've gathered some information on his whereabouts just prior to the accident and I'd like his comments before I quote any sources in my story.''

Lionel's eyes narrowed and he came a step closer, his coolly formal facade slipping an inch or two. ''Watch yourself, Rachel. Because if you don't, the whole town will. They'll watch you make a complete fool of yourself over my boy for the second time.''

She was stunned. But she knew there was no point in trying to convince Lionel Ludington that even though he'd insisted Eric call off the wedding, she had already made up her mind she could never marry him. Besides, she had a job to do.

She drew herself up. ''Is that on the record, Mr. Ludington?''

He hesitated for a moment, eyeing her coldly. Then he said, ''If you like, Ms. Gale. And you can also put *this* on the record. Tell Phillips that if he persists in letting his newspaper be used for revenge by a woman scorned, he's going to have a lawsuit on his hands.''

''Would that be *Grant* Phillips, Mr. Ludington?''

Rachel squeezed her eyes shut at the sound of Marcus's voice as he came up behind her. Of all the times for him to butt his nose-for-news into Rachel's business.

She slanted him a look. ''I thought I told you to wait in the car,'' she hissed.

''Oh, didn't I tell you? I don't take orders well,'' he said under his breath.

''Mr. Ludington,'' Marcus said, his voice taking on that impressive television journalist quality, ''do you have any knowledge of the whereabouts of your son at eleven this morning?''

Lionel's handsome face went dark red. ''Get out of here—now. Or I'll call the police!''

Marcus laughed dangerously. ''Yeah, do that, Ludington. And ask them to bring a breathalyzer because—''

The door slammed in their faces.

"Well that was certainly subtle," Rachel said, giving him a disdainful look. "If you'd calculated on how to get the door slammed in my face, you couldn't have done a better job." She turned and started down the staircase, stopping almost immediately to look back at him. "Unless, of course, you *did* calculate it?"

Marcus shrugged. "You weren't getting anyplace with him, were you?"

"We'll never know, will we?" she uttered as she started down the stairs again.

"And I suppose we'll also never know what Ludington was talking about when he mentioned revenge?"

She made her feet keep going, because if they stopped she'd end up looking at him, and that was the last thing she needed to do right now.

"That, Slade, is none of your business."

"Ahh, but it is. If it has to do with the story, it's my business."

"You're forgetting something, aren't you?"

"What's that?"

"This isn't *your* story. You don't work for the *Bark*."

That brought him up short, and he paused on the brick walkway and watched her walk the few steps to the car. "No," he muttered. "But I might very well own it soon."

She swung around. "What?"

He bit his bottom lip. "Nothing," he said, shaking his head and walking toward the car again. "Nothing at all."

Rachel seemed preoccupied on the trip back to town. Just as well, thought Marcus. Whatever was worrying her brow was keeping her from wondering about what he had said. He gave her a sideways glance. How much had she heard and what in the hell had made him say it? He had no intention of taking Grant up on his offer. He had only agreed to stay in Birch Beach a few days more to appease his old mentor—and to maybe get under Rachel's skin again.

He wasn't about to chain himself to a dinky little weekly in the kind of town that was poison to the soul. If he was around people like Eric and Lionel Ludington on a regular basis, he knew that somehow his fist would get buried more than once in their soft paunches. Their kind always managed to bring out the worst in him.

"Every small town has one, doesn't it?" he murmured.

"What?"

"A family like the Ludingtons. Father getting his power by walking over the backs of the rest of the town, mother always just vague enough to live in a constant state of denial, son that in any other family would be considered a loser."

Rachel's mouth twitched ruefully. "What did you do, Slade, research them?"

Marcus snorted. "Didn't have to. They're the same all over. And they make life hell for anyone who—" He stopped, not liking the sound of his own words, the self-pity too close behind the surliness.

He felt her looking at him. "Anyone who lives on the other side of the tracks?" she finished for him.

He gave a short, self-derisive laugh. "I sound like a kid who never grew up, don't I?"

"We all have things that are hard to let go of. Things that shaped our past."

He turned toward her. The sun and wind were in her hair again, the champagne streaks gleaming and stirring, keeping the brown from looking ordinary. Her sunglasses were sliding down her nose. He reached out his hand and pushed them back up with a finger. "Does Spinster Gale have secrets from the past that won't let her be?"

She gave him a look, a look that was self-evident even though he couldn't see her eyes. "None of your damn business, Slade."

"When you're on the trail of a story, everything is a reporter's business."

She waited until they pulled up behind a car at a red light before she turned to him. "But I'm not one of your stories, Slade," she told him. "There's nothing interesting enough about me to make me one."

His gaze moved lazily from her eyes to her mouth and back again. "Well, then, maybe we should work on that."

The light seemed to take forever to change. Which was just as well, thought Rachel. Her hands were actually shaking on the wheel. He had a voice calculated to stir the senses. A natural charm that he exploited to make people want to look at him, to make them not want to touch that dial. Men had envied him. Women had swooned over him. No doubt the body count left in his wake was high indeed. But whoever was doing the counting could just count her out.

"I think I can do without the kind of PR campaign you specialize in, Slade."

He laughed and tweaked her nose. She refused to acknowledge the shaft of raw pleasure that shot through her belly at the sound from his throat and the feel of his finger on her skin. With Eric Ludington she'd had enough of smug, self-satisfied men to last her a lifetime. And quick on the heels of that thought came the thought of Marcus Slade standing behind her while she'd talked to Lionel Ludington.

How long had he really been there? How much had he heard? How much had he guessed at? For all she knew he'd heard enough information to piece the entire story together. That's all she'd need to make his stay in the bedroom across the hall from hers even more enjoyable, she thought sarcastically, Marcus Slade with enough ammunition to bait her and make fun of her at every turn.

The light changed and she stepped on the gas, pulling

around the traffic lined up ahead of her and peeling out as fast as the car allowed.

She had a moment's satisfaction when Marcus Slade's hand came out to grip the dashboard.

HE COULD HEAR HER singing in the shower. She sang in the shower every morning—and it was driving him crazy. Not that she didn't have a sweet voice. She did. The part that drove him crazy was the image he had of her, her long hair dripping on her shoulders, her pale body soaped and slippery, water sluicing between her breasts.

He groaned and rolled onto his back just as the shower stopped running. Now she'd be climbing out, grabbing one of Frannie's fluffy white towels to pat her body dry. Then she'd be putting on one of those silky robes she was so fond of. And it would cling just a little to her slightly damp skin. He knew exactly how it would cling, too. He'd run into her on Sunday morning—and he vowed he'd never put himself through that again.

In fact, he'd been so shaken by the sight of her—and so seduced by the smell of country ham frying and the breeze drifting in with the scent of the crystal lake across the street—that he'd borrowed Grant's car and driven to the city, looking for action. He hadn't found any. Or maybe he just hadn't really wanted any. But this woman, this woman singing in the shower, this house, this town— this couldn't be what he really wanted, either, could it?

Maybe not, but you sure couldn't tell that by the reaction of his body. He had to will his limbs to stay put on the bed while the rest of his body stirred and hardened, the breeze that blew in the open window doing little to cool off his naked flesh.

What in the hell was he still doing here? True, the network didn't expect him back for weeks yet. But there *was* that redhead in Chicago. Hell, there were a lot of other places for him to go. He tried to tell himself he was staying on for Grant. Grant's news had made him feel mortal. Made him see how he'd missed the old man. Made him wish that he'd kept in touch more. Grant had cared about what happened to Marcus, believed in his ability and talent, urged him to go for all of it—and not stop until he'd gotten what he'd wanted. In short, Grant was the closest thing to a father Marcus had ever had. And he was staying in Birch Beach because he wanted time with his old mentor before it was too late.

"Yeah," he muttered, "so how come you're always trailing after Rachel? How come you're spending more time with Timmy than with the old man?"

He heard her come out of the bathroom, listened to her walk to the room across the hall from his.

"Shower's free," she called out to whoever might be wanting it next.

"And that would be you, Marcus, old boy. A nice cold shower is just what you need."

But once he'd gotten safely to the bathroom and shut the door, he found he wasn't safe at all. Her scent surrounded him, haunting the steamy air like a sensual ghost. That fresh, sexy scent she wore that fit her like it was made for her. His hand hesitated as he reached for her bottle of shower gel. But what the hell, he figured. He was already going through torture this morning. He picked up the bottle, flipped the cap open and breathed in the scent. While he stood there, the mirror started to clear of steam, and slowly his image came back at him.

"Marcus Slade, big-time war correspondent, perennial dodger of Cupid's arrows," he muttered to his image, "with his nose in a small-town spinster's bottle of shower gel." He flipped the cap closed and put the bottle back on the shelf near the shower. "Why don't you get the hell out of this town, man—before it's too late?"

THE DAMN BISCUITS smelled almost as good as she did. He sat across from her at breakfast, chewing one of Frannie's biscuits, deciding that today was the day. He was definitely getting out of Dodge.

He was just about to open his mouth to tell Rachel and Frannie the news when Timmy came shuffling into the dining room.

"Want some eggs, Timmy?" Frannie asked him.

"Naw," he muttered, his chin practically hanging low enough to touch his chest.

Marcus studied the boy for a moment. "Monday morning blues, soldier?" he asked.

Timmy just shrugged.

Frannie and Marcus exchanged a look.

"How about a biscuit, then," Frannie asked.

Timmy, staring at his plate, just shook his head.

"Well, Timmy, you've got to eat something," Frannie prompted. "You can't learn anything at school on an empty stomach."

"Ain't gonna be no learnin' today, anyway," Timmy grumbled. "Today's a special day. Gonna be sack races and baseball games and ice cream and hot dogs."

"Timmy, that sounds great," Rachel said. "Why the long face?"

"Yeah, soldier," Marcus put in. "When I was your age I would have jumped for joy at the prospect of a day of fun instead of learning."

Timmy kept his head down and kicked at the table leg. "Ain't gonna be no fun for me," he muttered.

"Nonsense," Frannie said. "You love baseball and ice cream."

Suddenly he looked up at Frannie—unmistakable, hopeful pleading in his eyes. "Can I stay home today, Aunt Frannie? I think I've got a tummy ache—yeah, that's it. I've got a tummy ache."

Frannie and Rachel exchanged glances. "Well, if you're sure you don't feel good, Timmy. But I hate to see you miss a day of fun with your school friends. And I'm sure they'll miss you when they're choosing up sides for a game.''

''Naw, they won't. 'Cause they're all gonna have their fathers with them.'' His blue eyes came up to look accusingly around the table, then his chin went to his chest again. ''And I don't have a father,'' he finished in a sulky mumble that was not like him.

Marcus looked up from his plate, a forkful of scrambled eggs halfway to his mouth, just in time to see Frannie giving him a look. When he shifted his gaze to Rachel, she was looking at him, too.

''Well?'' she asked, her brow going up, her eyes intent on not giving him a break.

''What?'' he asked back.

''You know what,'' she hissed at him.

He put his fork down and looked at Timmy's bent head. A cowlick stood out of the red thatch. If it hadn't been for that cowlick, he might have resisted. But it just made Timmy look even more vulnerable—even more needy. Would one more day in this burg kill him?

''Look, soldier, if you need a dad for the day, I'm free.''

Timmy's head came up, his face creased into a gap-toothed grin, and his freckles seemed to turn three dimensional.

''Really, Marcus?''

''Really, soldier. Now eat some breakfast so we can get over there and size up the other dads.''

THEY WON the sack race hands down.

''You wanna keep the trophy in your room, Marcus?'' Timmy asked.

''No, soldier, I think it should go in your room. After all, it *is* your school.''

Timmy was solemn for a moment, giving it some

thought, then he looked up at Marcus. "Okay. But you can come look at it whenever you want."

"Thanks, Timmy. I'll do that."

He didn't see any point in ruining the kid's day by telling him that he was leaving that night. They'd have this one last day in the sun together with no thoughts of the future.

"Looks like they're lining up for lunch, Timmy. Think your tummy ache can stand a hot dog and some chips?"

Timmy gave him a sheepish grin. "Sure, Marcus! Let's go!"

Heaped-up paper plates in hand, they turned toward the picnic tables.

"There's Stewie and his dad!" Timmy shouted as he headed over to a picnic table as fast as he could without dumping his hot dog.

Marcus followed more slowly. He wasn't looking forward to sitting around with some town yokel who probably would have a million questions about what really happened during the Gulf War, and then go on about how the war should have been fought. But this was Timmy's day, their last day together, and Marcus wasn't going to ruin it.

The man stood as Marcus approached and Marcus suddenly knew where Stewie got his big feet. The man was huge. Not fat, just built like a concrete block with a head perched on top.

He stuck out a huge hand. "I'm Stewie's dad, Kevin. How ya doing?"

Marcus shook the man's hand. "Great."

"Congratulations on the sack race. You guys were way out ahead." The man chuckled, and it sounded like rolling thunder. "Stewie and me went down three paces out. Maybe you heard the earth shake?"

Marcus laughed. "No, I was too busy trying to stay on my feet. You guys did great with the football toss, though. Was that your game in school?"

The man grinned. "Yeah, how'd you guess?"

"Never wanted to go pro?"

"Nah, I married my high school sweetheart, Stewie's ma. We own the Magic Mechanic down at the end of Main."

"Ahh, so you're the magic mechanic?"

The man grinned. "Yup. Never met an engine I didn't like."

Marcus snorted. "Wish I could say the same. I remember one in particular. A 348 that I'd dumped into a '67 Malibu convertible."

"Oh, heck, that 348 was trouble right from the start. I had a hard time liking her. But that Malibu—I remember that car—"

While they sat in the sun, munching hot dogs, the two men talked about cars, the benefits of fishing, Stewie's batting average at Little League and the excellent cherry pie down at the Buzzing Bee. It wasn't until they were choosing up sides for the softball game that Marcus realized Kevin hadn't asked him one single question about the Gulf War.

"Wow! Did you see the way Stewie's dad hit that home run! Man!"

They were walking home from the schoolyard, and Timmy was wound up and flying high on adrenaline.

"And then when you caught that fly ball that old Cindy Miller's dad hit, I thought the guys were gonna pick you up and carry you all over the schoolyard. Just like on TV!"

Marcus ruffled Timmy's red hair. "Yeah, it was quite a game, soldier. Quite a game."

He felt Timmy take his hand as his step slowed. He looked down at the boy.

"Thanks, Marcus. I never had a dad at Fathers' Day at school before."

And there was that lump in Marcus's throat again. That

warm feeling in his chest that he refused to acknowledge was entirely too close to a very vital organ. "Neither did I, soldier," he said.

They'd reached Knickerson's and Timmy stopped. "Let me buy you something this time, Marcus."

"What?"

"Come on." The kid tugged at his arm. "I got my allowance today. Seventy-five cents! Let me treat today!"

The smell of the place was becoming familiar to him. The wood of the floor, the candy behind the counter, Agnes Summers's overly sweet cologne.

Agnes came out of the back room, wearing shocking pink pedal pushers this time, with a blue flowered blouse and a yellow chiffon scarf tied around her neck.

"Well if it isn't the brigade from the Gale Guest House. What can I do for you today, boys?" she asked.

What she did for them was help them pick out a couple of balsa wood gliders—the kind that ran on rubber-band power—and ten cents' worth of burned peanuts. Only Marcus, as he hefted the white bag, suspected there was more like fifty cents worth in there.

They munched the peanuts while they walked home, chatting now and then about the baseball game and the sack race. When they reached the house they sat on the porch swing and put the gliders together. By the time Rachel walked up the sidewalk for supper, Marcus was sitting on the top step, his glider firmly stuck in a tree branch, while Timmy chased his around the yard.

"Got trouble, Slade?" she asked, shading her eyes to look up into the tree.

"Must have been some glitch in the engineering."

There was a glitter of amusement in her eyes when she looked at him. "Right."

"Well, Timmy's works well enough."

"That's what happens with things that say they can be

assembled by children, Slade. The brilliant mind can screw them up but good.''

''Very funny.''

''I'm surprised you're giving up so easily, though.''

''What does that mean?''

''Well, surely you were faced with more difficult situations in the Gulf. Seems like a glider up a tree would be child's play to you.'' A slight smile curved her wide mouth. ''Or maybe it just takes a woman.''

Before he could think of an answer to that, she'd kicked off her shoes and was on her way up the tree.

''Hey! Look at Rachel!'' Timmy shouted.

But Marcus was already busy doing that very thing. Her braid hung down her back like a little girl's, her trousers rode up as she climbed, revealing legs that were anything but. She seemed to know all the hand- and footholds.

''I see you've climbed that tree before,'' he yelled up after her.

''Of course,'' she called down. ''I grew up here, remember?''

''I guess I didn't picture you up in trees,'' Marcus called back, then wondered why he hadn't. Right now he was having no trouble at all picturing her in cutoff blue jeans and skinned knees, shinning up a tree to rescue a kitten or a kite. She reached the branch that had imprisoned Marcus's glider and stretched out her arm.

Her sleeveless shirt had pulled out of her trousers, revealing an inch or two of pale flesh, and Marcus, suddenly dry in the mouth, needed water.

''I can't quite reach it,'' she called. ''I'm going out.''

Marcus's gaze swung from the pale flesh to the limb. ''You're *what?*'' he called.

''She's going out on the limb, Marcus.''

Marcus looked down to see Timmy at his side, squinting worriedly up into the tree. ''Naw—she's not, soldier. She knows better.''

Then he heard the creak as she placed a foot on the old, frail limb.

"Rachel, are you crazy? It's a twenty-five-cent glider! That limb will never hold you!"

"This limb has held me lots of times. I just need to crawl out a ways and—"

There was a loud crack, the sound of shaking leaves, and Marcus found himself running forward, arms outstretched, hoping that by some miracle he'd catch her as she fell.

And Birch Beach must be the place for miracles, because he did.

She landed in his arms as if that's what she'd intended to do all along.

He threw back his head and laughed with relief. "Baby, if you wanted to get close to me you didn't have to go out on a limb to do it."

Rachel groaned. "Oh, very funny. Now put me down."

"Uh-uh, I don't think so. I think instead I should put you over my knee and give you a good spanking for pulling such a stunt."

"You wouldn't dare!"

"Wanna bet?"

"Marcus," she said in warning.

"I know, I know!" Timmy yelled, jumping up and down. "I know what you can do with her!"

"You got a better idea than a spanking, soldier?"

"Yeah! Take her across the street, Marcus. Dunk her in the lake. Girls hate that!"

Rachel gasped. "Whose side are you on, Timmy?"

"Marcus is my dad for the day," the boy said proudly. "Aren't you, Marcus?"

"Yup."

"So I'm on *his* side!"

"But who bakes you chocolate chip cookies, Timmy?" Rachel yelled as Marcus started for the street.

"You do," Timmy answered as he ran alongside. "But this is more fun."

They waited on the curb for a station wagon to pass. Rachel groaned again. "That was Mabel Harper. She'll have it all over town by supper time that you were hauling me around in your arms."

"Ah, small-town life. Isn't it wonderful, Rachel?" Marcus asked as he started across the street.

Rachel tried to wiggle out of his arms all the way to the water's edge.

"You ready, soldier?"

Timmy gave a peal of excited laughter. "Yeah!"

"Well, I'm not!" Rachel cut in. "Come on, guys, can't we do a little bargaining here?"

Marcus looked at Timmy. "What do you think?"

"No!" he shouted gleefully.

He looked down at Rachel, still wiggling in his arms. "You heard the boy."

"Ohh—I swear if you dunk me I'll never make another chocolate chip cookie as long as I live."

Marcus, who was just about to swing her out over the water stopped. "Hmm, that's a little harsh, don't you think?"

"No, I don't," she answered emphatically.

He looked down at Timmy. "How good are those cookies, soldier?"

Timmy thought for a moment. "They're mighty good, Marcus."

"Lots of chocolate chips?"

Timmy threw up his arms. "Thousands!"

"Hmm—"

"And I'll bake some this very night," Rachel put in.

Marcus made a show of chewing his lip for a moment. "Gee, I don't know, Timmy. That seems like a pretty good offer, don't you think?"

Timmy nodded solemnly. "Yeah, Marcus, I don't know

if I'd want to go through the rest of my life without one of Rachel's chocolate chip cookies.''

"Okay, Timmy, it's up to you. Do we take the bribe? Get the cookies and let her go?''

Timmy suddenly brightened. "Yeah! Let's do it!''

"Good boy, Timmy," Rachel said. "Now put me down, Slade.''

"Wait!''

They both turned to look at the boy. "Something else you want, soldier?''

He nodded so fast the cowlick on top of his head shook. "Yeah! I want you to kiss her!''

They looked at each other, then at Timmy, saying in unison, "What?''

"Kiss her!'' Timmy yelled as he jumped up and down on the sand. "Kiss her!''

Rachel narrowed her eyes at Marcus. "Did you put him up to this?''

"Of course not.''

"Then where would a seven-year-old boy get such an idea?''

"From TV, Rachel!'' Timmy cried. "Moms and dads always kiss on TV!''

"But...but,'' Rachel sputtered, "I'm not your mom.''

"Aww, just for today, Rachel. Please?'' he pleaded. "Marcus is my dad for today. You be my mom.''

Rachel looked down at his blue eyes squinting up at her, at his mussed red hair. But it was his hands that really got to her. He was crossing his fingers so tightly, the tips were turning red.

"Oh, all right, Timmy. Chocolate chip cookies, a mom for the day—''

"And the kiss! Don't forget the kiss!''

She rolled her eyes toward the blue sky, then looked at Marcus. "Well, what do you think?''

He shrugged. "It's not like we haven't done it before.''

"Don't remind me."

A slow, lazy grin spread across his mouth. "I bet I don't have to."

"Oh, shut up and kiss me. Let's get this over with."

"Well since you insist—"

He bent his head and placed his mouth on hers. Timmy's peal of laughter and clapping of hands filled Rachel's mind with sweetness. Then just as she was about to pull her mouth away, Marcus's mouth changed.

His lips parted, his tongue made a lazy stretch into her mouth. When it touched hers, she started to tremble so that she had to tighten her arms around his neck. And then his arms moved upward, letting her body slide down his, till her feet nearly touched the sand, pulling her in closer to him while he moaned into her mouth. And that was all it needed for her mouth to open wider, for her tongue to seek out his, for her hands to move up into his hair.

"Oh, yuck!" Timmy yelled. "That's not the way they kiss!"

They both started to sputter with laughter at the same time. "It's not?" Marcus asked against her mouth.

"No!"

"Should we try again?"

"No!" It was Rachel who'd yelled this time. One more kiss like that and she might forget that a seven-year-old boy was watching. Might as well be honest, she'd forgotten *that* time, too. And she'd wanted to forget that they were in a public park, the sun still fairly high in the sky. She'd wanted him to drag her down to the cool sand and—

His arms were still around her, his shirt in her fists, his mouth too close, his eyes too watchful. She started to pull away from him but his hands remained firm and hard at her waist. "I think you can let me go now, Slade. We've fulfilled that part of the bargain."

"Have we?"

She thrust her chin up, but refused to look at him. "Yes, we have," she answered firmly.

"Okay, Mom," he said, finally letting her go. "Let's go bake those cookies."

## Chapter Six

"Timmy? Don't you have homework to finish up?"

Timmy stuck his finger into the crockery bowl of cookie dough again, snagging up a huge hunk and shoving it into his mouth. "Mmm-hmm."

"Then why don't you get to it while the cookies bake? Then we can sit out on the porch and have some."

"But, Rachel, it's geography," Timmy wailed. "I hate that stuff! By the time I finish drawing that stupid map, the cookies will be cold."

Rachel straightened from digging out the cookie sheet from a lower cabinet. "Geography?" She grinned over at Marcus where he was sitting at the kitchen table chopping walnuts. "I bet 'Daddy for the Day' is good at that."

"Hey," Marcus protested, "I'm already working here."

Rachel came up behind him and peered over his shoulder. "I think that's enough walnuts, Slade. So, unless you want to do the dishes—"

"Yeah, Marcus! You don't want to do dishes! Besides, dads are supposed to help with homework. I'll go get it!"

Marcus shook his head as Timmy ran out of the room. "When does my stint as dad for a day end, anyway?"

"Midnight, I imagine," Rachel answered, picking up the bowl of nuts Marcus had chopped and dumping them into the cookie dough.

Marcus stood. "And what time does *our son* go to bed?" he asked.

Keeping her eyes on the nuts and chocolate chips swirling around her wooden spoon, she answered, "Usually between eight and nine."

He came up alongside of her, leaning against the kitchen counter. "Where's Frannie tonight?" he asked.

"Out with Grant." She was still careful not to look at him.

"Let's put him to bed early tonight, Mommy," he said in a voice that was too low, too suggestive for her peace of mind.

"Wh-why?" she managed to croak as she felt the back of his finger make a lazy, erotic trail along her bare arm.

He leaned in close enough for her to feel the heat of his breath against her cheek. She stopped stirring.

"So Mommy and Daddy have plenty of time to play before midnight," he answered. The words, more breath than sound, were followed by a stillness in the room where the only thing that seemed to exist was that almost painful, minute brushing of her flesh and the erratic beat of her heart.

Then suddenly sound and Timmy burst into the room.

"Got it!" he yelled, hoisting his geography book high into the air. "Come on, Marcus. Let's get this junk done so we can eat cookies!"

Rachel grinned and slanted a look up at Marcus. "Go on, *Daddy*. Homework time."

He leaned even closer. "Yeah. But even if the kid stays up till nine, that's still three hours till midnight, Rachel." His lips brushed her jaw line. "Think about it," he whispered.

And she found she could think of nothing else.

THE WIND HAD STARTED to pick up, dark clouds scudding across the evening sky, the porch swing rocking crazily.

A plate of cookies rested on Rachel's knees where she sat between Marcus and Timmy on the top step of the porch.

"Wow—gonna storm, huh, Rachel?" Timmy asked, breaking one of Frannie's rarely enforced rules and talking with his mouth full.

Rachel looked up at the sky. "Looks like it."

Marcus picked up another cookie and studied it intently. "Know something, soldier?"

"What's that, Marcus?"

"You were right about these cookies."

"Awesome, huh?"

"Yup, just like the lady who made them."

Rachel felt heat flood her body. "Knock it off, Slade," she muttered. "I've decided that your stint ends at bedtime, so you can just get that gleam out of your eye."

"Hey, you can't go changing the rules without a vote, can she Timmy?"

Timmy wrinkled his brow in a moment's deep thought. "I don't think so. What we gonna vote on?"

"When my tenure as Daddy ends. What do you think, soldier? Bedtime or midnight?"

"What's tenure?" Timmy asked while he licked chocolate from his fingers.

"Time. We're voting on when my time is up for being your dad for the day."

Timmy nodded emphatically. "I vote midnight."

Marcus grinned. "Me, too."

"Wait a minute," Rachel hurried to put in. "Why midnight, Timmy?"

Timmy stood up and skipped down the steps, running inexplicably out to the front walk and back again before answering. "'Cause," he said, "he's my dad for the day and the day ends at midnight. And you're my mom for the day, so that ends at midnight, too."

Marcus cupped her cheek and forced her to look at him. "The simple logic of a child," he said. But there was nothing simple·at all about what the look in his eyes was doing to her.

She avoided looking at him the rest of the evening. But when they both stood beside Timmy's bed and Marcus bent down to tuck the child in, it was, finally, impossible to avoid it. He was rangy and rough looking, scruffy five-o'clock shadow and hair in need of the attention of a barber. But when he straightened from giving Timmy a kiss on the forehead, a look of such tenderness passed over his face that her heart was affected where it had only been her body before. Something caught inside of that organ and held the beat until she thought she'd choke with the powerful emotion that welled up inside of her. She was more than relieved when he didn't even look at her, just left the room without a word.

"He's a cool daddy, isn't he, Rachel?" Timmy asked as she bent to kiss his cheek.

She brushed his carrot hair back off his forehead then straightened to cross the room and switch out the light. "Yup, Timmy. He makes a great dad for the day."

"Maybe if I wish hard enough..." The childish voice trailed off into the darkness.

"What, Timmy? Maybe if you wish hard enough, what?"

"Maybe he could be my dad forever. And you could be my mom."

Her hand came out to clutch at the door frame. "You think you'd like that, huh?" she asked in a surprisingly steady voice.

"It would be the coolest," he murmured, sleep already claiming him. She stood in the doorway until his breathing fell into an even pattern and then she walked down the hallway to her room.

Inside, she shut the door, grateful not to have to face Marcus again. The boy's words were still heavy in her chest. Timmy knew the precariousness of his situation. If something happened to her mother, if Frannie was no longer here for Timmy, Rachel could apply for foster-care status. But it would take time—and the child welfare services might take some convincing that a woman who'd never been married, who'd never had a child and who worked all day—and sometimes into the night—would be a fit caregiver for a seven-year-old child. And worse, since Timmy was part of an exchange program with the city of Milwaukee, if Frannie had to give him up for some reason, he'd be shipped right back there. Rachel hated the idea of him having to give up everything that small-town life could offer him. Hated the idea that she might no longer be a part of his life.

But when she undressed and crawled between the cool sheets of her bed, it wasn't only Timmy she was thinking about. It was Marcus. Not the sexy television journalist who had a way of maddening her even while he was tripping up her heart—but the man who took Timmy to a five-and-dime he claimed to despise every day, the man who'd won the sack race at Fathers' Day, the man who'd sat on the front porch steps and eaten chocolate chip cookies hot from the oven, the man who'd looked at a sleepy little boy with such tenderness.

And somehow Rachel knew, as she lay in bed and listened to the faraway thunder of a spring storm a county away, that the second Marcus Slade might be even more dangerous than the first.

THE CRACK WOKE HER, and her eyes shot open only to squeeze shut again against the bright flash of lightning that filled the room. The storm had moved into Birch Beach.

She opened her eyes again, feeling a damp wind on her skin. The rain was blowing into the room right along with the sheer, ruffled curtains.

She threw back the covers and got to her feet, crossing the floor to lower the window halfway. Smoothing the damp curtains down, she wondered how many other windows in the house were open. She decided she'd better check, or the whole place would smell damp tomorrow.

She worked her way through the house, closing windows as she went. When she reached the kitchen, she stopped abruptly. The door leading to the back screen porch was open. The chill going down her spine was caused by more than the wind that was blowing into the room.

Then she thought, *Of course.* In an effort to avoid Marcus, she hadn't come back down after tucking Timmy in. She was the one who had left the back door open.

Another crack of thunder sounded, shooting light in for a split second, before the room was plunged into darkness again. She crossed the floor on bare feet, her long, cotton gown billowing around her, then reached out to close the back door.

Something stopped her. A sound? Her skin felt alert and charged, while her body quickened. It was just the excitement of the storm, surely. But she decided to push open the screen door and take a look.

Just then thunder rolled and the sky lit for a heartbeat and she saw him standing there, silhouetted against the night.

SHE WAS WEARING that damn cotton nightgown again. The one that should have looked innocent. The one that should have made her untouchable, should have screamed *small town.*

But it didn't. It stirred him like nothing sheer and black ever had. Or maybe it was just Rachel that stirred him. Her streaked hair blew in the wildness of the storm. The gown billowed around her, tossing the skirt, molding the bodice against her soft breasts.

"I didn't know you were out here," she said.

He pushed himself off the railing and started toward her.

"I don't think it's quite midnight, yet, Rachel," he said boldly, half hoping that she'd turn tail and run. But she'd either lost all sense of self-preservation or else she just didn't give a damn.

"Oh—" was all she had time to say before he decided that he didn't give a damn either. He snaked an arm around her waist, pulled her up against his body and covered her mouth with his own.

Instead of resisting as he thought she would, she moaned, her sweet mouth opening to his—moist, tender and needy. So damn needy it sent a jolt through him like nothing he'd ever felt before.

He tore his mouth away from hers and looked into her face, her dark brown eyes, her wide, wet mouth, her pale skin glistening with misty rain. "Rachel," he murmured roughly, "I want you. I want you tonight—here, now."

"Oh," she said again, the sound a little surprised, a little trembling, but then she smiled, shyly, triumphantly, sweetly. And offered her mouth again.

And he wanted. Wanted to taste her tongue, feel her teeth, drink her breath. But he wanted her to know—without a doubt—that this night was all it would be. That he was leaving—and soon. That he had to.

His hand came up to cup her cheek. He looked into her eyes, deep and dark, yet somehow clear—shining with some sort of serenity.

"You know I'm leaving," he told those eyes. "You know this is for tonight—that I couldn't possibly stay here."

Her eyes smiled at him. "Don't worry, Slade, we don't own a shotgun."

He laughed then, his forehead resting on hers, his eyes caught in her gaze. And then the soft laughter stopped, and his hands tightened at her waist as he lifted her and spun her until he had her back pressed against the screen of the porch, holding her there with his body pressed into hers.

Their mouths couldn't seem to get enough of each other. The rain misted through the screen, wetting their flesh, their lips sliding, their tongues tangling. Slowly he loosened his grip, letting her slide down his body, till her feet touched the porch floor. And then his hands were on her breasts, feeling the heat of them through the damp, thin cotton of her gown, feeling her nipples leap to life as his thumbs found them. She gasped into his mouth and he smiled.

"You like that?" he murmured against her lips.

She nodded her head crazily. "Yes," she whispered.

"And do you like this?" he murmured again while one hand slid lower, down her hip, over her belly, till he cupped her between her thighs. He felt the jolt go through her then heard her ragged whisper. "Yes."

"Rachel," he murmured, his voice barely audible above the storm, "do you know what you're doing to me?"

She nodded her head, the smile in her eyes again. "The same thing you're doing to me, I hope," she whispered.

His hand moved on her, the heel of his palm moving slowly and deeply. "Tell me you want this as much as I do," he said. "With no chance of tomorrow, tell me you want this."

She gasped when his palm moved again. "Yes, I want this. And the hell with tomorrow."

That was all he needed to hear. Thunder rolled in, crashing spears of light to the ground while he took her down to the sisal rug on the floor of the porch and started to make love to her.

HIS HANDS FELT HOT through the cool damp fabric of her gown as they surprised her body in ways that were new to her. Her arms circled him, moved down his back, feeling taut muscle, while his hard body pressed hers into the porch, his mouth and hands seeking, caressing, making magic.

The rain misted over them as she found the hem of his T-shirt and swept her hands up the firm, smooth flesh of his chest. She was rewarded with his breath coming hard and fast against her neck and his sweet, raw words, "Rachel, touch me."

And she did. She moved her hand down his chest again and lower, till she'd found his zipper, inched it down and freed him. He was in her hand, heavy and hot, smooth and hard—so hard—

He gasped and his mouth found hers again, stealing her breath with a fierceness that should have scared her, but didn't. Instead it made her want more of it.

She stroked him, cupped him and every time her unpracticed hand moved she felt the breath tear through his lungs, felt renewed hunger in his mouth.

"Rachel—" He gasped, pulling away, getting to his knees and looking down at her. "I've got to have you, you know that, don't you?"

She looked up at him, at the smooth, tanned beauty of his body, at the fierce glitter of desire in his eyes. And she knew. Because it was the same for her. "Yes," she whispered. "Yes I know that. I have to have you, too."

He squeezed his eyes shut for just a moment, letting out a breath held so deeply she could see it move in his chest. Then his eyes were open again and his hands went to the tiny buttons down the front of her gown. But the same impatience that was making her move restlessly under his gaze fired him, and he tore at the buttons, finally taking hold of the low scoop of the gown and ripping it until her flesh was bare to him. His gaze swept her.

"You are so lovely," he whispered.

And in that moment she felt lovely.

He pulled off his T-shirt, his eyes only leaving her long enough to yank it over his head. He shucked down his jeans and then he was there with her, her legs parting to cradle him while he thrust into her.

And there was no stopping, no gentleness. Just a hot, hard thrusting that seemed to enter her soul and turn her body as wild as his. She answered every thrust, every kiss, every murmured word of need and desire. Thunder rolled. The storm moved over them across the sky. And when she cried out, her body convulsing around his, her soul shattering, she heard him roar, felt him shudder and knew he was shattering right along with her.

HE SHOULD HAVE BEEN relieved that he woke up alone. And he was, for just an instant. But by the time he'd gotten to his feet and walked over to his bedroom window he was wondering where the hell she was. Then he heard her sweet voice over the sound of the shower and he suddenly felt calmer. Of course. She had to get in to the paper. It was Wednesday. Deadline day for the weekly.

He threw himself back on the bed, grinning as he pictured her coming through the door at any second, dewy and fragrant from her shower. She would come over to the bed and bend to kiss him good morning. He'd take hold of her and pull her down alongside of him where he could taste her mouth, touch her softness, maybe make a little quick morning love before he reminded her again that he'd never said anything about forever.

He heard her come out of the bathroom. But it wasn't his door she went to. It was her own. He felt a moment's frustration until he remembered that the house bustled in the morning. She would be shy being seen going into his room. Shy about the wild passion they'd shared on the screen porch and the slower passion they'd shared for most of the night once she'd taken his hand and led him to his room.

He waited until he heard her go downstairs, then headed for the shower. Wouldn't do to appear too eager, give her any false hope. When he sauntered down the stairs himself, he figured she'd be in the dining room, waiting for him.

She wasn't.

Frannie murmured a good-morning while she made a list on a pad of paper over coffee. Timmy's place was empty, showing signs of a breakfast gulped hurriedly while Stewie had probably waited on the front porch.

He looked at the kitchen door. That was it. She was probably in there making him a special breakfast. Something calculated to make him remember not only last night but the morning after, too. Something like French toast or waffles.

Grinning, he sauntered over to the kitchen door, shoved it open and peered in.

It was empty.

"You looking for someone, Marcus?" Frannie asked from behind him.

"Where's Rachel?"

"She left for work already. Deadline today. She'll be busy."

He let the door swing shut again.

"Biscuits are still warm, Marcus. And Molly Finch sent over some of her homemade strawberry preserves just for you."

Marcus told himself that he was glad she was gone. Glad he didn't have to face her on the morning after, glad that he didn't have to remind her again that he was leaving, that last night had been merely an interlude—an isolated moment in the lives of two adults who'd taken what they wanted and were moving on.

He told himself all of that. But it didn't keep him from wondering how the hell the town spinster had moved on so damn fast.

"I THOUGHT he'd be gone by now," she muttered.

"Who?" Grant asked from inside an office.

"You know very well who," she answered testily, as she stood at the window in the *Bark* office and watched

Marcus come out of Crawford's Bakery across the street, munching a sugar doughnut. After his warning last night, she thought he'd get going while the going was good. She thought she'd never have to lay eyes on him again. She thought she'd be left with a sweet, hot memory, and not an uncomfortable flutter in her belly at the thought that maybe he'd decide to take his doughnuts for a walk across the street.

Grant walked up behind her to peer over her shoulder. "Maybe he just likes Hattie Crawford's doughnuts."

"Uh-huh—"

Grant chuckled as he headed back to his desk. "Well, they're damn good doughnuts, Rachel."

"Then why haven't you eaten any lately?"

"Maybe I'm watching my waistline. Trying to get your mother to give me a second look."

"And maybe I'm not going to get a straight answer out of you about anything today."

Grant just chuckled again but Rachel was seriously considering the changes in her boss lately. She hadn't seen him mosey over to Crawford's for over a week. The smell of herbal tea had replaced the stench of overboiled coffee in the office—and her mother had even laid in a good assortment of it. And he'd suddenly taken to eating soup and salad for lunch at the Buzzing Bee instead of his usual meat-loaf plate or stuffed pork chops. But strangest of all, Grant, who believed that you couldn't be a newsman without a bottle of Jim Beam in the bottom drawer of your desk, had gone on the wagon. That last late night with Marcus seemed to have been his swan song.

"You decided what you're going to do about that story on Eric, yet?" Grant asked.

Marcus had chosen a bench outside of Crawford's and was sitting there casually, munching on doughnuts from a white bag. Relieved, Rachel turned from the window.

"No. It's only speculation."

"But you do have the testimony of the bartender at the Shady Tree Pub."

"But that's all I've got that even comes close to resembling concrete. We could get crucified on it."

Grant shrugged. "You know how I feel. If we get sued…we get sued. Sells papers either way."

"So, basically, you're leaving it up to me?"

Grant took a sip of tea and nodded. "Yup. Your call, honey. Just make sure you make that call by noon deadline."

Luke Watkins breezed out of the layout department. "Front page is almost set, Rachel," he said. "You've got to make up your mind."

Rachel blew out a breath. "I know. I'll let you know soon, I promise."

"I'll hold off with the final layout until ten tomorrow morning," Luke said as he paused at the door to the layout room, "that's all I can promise. It's got to go into production by noon tomorrow," he added before shutting the door behind him.

"Holding the presses for a big story?"

She didn't have to turn her head to know that Marcus Slade would be lounging in the doorway with his usual scruffy elegance.

"Did you get your degree from the Lurk in Doorways School of Journalism, Slade?" she asked without looking at him.

"Hey, whatever gets the job done."

"So I hear," she muttered.

He strode over and sat on the edge of her desk, holding out the white bakery sack.

"Doughnut?"

The aroma from the bag was divine, but in the end her decision was based more on giving herself something to do rather than sit around while her body forgot that last night was a once-in-a-lifetime shot. "Thanks," she said with exaggerated sweetness. "I think I will."

She took one and bit into it. It was still slightly warm. "Mmm," she murmured.

He sat on the desk, watching her chew, an amused expression in his eyes. She tried to keep her gaze focused there, but it wanted desperately to slide down to his mouth. And she definitely didn't want to go that route. Definitely didn't want to look at that mouth and remember all the things it had done to her the night before.

"Don't you have something to do, Slade?"

"Yeah," he said. "You've got a little bit of sugar right at the corner of your mouth. I think I should—"

Before she became fully aware of what he was about to do, he leaned forward and ran his finger over her mouth, then brought the finger up to his own mouth and licked it.

And Hattie Crawford's lighter-than-air doughnut almost got stuck in Rachel's throat. She gulped it down and stood. "I've got to go."

"You going down to the town meeting?" he asked, following her to the door.

"None of your business."

"Good. That's where I'm headed. I'll walk with you."

She stopped and faced him. "I thought you were leaving town today?"

"I was. Then I heard about the town meeting from Frannie. Can't leave till I find out if they're going to lower the boom on Knickerson's, can I?"

She put her hands to her waist. "A few days ago you could have cared less what happened to the five-and-dime."

He watched the flash in her eyes and knew what she said was the truth. But the few days in this town had changed him. Suddenly he cared a lot that Knickerson's would be around to supply Timmy with marbles and gliders. And he hoped they'd be around for a long time to come. "People change," he told her, before he had a chance to stop the words.

Her eyes searched his, and for an instant he was almost afraid of what she would find. Then she turned around and left the office.

He stood there and watched her leave, then he crumpled the last doughnut in the bag and tossed it toward the garbage can, swearing when it missed.

"Something bothering you, hotshot?"

"Yes—no! Hell, I don't know!"

Grant chuckled. "I think you've met your match, boy. You intend to do anything about it?"

"Yeah," Marcus said over his shoulder as he headed for the door. "I intend to get the hell out of this town."

But once he was out on the sidewalk, he didn't turn toward the Gale Guest House to pack his bags. Instead he turned the other way and started after Rachel. By the time he'd caught up to her, she'd gathered a small entourage of town folk on their way to the meeting.

"It's scandalous," Miss Huffington from the library was saying.

"Worse," said Mabel Harper with her usual need to one-up Ariel Huffington. "I don't know what those Ludingtons are thinking of."

"Their pockets, as usual," Olive said as she jingled change from tips in the scalloped pocket of her waitress uniform.

Marcus listened with an attentive ear, then asked Rachel, "Are the Ludingtons involved in this, too?"

"They're involved in just about everything that goes on in this town. In this case it's their land the town council is considering rezoning so they can lease it to Big Bill's."

"Sounds like most people aren't in favor of it, though."

"Right. But the Ludingtons carry a lot of weight in this town. The people who matter listen to them."

The town meetings were held in the American Legion Hall just north of the band shell.

"Norman Rockwell strikes again," Marcus murmured as the small procession filed up the redbrick walk to the white clapboard structure, with its wide porch and American flag whipping in the breeze from its pole. The town was unbelievable. There were so many houses painted white that Marcus wondered if the town fathers owned stock in Sears. All that white wood looked to him like it was painted every spring. The beach was so clean it was a wonder the sand was allowed to show footprints. And the people were so homey and friendly he was becoming suspicious that he might be in a Stephen King novel, and Molly Finch, who looked right at home on the Legion Hall's wide, white porch with a gardening hat perched on her head, would suddenly turn into something evil. Maybe she merely wore those huge hats to hide the horns sprouting from her skull.

"Yoo-hoo, Mr. Hunk!" she chirped when she saw him. "I'm so glad you're here. Have you heard what they're trying to do to Knickerson's?"

Miss Finch put her tiny hand in the crook of his arm, and Marcus allowed himself to be led into the hall. Where, in the next two hours, he found out exactly what they were trying to do to Knickerson's.

THE AIR WAS FILLED with chatter as the crowd tumbled out of the Legion Hall after the meeting. Rachel had every intention of heading right back to the office. In fact, she'd rushed out of the hall so fast that she'd completely lost sight of Marcus—which had been the plan all along.

She drifted down the steps with the crowd, finding herself imprisoned by people swarming around her, making comments, asking questions. Ordinarily, she'd have been all too happy to linger—drawing people out, looking for quotes. But today she just wanted to put space between her and the man who'd held her in his arms half the night.

. Suddenly her hand was snagged and she found herself being pulled from the crowd. The relief of breaking out lasted just long enough for her gaze to run from the hand holding hers, up the arm and into the face of Marcus Slade.

He started to drag her toward the park.

"What do you think you're doing? I've got to get back to work. Let go of me."

He held fast to her hand as she tried to twist it free.

"We need to talk," he told her.

"Who says?" she asked belligerently.

"I do," he answered, leading her under a spreading oak to a bench and pushing her down onto it. "Now just sit and cooperate for once."

"Last night you said you didn't want to rehash—"

"This isn't about last night," he cut in.

"Oh," she said, feeling chastened and slightly stupid. "What do you want to talk to me about, then?"

"Knickerson's."

*That* got her attention—well, not completely—off the sight of his thick, dark hair blowing in the sun. Maybe nothing would, considering she now knew what that hair felt like clutched in her fingers. She swallowed, and it hurt her throat.

"What about Knickerson's?"

"I think you might have the power to save it."

Her mouth dropped open. "Me? But how? And since when do you care?"

WHEN HAD HE STARTED caring? Had it been the first time Timmy had taken his hand and led him into the cool, dim, fragrant oasis of the dime store? Had it been the time Timmy had bought him the glider?

He looked up into the tree branches and stared at the clear blue sky through the leaves. He blinked. It was an aberration, of course. A fantasy he was allowing himself to live in for a few days before he went back to reality— his reality. Which would be some Eastern European country where the dime store was being more than just forced out of business. It was being bombed off the face of the earth.

"Tell me how you think I can save Knickerson's?"

Rachel's voice brought him back with a jolt. He'd been back in Bosnia, watching a street all but destroyed by firebombs, hearing a little boy cry for his mother.

His jaw tightened. He'd seen enough destruction to last a man more than one lifetime. And all he'd been able to do was report it. His gaze scanned the crowd lingering outside the Legion Hall, then came back to rest on Rachel's questioning face. It came to him that in Birch Beach he might be able to do something to change the path of destruction.

"Are you planning on running that story on Eric Ludington in Friday's paper?"

Rachel blinked, then looked away from him so quickly that he knew he'd hit on something. A million questions rose on his tongue, but he kept silent, watching her carefully.

She stood up and paced a short distance away from him. She wore trousers today, tailored linen trousers, and a soft, cream-colored short-sleeved shirt, her bare arms freckling in the sun, her breasts outlined by the breeze off the lake molding the shirt to her body. How could a woman who dressed like this, who acted like this, get to him so? How could it be that instead of getting out of Birch Beach as fast as he could, all he really wanted to do was take hold of her hand and stroll beneath the trees with her, down to the water's edge, and watch the breeze trying to tug her hair free? All he wanted to do was tell her to forget what he'd said the night before if she would just promise to come to his bed again that night.

Finally she answered him and what she said made him forget all about the longing in the pit of his gut.

"I don't know," she said.

"*You don't know?* But if you wait another week—"

She paced back to him, looking up at him with some sort of sad determination in her eyes. "I might not run it at all, Slade."

"Are you crazy? Do you realize what you've got? You've got a prominent citizen who caused several injuries because he was driving drunk. You've got a sheriff's department that spirited him away and helped cover up that fact. You've got—"

The look in her eyes hardened. "I know what I've got, Slade. What I've got is a lot of unsubstantiated conjecture."

"The bartender at the Shady Tree?"

She shook her head. "Not a reliable source. He's an outsider. His job—"

Marcus thrust his hands into his hair. "His *job?* What is this, the dark ages?"

Rachel glared at him.

"Oh, yes," he said, barreling on, "the place where time stands still. That's Birch Beach. The place where outsiders are shunned and bartenders are—what, Rachel? What are bartenders in Birch Beach classified as?"

"Slade, you don't know what you're talking about."

"Oh, yes I do. Listen, I've spent my career reporting things with no bias—watching, listening, never doing. This could make a difference, Rachel."

"In what?"

"In what happens to Knickerson's. Print that story and the people who have power in this town will think twice about going along with Eric Ludington."

She stared at him. He thought for a moment he had her. Thought that she would say, Yes, of course—he was right.

It seemed so damned right! And out here under the clear blue sky, possible—entirely possible.

When she opened her mouth to speak, he thought he knew what she was going to say. He was wrong.

"It wouldn't work that way, Slade. It should, but it wouldn't. Not this time."

Marcus Slade found himself in a position he'd rarely been in: his mouth hanging open with nothing to say. She turned and started to walk away.

He started after her. "Why wouldn't it? Isn't it worth a try? Don't the Knickersons deserve—"

She swung around on him. "Don't you tell me what the Knickersons deserve. You've been here five days—I've spent my life in this town. Sure, you've had your kicks taking Timmy over there every day and spending some money on him. But when you're gone—which we both know will be soon, now—Timmy and I will still be here."

"And so should the five-and-dime, Rachel. I thought that's what you wanted."

"It is. But it's more complicated than that."

"Then tell me about it. Talk to me, Rachel."

She stared at him for a moment, then shook her head and turned and walked away.

This time he let her go.

## Chapter Seven

"Hey, Marcus!" Timmy came running down the school steps, a huge sheet of paper in his hand.

"What have you got there, soldier?" Marcus asked him.

"It's one of your helicopters. See?"

Marcus took the paper and held it in both of his hands. "Hey, Timmy, it certainly is. You draw this all by yourself?"

Timmy nodded. "Yup. Made it just for you."

Marcus looked down at the boy, his bright carrot hair ruffled by the wind, his blue eyes squinting in the sun, the pride clearly visible in them. And something more. The need for acceptance. The need for love.

Marcus recognized that need. It had been inside of himself for a long, long time. But he'd always brushed it aside, refused to look at it, refused to take it out and let it be trampled on by someone who didn't give a damn. With Timmy he felt safe—for maybe the first time in his life. He took the boy's hand.

"I'll keep it forever, Timmy. Wherever I go, it'll be with me."

Timmy wrinkled his nose. "You talking about leaving again, Marcus?"

Marcus laughed. "I've been talking about leaving since I got here, haven't I?"

Timmy nodded again. "Yup. But you keep stayin'."

"Yup," Marcus answered. "I keep staying."

But tomorrow would be it. He'd promised himself that. As soon as the deadline for the *Bark* arrived, as soon as he knew that Rachel had done the right thing and printed the story on Eric Ludington, he was gone. And she *would* do the right thing. She had to. If she was genuine, if this town was genuine, then it would work out. She'd print the story, the five-and-dime would be saved. He'd never believed in fairy tales—or miracles. But when he'd caught Rachel in his arms as she'd fallen from the tree trying to rescue his glider, for that one moment he'd believed that maybe miracles did exist. He was going to hold out for another one.

And then he was getting out, before he allowed himself to dream of something that might come true.

"Come on, Timmy. Let's head over to Knickerson's and see what we can find today."

When they left Knickerson's, Timmy had a book on birds under his arm and another idea in his head.

"I bet we can find some of these birds right in the yard, Marcus. What do you think?"

"I think you're probably right. Heck, if I was a bird, I'd sure hang out at the Gale Guest House hoping for a few of Frannie's biscuits."

Timmy chortled. "Hey! Let's see if she has any left from this morning, okay, Marcus? We can feed the birds with them."

"Sure, Timmy," he said. And Timmy chattered the rest of the way to Elm Street, talking about the teacher he would have next year, and about how Stewie's dad had an autograph from a Green Bay Packer.

They'd almost reached the guest house when Molly Finch called out from her front porch.

"Yoo-hoo, Mr. Hunk!"

Marcus grinned and shook his head before saying, "Yes, Miss Finch? What can we do for you?"

"I've got a potted plant that's just dying for some fresh air but the Lord knows I can't lift it myself. Would you—"

"Sure, Miss Finch. I'd be happy to."

Molly Finch's house was so full of furniture and bric-a-brac that Marcus had to walk sideways. But it was clean and the smell of something freshly baked wafted through the house from the kitchen.

"That big fern over there, young man," she said, pointing into the dining room.

And it *was* big. Gigantic. "That's a beauty, Miss Finch."

"My, yes. Isn't it? That plant is over twenty years old. A gift from my last gentleman caller."

"Why, Miss Finch, you don't mean to say that you haven't had a gentleman caller for twenty years? I would think the bachelors in this town would be pounding your door down."

Molly Finch tittered and fluttered. "Oh, go on with you," she said, tapping his arm lightly. "A town this size doesn't exactly attract fun-loving, unattached men, you know."

"Then they don't know what they're missing."

She tittered again and blushed. "Why, Mr. Hunk, I do believe you're flirting with me."

He leaned over and brushed her cheek with his lips. "I do believe you're right."

Her peel of laughter filled the house and his senses. Who would believe it? Marcus Slade spending the afternoon flirting with an eighty-year-old woman? If he didn't leave this town soon, he might end up taking her to an ice-cream social. And even worse, he'd probably enjoy it.

"Now you get your mind on business, young man. That fern belongs out on the front porch. Likes to spend its summers there."

"Then we better give it what it likes, hadn't we?"

"Oh, indeed," she said, smiling and blushing while she led the way back outside and showed him where to set the wicker fern stand.

Timmy was on the porch steps looking through his new book.

"Would you boys like some lemonade for your trouble?"

Marcus was about to say no...but what the heck. He had another day to kill in Birch Beach, and Molly Finch's front porch, with its ancient wicker furniture heaped with colorful cushions was looking like a good place to kill part of it.

"That'd be great, Miss Finch."

"And pound cake? Do you like pound cake, Mr. Hunk?"

"So that's what smells so good."

"I like pound cake!" Timmy piped up.

Miss Finch giggled girlishly. "All right, then. Pound cake and lemonade all around. I'll be right back."

After she'd gone back into the house, Marcus settled into a wicker rocker. The spring day was warm and fresh. He thought he'd never smelled air so fresh. The countryside of some of the places he'd covered was beautiful, but it had always been marred by the war or skirmish just miles away. He rocked and listened to the breeze and much to his surprise, he didn't feel a bit restless. No, at the moment he felt as though he could sit on this porch forever and watch the fern fronds dance in the sun and wait for a piece of Molly Finch's pound cake.

"Here we are," she said, and Marcus stood and took the tray from her, setting it on a wicker table.

Timmy came and got his cake and lemonade, pointing out a few birds to Miss Finch, asking questions, then went back to sit on the steps again.

"He's a sweet child, isn't he?" Miss Finch asked.

"Yes, he is," Marcus answered.

"He's lucky to have Rachel and Frances to look after him."

"Yes, he is," Marcus said again.

"Just think, if Rachel had married Eric Ludington she'd have children of her own almost as old as Timmy."

Marcus suddenly found it difficult to swallow the pound cake he'd been chewing.

"Rachel is the kind of woman that should have been a mother," Molly Finch went on.

The cake stuck in his throat. Marcus grabbed his glass of lemonade, gulped a mouthful then set his glass carefully down. "Eric Ludington and Rachel Gale?"

"Why, yes. Didn't you know?"

"Didn't I know what?"

"They were engaged. Years ago."

"Engaged?"

"My, yes. Almost made it to the altar, too. But Eric always was a willful boy."

"What do you mean?" Marcus asked.

"Why, he jilted her. One of the town's biggest scandals. Well, except of course for the time that Wendell Craft, rest his soul, decided to go skinny-dipping right in the middle of the day. But that was Fourth of July," she said, giving a knowing little nod, "and everyone knows Wendell was a little too fond of spiked lemonade."

Miss Finch went on, but Marcus wasn't really listening. Rachel and Eric? Engaged? And Eric had jilted her?

He leaned back in the rocker and looked up at the porch ceiling. He couldn't even imagine it. How could Rachel have ever loved a man like Eric Ludington enough to want to marry him?

And then he was sitting bolt upright because the next thought was even more unsettling. Was she still in love with him? So in love with him that she would compromise her integrity as a reporter and refuse to expose him?

No. Not the Rachel he knew. Not the Rachel he'd made love to the night before. Not unless he was very wrong about her.

He got up and walked over to the porch railing, looking out at the town. And why should that surprise him so much? He knew better, didn't he? He knew people were capable of just about anything. And he knew that towns like he'd begun to believe Birch Beach to be didn't really exist. He'd just forgotten for a while.

THE BIRDS in the Gale Guest House backyard loved Frannie's biscuits. The sound of Timmy's laughter floated to Marcus where he sat on the glider on the back screen porch. The same screen porch where he had made love to a woman who was still in love with another man.

A man who wore white shoes and a white belt.

Man, oh man. Could he pick 'em.

Well, he hadn't really picked Rachel. She'd just sort of happened along—just like all the love songs warned.

Love? No, he wasn't in love with her.

Was he?

Well, it didn't matter either way. Because Rachel obviously had her affections tied up elsewhere. He looked at the porch floor and remembered her lying there, remembered her pale skin misted by the rain. Remembered the effect her soft cries and gentle hands had on his heart as well as his body.

He stood up suddenly. Why wait till tomorrow to leave? Why stick around to be let down by the woman and the town? Why not go upstairs right now and get his gear together and split?

But when he turned toward the kitchen door, he ran right into her. Rachel.

"Oh...sorry." He gave her a hard look, then started around her.

"Are you coming tonight?" she asked.

He stopped. "Tonight?"

"The concert across the street. It's the first of the season. The Fire House Band is playing."

Timmy banged through the screen door. "Sure he's coming, aren't you, Marcus?"

"Well..."

"Aunt Frannie made fried chicken for a picnic, didn't she Rach?"

Rachel smile at the boy. "Yup. And I've got some apple cobbler in the oven."

Just as she said it, he smelled it. The sweet, spicy scent of apples coming from the kitchen. But it couldn't wipe out the scent of her, standing next to him, fresh, sweet and uncomplicated. Another deception of the senses. Because Rachel Gale wasn't uncomplicated at all. Rachel Gale was possibly a woman so much in love with a man who jilted her years ago that she might help in a cover-up that, if the truth came out, could help save a town from dying.

And he couldn't help it. He wanted her. Still.

And he wanted to sit in front of that band shell across the street and eat fried chicken and laugh with Timmy and listen to corny music from another time.

"You're gonna come, aren't you, Marcus?" Timmy asked again.

"Yes," he answered, before he could talk himself into reason. "I'm gonna come."

RACHEL MOVED OVER on the blanket to make room for Adelaide and Sam Cheevers. Adelaide was looking like her old self again, a big bowl of her potato salad in tow. Sam had brought cold cuts from the market to go with Molly Finch's home-baked rolls. Olive, who, everybody said, couldn't bake a pie that somebody else had put together, had brought a box of Twinkies and her teenage daughter and her boyfriend seemed to be making a meal of them.

The evening breeze was just cool enough to be comfortable, and the boys from the firehouse were giving a peppy rendition of "And the Band Played On."

It should have been a perfect evening. And it would have been, thought Rachel, if it hadn't been for Marcus Slade sitting up against an oak tree glowering at her.

"Marcus," Frannie said, "that look on your face could flatten an angel food cake."

"Yeah, hotshot," Grant added. "What's the matter, don't you like the music?"

"The music is just fine," Marcus answered, his dark gaze still on Rachel.

"Well, hotshot, it can't be the food. The ladies of the town have outdone themselves."

"The food in this town is the one thing you can count on," Marcus returned.

Rachel had had just about enough of him. She didn't particularly care why he was in a mood, and she sure wasn't going to waste a beautiful evening trying to figure out just what that mood was. She stood, smoothed down her denim skirt and said, "I'm taking a walk," then headed toward the water.

The moon had risen and a few stars had joined it in the darkening sky. As she reached the water's edge the band behind her hit a few sour notes and she smiled. The Firehouse Band never would be perfect. But then what was?

"Rachel—"

She stiffened at the sound of his voice.

"We need to talk."

She shook her head, refusing to turn and look at him. "No we don't. We have nothing to talk about. No future, remember?"

His hand touched her hair and she shivered, pulling the sweater draped over her shoulders more tightly around her. "Don't," she said.

"I still want you, Rachel."

The words were as soft as the water lapping so near her feet.

"Tell me you still don't want me."

She closed her eyes. "You ask for too much, Slade. Maybe you always have. Maybe that's why nothing has ever lived up to your standards."

He gave a short, bitter laugh. "I thought *you* might."

She did turn to look at him then. "Me? Haven't I done just what you wanted? One night? No regrets. No expectations."

He made a small, impatient movement with his head. "That's not what I'm talking about."

"What then?"

Eric Ludington, he wanted to say. The story that could save the five-and-dime, he wanted to say. But when he looked down at her, looked at her sun-streaked hair blowing in the moonlight, looked at her clear brown eyes and that wide mouth that he knew could drive him crazy, he wanted nothing more than to take her into his arms.

"Dance with me," he said.

Her mouth dropped open. "To the Firehouse Band doing 'Stars and Stripes Forever'?"

"To anything and nothing, Rachel. Just come into my arms."

And she did. She took two steps, and then his arms were around her, swaying with her to a music he knew that only the two of them could hear.

He nibbled her ear, traced it with his tongue and felt her arms go around his neck, her fingers run into his hair.

He pulled back and looked down at her. "I need to kiss you again, Rachel."

She smiled a little sadly. "I know. I need that, too."

And so he let his lips touch hers while the night came the rest of the way down and the music played and the crowd behind them ate and sang and laughed. And it was enough, just that sweet, simple kiss. He put his arm around her shoulders and started walking along the shore.

"It's funny," she said.

"What is?"

"I always dreamed of this. Of being with a man on a night like this, of a few quiet kisses and a moonlight stroll."

He'd never dreamed of it. Ever. And yet it seemed so right. With all the differences that lay between them, with disillusionment maybe just around the corner, this night, this park, this moonlight, this woman—it all somehow felt right.

"See that tree over there?" he said, pointing at a huge oak tree.

"Mmm…the oldest oak in town."

"I want to stand under it with you and neck."

"In front of all these people?"

"Part of the fun, Rachel. Trying not to get caught. Maybe not giving a damn if we do."

She laughed softly, and he took her hand and started to run. By the time they reached the oak on the far side of the park, she was laughing breathlessly along with him. He pressed her back against the tree, kissed her nose, her chin, her eyes. And suddenly she wasn't laughing anymore.

"Oh, Marcus," she whispered. And he knew the yearning was inside of her, too. The yearning for something simple and sweet and carefree.

And he gave it to her. His mouth covered hers, sweetly, almost chastely, until he heard her sigh, felt her heartbeat quicken. He deepened the kiss, just enough to drive them both to the edge of craziness, but not over it. Then his mouth was buried in her neck, his arms holding her tightly, not allowing himself more. Creating sweet torture for them both.

She laughed softly again. "I feel like a teenager," she said.

"Me, too. Only not the teenager I ever was. Something better."

He looked down at her again and brought up a hand to trace her mouth with his fingers. "Maybe Birch Beach really is the place for miracles," he murmured.

"Maybe," she whispered back. "Maybe."

And then she pressed her lips to his and his mind no longer wanted to think.

It was Timmy who found them in the end.

"Come on, you guys! The concert is over. Aunt Frannie says it's time for bed!"

"Does she?" Marcus asked, his gaze still caught in Rachel's. It seemed like they'd been doing nothing but gaze into each other's eyes and kiss softly for hours.

She smiled. "Behave yourself, Slade."

"Gonna make me?" he asked.

"Yes," she answered simply. And he knew she would. He knew he could go to her room tonight and she wouldn't let him in. But he also knew that he wouldn't try. Because this short, sweet time meant more to him than any hot, sweaty roll in the hay could.

"Come on!" Timmy called again, before he started to run toward the others.

Marcus took her hand and held it all the way back to the house.

HE LAY IN BED for hours—sleepless, mind cluttered with thoughts. She would do the right thing. By tomorrow at noon, he'd know. But then what? Could he stay here? Could he fall in love with her?

Had he already?

Tonight under the stars, he'd kissed her like some innocent schoolboy. Not that he hadn't wanted more. He had. But, just like a schoolboy, he'd held himself back, drawn by the desire and the sweetness of holding it in check.

He laughed softly into the darkness. Marcus Slade, original bad boy, cold, accurate reporter of "Just the facts, ma'am," the man who always moved on before things got messy. Marcus Slade, staying in a town like Birch Beach. For a woman like Rachel Gale. A woman who still lived with her mother, baked apple cobbler and dressed like a prude. But she wasn't a prude. She was innocently passionate, able to meet him more than halfway.

But she was also a woman who might very well be in love with another man.

And maybe always would be.

IT WAS ALMOST ten o'clock the next morning when Rachel walked into the newspaper office.

"Of course you know that Luke is going crazy," Grant said the minute she'd cleared the door.

"I'll go see him right away."

She headed toward Luke's office in layout.

"Rachel?"

Rachel stopped but didn't turn around. "Yes?"

"Have you decided what to do about the story on Eric Ludington?"

She turned. "You said it was up to me, right?"

Grant nodded. "Right."

"Then, yes—I've decided."

If Grant wanted more, he wasn't going to get it. She wasn't in the mood to discuss her decision with anyone. She headed again for layout so she could tell Luke Watkins what to do with the front page.

Luke looked at her strangely, but didn't ask any questions, for which she was grateful. Back out in the front office, she grabbed a notebook and a camera from her desk and started for the door again.

"You leaving?" Grant asked.

"Yup. Gotta cover the luncheon over at the Garden Club."

Grant snorted. "I take it you're not in the mood to discuss this."

"That's right."

Grant nodded. "Fair enough. Then get going. Molly Finch wants a picture of the tables before the group gets there."

"Right, Boss. And thanks."

Grant gave her a light grin and waved her out the door.

It was another beautiful day in Birch Beach, but Rachel scarcely noticed as she walked over to the library where the Birch Beach Garden Club held its annual luncheon in their pride and joy—the gardens in back of the library.

She hadn't slept well the night before. And it wasn't only the decision about Eric Ludington that had kept her tossing and turning. Another man had been on her mind even more. The man across the hall.

She prayed he'd leave today. She prayed he wouldn't. She'd lain in bed last night and let the fantasy that he would ask her to leave with him play out in her mind. But she knew that would never happen. And even if it did, she didn't know if she could go with him. Small-town life was what she wanted. A white picket fence and two or three kids in a sandbox was what she wanted.

Oh, hell, Marcus Slade was what she wanted. But she knew she wasn't going to get him. Because even if he cared enough to ask her to go with him, she couldn't. It would burn her out. For him to stay would bury him. They would kill each other's dreams, and anything they felt for each other would die right along with them. So she'd stayed in bed, not to catch up on sleep, but to avoid running into him that morning. Not until she'd heard him leave the house, had she gotten up and headed for a shower.

"Yoo-hoo!" Molly Finch called from in front of the library across the street. "Over here, Rachel!"

Rachel waved and smiled. "Hi, Miss Finch! You ladies certainly have a lovely day for your luncheon."

"Don't we, though?"

Rachel crossed the street and let Miss Finch take her arm and lead her back around the library to the gardens. Early perennials were already blooming, along with hydrangea bushes and tulips and daffodils. Roses were starting to bud. Four round tables were draped in pink and decorated with the last of the lilacs from Molly Finch's bushes.

"Everything looks beautiful, Miss Finch."

"My, yes. Doesn't it?"

The tiny, old woman had her hands clasped under her chin, surveying her handiwork, her sweet, weathered face shaded by a bonnet festooned with violets. Rachel raised her camera and snapped a shot of her, capturing her forever in time just as she was that day—happy, hopeful and content.

Just the way Rachel herself had always felt. Or at least until the morning she'd awakened to find Marcus Slade in her bed, stirring her senses in a way that was new to her—and that seemed to give her no peace.

Behind her the birdsong in the garden was broken by high, chattering voices and small, almost girlish giggles. The other ladies of the club had arrived. Miss Finch patted Rachel's arm and went to greet them. Rachel wandered over to stand under a magnolia tree to watch them, wondering if she would ever feel content again.

"SHE WHAT?" Marcus bellowed.

"She killed it," Luke Watkins repeated. "Filled the space with the Garden Club Luncheon story."

Marcus thrust a hand into his hair. "The *what?*"

"Over at the public gardens behind the library. Every year they—"

Marcus held up a hand. "No, don't tell me. I don't want to know."

Besides, he already knew. Molly Finch had waylaid him on his way over to the *Bark* office and told him all about how Agnes Summers had refused to sit anywhere near her and how, in the ensuing shenanigans, the topping for the fruit salad had wilted and run. It was a hot breaking story, all right. Marcus could just see the headlines: "Whipped cream melts while the ladies of the club skirmish."

Lord, what was Rachel thinking of?

Hell, she was thinking of Eric Ludington, that's what she was thinking of. Protecting him along with the sheriff and the rest of the Ludingtons.

"Where is she?" Marcus asked Luke.

"Rachel?" Luke shrugged. "Probably went to the city to get the film developed. She wants a picture of the gardens on page one."

"What every seasoned reporter wants," muttered Marcus. "Lilacs and fruit salad."

"Huh?"

Marcus gave a disgusted snort. "Never mind. Where's Grant?"

Luke shrugged again. "Said something about taking Frannie out for lunch. Ain't back yet."

Marcus stormed into the outer office. Deadline, and the place was empty. The star reporter off on a hot breaking story about tulips and the editor off joyriding with his lady love. Maybe he was beginning to be seduced by the peaceful pace of a small town, but this was ridiculous.

He headed out onto the sidewalk, but once out there he didn't have a clue as to what to do. Sugar doughnuts beckoned from across the street at Crawford's. Burned peanuts whistled at him from over at Knickerson's. But in the end it was the Buzzing Bee Diner he headed for, picking a seat by the window and succumbing to the meat-loaf plate while he waited for Rachel's car to pass by.

He thanked Olive for a second cup of coffee knowing that he shouldn't be contemplating a piece of pie but should be headed back to the guest house to pack. Leaving this town seemed to be taking him forever.

"Anything else, hon?" Olive asked.

"Yeah," he answered. "Give me the pie, Olive."

"À la mode?"

"Absolutely."

What the hell. He wasn't leaving yet, and he knew it. Not until he had it right from Rachel's wide, sexy mouth. Not until he'd heard her say the words that would make him understand once and for all that he'd been right about small towns and their people. Once he'd heard her say them, he could head out of here without looking back.

"THAT'S IT, LUKE. Send it out of here."

"Right, Rachel. I'll drive it into the city myself."

The *Bark* was printed in Milwaukee and sent back for Friday distribution to Birch Beach and its outlying neighbors.

"Thanks, Luke. Sorry for the delay. I appreciate your staying to work on the front page."

"No problem, Rachel. That picture of Ariel Huffington gettin' stung by a bee right on her nose is priceless. AP just might pick that one up."

Rachel groaned. "Miss Huffington will have a fit."

"She'll love it," Luke said with a laugh. "Especially when I tell her that her hat was the prettiest one there."

"Luke, I can see why Daisy is in love with you."

"Aww, shucks."

Rachel laughed at Luke's imitation of country modesty. But it was a fact that he could lay out a heck of a front page and keep Daisy coming into advertising every morning with a smile on her face.

She took one last look at the pasteup with its three pictures of the Garden Club luncheon, Ariel's front and center. The ladies would be pleased, indeed.

"Okay, Luke. Get it out of here and get home to your wife."

"Nice night. Think I'll pick Daisy up first, drive her into the city with me." He winked. "Maybe do a little parking on the way home."

"That should make up for me keeping you so late," Rachel said. "'Night."

"'Night, Rachel."

She walked through the darkened front office and out onto the sidewalk. It was only nine o'clock, but Main Street was all but deserted. The spring breeze was warm and gentle. The night sky full of stars. Lucky Daisy, she'd be in the arms of the man she loved tonight.

Rachel reached Elm and turned toward home, wondering if Marcus had stayed or gone. Not knowing which way to hope. If he was there, in the room across from hers, she just might surprise him. Just might knock on his door and invite herself in. One more night with him to take out and remember on all the nights like this in her future. On the nights that she wanted him with an almost unbearable sweetness and longing. And she knew there'd be nights like that for the rest of her life. Even if she eventually married, and heaven knew the pickings for that were slim in a town like Birch Beach, some part of her—the wild part he'd helped let out, the nurturing part that still wanted to do something for that little boy who'd stolen the candy bar—would always yearn for him.

She turned up the front walk to her mother's house and went up the steps, quietly letting herself in through the unlocked door. She was hungry, she decided, and headed for the kitchen to see if anyone had left her some apple cobbler.

The kitchen was dark. She left the light off and went to the refrigerator, opening it and bending to peer inside.

"And you call yourself a newspaperwoman."

She jumped at the sound of the words coming from behind her. Whirling around, she found him sitting there at the kitchen table, the light from the refrigerator just bright enough for her to see that Marcus Slade was mad as hell.

# Chapter Eight

Rachel's hand shot to her pounding heart. "Marcus! You scared me!"

"You're the scary one," he said.

"Me?"

"Yeah, you."

She shut the refrigerator door. "What's this about?"

"You killed the story on Eric Ludington."

She could barely see his face in the dim moonlight filtering through the ruffled, checked curtains, but she didn't really need to. His tone of voice clearly conveyed the grim lines she'd find there.

"Yes," she said. "I did."

"I thought you cared about what happened to Knickerson's. About what happened to Agnes—this town."

She thrust her hands into the pockets of her skirt. "I do."

"Bull!" he shouted, standing up with such force that the chair he'd been sitting in skiddered backward, crashing into the wall.

Rachel looked nervously over her shoulder. "Keep your voice down, Slade. Everybody is asleep."

"You think I give a flying—"

He stopped short but she knew the expletive he'd been

about to utter. She stared at him for a moment before saying, "I'm going to bed."

He caught hold of her arm before she had a chance to move. "The hell you are. Not until you explain to me how you could do it."

"Do what? Marcus, what is this about?"

"This is about a woman who said she cared what happened to this town. About a woman who has the power to make a difference. About a woman who chose not to. But mostly it's about the reason she chose not to."

She thrust her chin up. "And what do you think that reason is?"

"You're protecting him."

Her eyes narrowed, and her mouth twisted. "Who? I'm protecting who? Eric Ludington?"

"Yes."

"That's crazy. Why would I—"

He let go of her then, stopping her words with the energy of his body moving swiftly around the kitchen, his hands raking into his hair. He stopped at the counter, bracing himself, his back to her, his corded arms stretched to their limit. "Because," he growled, then spun around. "Because you're still in love with him!"

"What?"

"You know what," he said harshly, his words vibrating off the walls.

"Shhh, Marcus—you'll wake the house up!"

"Good! Let's wake 'em up! Let's wake the entire block up! Let's shout to the rooftops of this storybook village that Rachel Gale is as fake as the town!"

"Have you lost your mind?"

He hooted bitterly. "Almost, baby, almost!"

"Will you keep your voice down?"

"No!"

"Then we're taking this outside," she said, giving him a shove toward the back kitchen door. "Get out on that screen porch and tell me what the hell you're talking about.''

He went, much to her relief, and she shut the door behind them. The night was filled with the sound of crickets, the sight of fireflies winking in the darkness, the smell of evening dew on freshly mown grass.

She pushed it all aside, along with the feeling growing inside of her that this was not what she wanted to be doing with Marcus Slade out on this screen porch on a spring night. She would far rather be doing what she'd done with him out here before—making love. She pushed the thought aside, because that definitely wasn't what Marcus had on his mind.

''I am not now, nor have I ever been in love with Eric Ludington.''

''Come on, Rachel. You were going to marry him.''

''Yes. Yes, I was. But you're old enough to know that people marry for all sorts of reasons that have nothing to do with love.''

''Save that bull for someone who still believes in fairy tales.''

Her hands went to her hips. ''You've got a lot of nerve, calling me a liar. If I say I wasn't in love with him, then I wasn't in love with him.''

''Then why are you protecting him?''

''I'm not!''

''The story, Rachel. You killed the story. Grant left it up to you, and you killed it.''

''It was nothing but conjecture, and you know it.''

''It would have been enough—''

''Enough for what?''

''To get the council to vote against him.''

''If you believe that, Slade, then you really do believe in fairy tales. It wouldn't have been enough—not to stop the Ludingtons from getting what they wanted... And do you know why?''

His mouth looked hard when he asked, "Why don't you tell me?"

"For the same reason you're accusing me of protecting him. Because I was once going to marry him. The whole damn thing could have backfired. Blown up in our faces. Eric and his father would do their best to convince anyone who mattered that the story was just another effort on my part to pay Eric back for jilting me. That's why I didn't run it, Slade."

"Your journalistic integrity stinks."

She stared at him for several heartbeats. Was he right? Had she somehow sold out? No, she'd done what she thought was best for all of them. She'd held off on the story, hoping that the information could be used to better advantage. Somehow. Somewhere. But she'd be damned if she was going to stand here and try to make the arrogant, righteous Marcus Slade understand.

"Go to hell," she told him.

"I'm already in it," he shot back. "This damn town has been playing hell with me ever since I got here. The place is as seductive as the devil. Molly Finch's lemonade, Hattie Crawford's doughnuts, your mother's damn kitchen and her porch swing, Timmy's innocent blue eyes, Knickerson's damn candy counter."

He stopped and stared at her for one hard, silent moment.

"And most of all you, Rachel," he finally said. "Most of all you."

And then he pulled her into his arms and took her mouth with enough force to drive the breath out of her. The kiss held anger and lust and a need she thought might kill her.

She twisted her lips from his. "Marcus—"

But he wouldn't listen, wouldn't stop. His mouth covered hers again, his hands shooting down her back to her hips, pulling her tight against him. Tight enough to feel the hardness of his need, making the need soar inside of her own body.

Her hands thrust into his shirt, feeling the heat of his skin, renewing the hunger in his mouth. She wanted his hands on her breasts. She wanted them badly. And then they were there, kneading her flesh, brushing her nipples, making her gasp. He bent his head and suckled through her cotton blouse, and she ran her hands into his dark hair, holding him there. And then she felt his hand on her bare thigh, and higher still, finding the heat of her need for him, the center of her existence—her only existence, for this wild, searing moment.

His hand stroked, and she cried out, her hips bucking, her body straining toward his. His mouth left her breast and he buried it against her neck while his fingers found their way into her. And that was all it took. That one thrust. That one sweet invasion, and her body gave over to it while her mind grappled for reason. Wave after wave slammed through her, stunning her. "Marcus," she moaned.

"Rachel," he whispered into the curve of her shoulder.

She thought it would go on forever, this sweet, wild release. And then he spoke again.

"Make me believe it, Rachel," he whispered harshly. "Make me believe that you're not still in love with him."

She pulled away from him. "Wh-what?"

His breath came harshly from his throat. "Make me believe that you're not still in love with Eric Ludington."

She stared at him for a moment before asking, "How? By printing the story? You are incredible! You make love to me, get me going in a way only you can, and then you lower the boom. Marcus Slade's custom-made variation of the age-old line: 'If you love me you would!'"

He took a step toward her. "Rachel—"

"No! The answer is *no,* Slade. I didn't kill the story.

because I was in love with Eric, and I won't print the story because I'm—''

''Because you're what, Rachel?''

The night seemed to go suddenly still, except for some weird current of energy that flowed between them. And caught up in that energy was the word *love*. It bounced between them like a spark frantic for a piece of kindling. Or one of the fireflies out in the yard, looking for its mate.

But she wasn't going to let the word land—ever. No matter how much it clamored. And it *was* clamoring. So damn hard that something inside of her snapped.

''You are without a doubt the most infuriating man I have ever met!'' Frantically she looked around her, uncertain of what she hoped to find. But when she found it, she knew. She picked up a wicker basket and threw it at him.

He put up his arms in time to deflect it, but what really got to her was the laugh that followed.

''Oh, you think that's funny, do you?'' She picked up another one—her mother collected the things—and aimed it at something other than his head.

He kept laughing. ''Watch it, Rachel. You could injure something vital.''

''Huh! The only thing I see here that is vital is that you get out of town as fast as possible. It's what you've wanted, isn't it?'' she asked, picking up another basket—this one in the shape of a rabbit. ''Ever since you got here you've talked about leaving—'' she pitched the hapless wicker rabbit at him ''—why don't you?''

He grinned, the white flash of teeth quick and lethal. ''Why? You want me to leave before you start begging me to stay?''

''Ohh! You, you—'' She looked frantically around for something more lethal to throw, spied a clay planter full of philodendron and picked it up.

"Now, Rachel," he said, backing toward the door. "Come on. That could really hurt someone—"

"Nothing could possibly hurt that insufferable ego of yours!" she said, lifting the plant high. "So I'll settle for a few broken bones, instead." She aimed the planter, but he was quicker. He was out the back door in a flash, nearly tumbling down the steps, landing on his back on the grass below.

She started down the steps after him.

"Well, well, the great Marcus Slade felled and helpless." She stood over him, planter still in hand.

"Don't you dare," he began.

"Oh, yeah? And how are you going to stop me?"

He grabbed her ankle and she toppled on top of him, the planter flying out into the dark yard, the wind going out of her. Just as swiftly, he rolled her until she was on her back, under him.

"I'm going to stop you," he said, gazing into her face, "by making love to you again."

There was a nasty retort right on the tip of her tongue, but she swallowed it down, nearly choking on the words she did say in a breathless whisper. "Oh, Marcus…"

She felt his taut muscles relax, felt the breath go out of his chest while his gaze swept her face, the glitter of combat switching with devastating suddenness to something she had to push out of her mind. "Rachel" he murmured.

She took a deep breath and flipped him.

"Umpf!" he gasped when his back hit the hard ground.

Still using surprise against him, she pinned his arms above his head while she straddled him. "You were about to say, Slade?" she asked him sweetly.

Instead of the anger she expected, he grinned again. "I was about to say that if this is the position you wanted me in, Rachel, baby, all you had to do was ask."

"No, Slade, this isn't the position I want you in. The position I want you in is the one that finds you out on the highway with your thumb out." She let go of his arms and jumped to her feet. "Or any other position that gets you out of this town. The sooner the better," she added as she turned away from him and started for the house.

She stomped up the back steps, flung open the screen door and let it bang shut behind her. But nothing could drown out the infuriating sound of his laughter.

HE LAY THERE in the darkness, the dew from the lawn seeping into his clothes, the smile dying on his lips.

He'd wanted her to say the words. With the scent of her still on his fingers and the need of her in his brain, he'd wanted to hear that she was in love with him.

"You are going insane," he muttered, staring up at the stars filling an impossibly clear sky. "And if she had said them…" he asked himself and the moth hovering over his head, "what would you have done?"

Would he have taken her in his arms, declared his own love and asked for her hand in marriage? Was he in love with her? No, of course not. With her moving like a wild thing against him, his fingers inside of her, her cries filling him like the night filled the sky, he'd mistaken lust for love. But only for a moment. Bless Rachel and her temper and her leftover tomboy ways. She'd knocked that moment out of him as effectively as a pail of cold water on a rutting dog.

He got to his feet, then thrust his hands in his pockets and sank down onto the bottom step of the back screen porch.

"Slade," he muttered, "she's right. It's time for you to leave." He'd never been a crusading reporter. His specialty had always been to get the story no one else could. To put himself in jeopardy to do it, if need be. But it was always life and limb he'd risked in the past. Never his heart.

But here he was, in a nowhere town in Wisconsin, contemplating a crusade to save a five-and-dime. And wishing to hear words of love from a stubborn, uptight spinster.

It was definitely time to move on. Because, although he thought he might be able to win the crusade for Knickerson's, winning Rachel wouldn't be nearly so easy.

"HE'S GONE?"

"Yup," Frannie confirmed. "Didn't even hang around for a final biscuit."

Rachel looked at the biscuit hovering halfway to her mouth. She set it down carefully on the plate in front of her, her appetite gone out the open window.

"How is Timmy taking it?"

Frannie sighed. "He doesn't know yet."

Both women looked toward the front hall as they heard Timmy clamoring down the stairs.

"What do you think?" Rachel asked her mother.

Frannie shrugged. "I think we're going to have a mighty unhappy boy on our hands."

Timmy came bouncing into the dining room. "What's for breakfast? Can I stay at Stewie's after school? Where's Marcus?"

The questions ran together, vibrant with the energy special to a seven-year-old boy.

Frannie and Rachel looked at each other.

"French toast for breakfast. And yes, you can play at Stewie's after school."

"Cool!" Timmy shouted, shooting a fist into the air, a gesture he'd taken to after spending the afternoon with Stewie and his older brother.

"Mother, why don't you go get Timmy some French toast?"

Frannie gave her daughter a pointed look. "You sure?"

Rachel nodded, but she wasn't sure at all. She only knew that Timmy's pain was going to be equal, at least, to her own. They might as well share it.

She stood and went to Timmy, stopping behind his chair, putting her hands on his shoulders.

"You asked where Marcus was, Timmy."

"Yeah. Doesn't he like French toast?"

Did he? How the hell did she know? She really knew almost nothing about him. Except that he was a charming scoundrel. The fact that he was able to leave Birch Beach without so much as a brief goodbye for the small boy who had seen him as a friend and a hero only reinforced that knowledge.

"I don't know if Marcus likes French toast or not, Timmy."

"I bet he would if he tasted Aunt Frannie's," Timmy said, nodding with assurance.

Rachel moved around to the side of his chair, hunkering down and smiling at him. "I think you're right, Timmy. But Marcus had to leave early this morning, so I guess we'll never know."

The knowledge of what she'd just told him slowly clouded the boy's eyes and took his smile.

"Marcus left?"

She nodded. "I'm afraid so. But remember, we knew he was only visiting, Timmy."

Timmy stared at her for a moment, his lower lip quivering dangerously before he seemed to get hold of himself. "Yeah, I know," he said. "Everybody always leaves."

After doing her best to comfort Timmy, Rachel stormed into the kitchen.

"Damn him! I wish I'd decked him with that flowerpot last night!"

"What are you talking about?" Frannie asked her.

"Marcus Slade, what else? He's managed to break Timmy's heart, and I wish I had him here right now so I could—so I could—"

Frannie calmly put two slices of French toast on a plate.

"So you could tell him he's broken yours, too?" she asked softly.

"Mother, you're talking nonsense!"

"Am I?"

"Of course! You know I loathe the man. He didn't even have the decency to say goodbye to that boy in there."

"Or to you."

She thrust her chin up. "Oh, I knew he was going—I'm the one who told him to. Just last night. So it comes as no surprise to me that he did." She was lying through her teeth and she knew it. But she'd never let anyone else know it. She took a deep breath. "What surprises me," she said, hoping her indignation drowned any sign of her slightly cracked heart, "is that he couldn't even stick around long enough to say goodbye to Timmy. That boy's been left enough in his young life. He didn't need to be left again."

Frannie, plate of French toast in hand, paused at the swinging door that led to the dining room. "And neither did you," she said.

Rachel bit her lower lip and blinked back what couldn't possibly be tears. Well, she thought, dashing at them with the back of her hand, if they were tears, they were for Timmy. For a sweet little boy who'd been left by his father and by his mother—and now by a man who'd made him care. Made him want.

She pushed open the back door and went out onto the screen porch. The wicker rabbit lay where she'd thrown it. The lump in her throat grew. Because Marcus Slade had made her want, too. And then he had left. Okay, so it was what she'd wanted him to do. But since when had Marcus Slade ever done anything she'd wanted him to?

"Slow down, Grant."

"What's the matter, hotshot? Thought you liked speed."

"That's a Big Bill's Bargain Palace right up ahead, isn't it?"

"Yup, that's it."

Marcus glanced at his watch. "We've only been on the road for fifteen minutes."

Grant nodded. "Thereabouts."

"Where's the site owned by the Ludingtons?"

Grant jerked his head back. "The other way. North of town."

"Show me."

"What?"

"Take me to the site where Big Bill's wants to build in Birch Beach."

"I thought you were in a big hurry to put Birch Beach behind you?"

"I am."

"So now you wanna go back?"

"Humor me, would you, old man? Something's been bugging me about this thing from the beginning. It's gnawing at me."

Grant snorted. "And how will checking out the site help?"

"I don't have any idea. I just know I need to do it."

Grant slowed the car, waited for a truck to pass, then made a U-turn. "Hell," he said, "who am I to argue with you? I taught you everything you know."

Marcus laughed. "Yeah, old man, arguing with me would be like arguing with yourself."

Grant slanted him a look. "Almost, hotshot. And it means I win every time."

GENERAL MITCHELL AIRPORT on the south side of Milwaukee, was nearly deserted. Lots of pacing room. And Marcus needed it. Because the drive past the proposed site for the new Big Bill's hadn't answered any questions. It had only piled new questions on top of the old.

Marcus had clocked it. The drive from the Big Bill's in Pine Village to the new site took less than twenty-five minutes. If one Big Bill's didn't have the size wrench you needed you could hit the other one and still be home in time for Saturday lunch.

It made no sense. Why would they want to build them so close to each other? Wouldn't they end up competing with each other? Could there possibly be enough of a customer base to warrant two stores less than a half hour away?

And why the hell did he care?

He scraped a hand over his chin. He had left the Gale Guest House and Home for Exasperating Spinsters so quickly that morning that he hadn't taken the time to shave. He'd stuffed his gear in his duffel bag and made a run for it like a scud missile was pointed at his backside.

The speaker system crackled, and he heard his flight to D.C. announced. He headed for the gate, ticket in hand. The attendant was blond and built with a megakilowatt smile and a perky voice.

"Mr. Slade," she chirped as she took his ticket, "enjoy your flight."

She was handing the ticket back to him. He stared at it, but he didn't touch it.

"Mr. Slade? Is anything wrong?"

"Yeah," he answered. "Something is definitely wrong."

He turned around and started down the corridor from which he'd come.

"Mr. Slade?" the attendant called from behind him. "What's the matter?"

"I don't know," he threw over his shoulder. "But I intend to find out."


IT WAS DARK when Marcus pulled the car he'd rented at the airport into the shallow, circular driveway in front of the Ludington house. He flung open the car door, slammed it shut, then stalked up to the front door and pounded.

When the door opened, an immense middle-aged woman growled, "Yes?"

"Eric Ludington, please."

"Mr. Ludington isn't seeing visitors this evening."

Marcus stepped inside and strode to the center of the foyer. "He's seeing me tonight if I have to search this mausoleum and find him myself."

"Well!"

"Get him for me—or I'll get him myself."

The woman stared, mouth open for a few seconds, then her mushy lips thinned and hardened. "Wait here," she said.

"Don't worry, sweetheart, wild horses couldn't drag me away."

The woman snorted and started to trudge up the stairs. Marcus prowled the foyer, touching this and that, surprised that he didn't find a coat of arms above the door or a suit of armor stashed in a corner. The place had that kind of feel to it, and somehow he couldn't imagine Rachel part of it all.

He turned away from a painting of someone's sour-looking ancestor in time to see Eric Ludington, in a sky blue dressing gown, coming down the impressive staircase.

"Mr. Slade," he said. "Alice says you were quite adamant about seeing me."

"That's right. I've got some information about Big Bill's that I thought you should know about."

Eric's pale blue eyes took on a sudden alertness. "Is that right? Look, Slade, I've got lawyers and business managers to sort out things of such nature. I don't see what you could tell me that I don't already know."

"Then do you know that if you lease that site to Big Bill's and build to suit them, you're gonna end up with an empty building in less than two years?"

Eric narrowed his eyes. "What are you talking about?"

"I've been in Milwaukee all day, Ludington, at the newspaper morgue and at the library. Big Bill's has a habit of saturating an area with stores, forcing smaller, locally run businesses out, then, when they've cornered their customer base, closing down half the stores in the area. Your store will probably be one of them."

Eric stared for a moment, then started to laugh. "For an international newsman, you are incredibly naive. Did you really think I didn't know that? And do you really suppose that I care?"

The man before him was pale and ineffectual looking, but Marcus knew enough to never underestimate the type. Not when they had the power of money behind them.

He looked down at the man's pale legs sticking out of the dressing gown, his narrow feet thrust into maroon velvet slippers, then back up into his bland, arrogant face.

"Why don't you educate me, Ludington?"

Eric laughed. "Someone should. Big Bill's will be the anchor store to attract other businesses to a strip mall we'll be building alongside of it. By the time Big Bill's closes their Birch Beach store, the strip mall will be full and thriving."

"Because," Marcus said carefully, "the owners of those businesses have no idea what will happen."

Eric shrugged. "If they don't, it's their own fault. You found the information, figured it out. They could, too."

"Survival of the fittest?"

"Exactly, Slade. It's a jungle out there—even in Birch Beach."

"But you could lose out in the end, Ludington. If Big Bill's pulls out, those other businesses might fail."

Eric laughed again. "You really are naive when it comes to business, aren't you? You see, Slade, we can't lose. The tax breaks we'll get from an empty strip mall will exceed what we'd get from rent. We could care less if Big Bill's or any of the other places make it.''

It took a moment for Marcus to digest this information. But only a moment. It tasted lousy in his mouth, left a cold lump in his gut. ''And the people?''

Eric looked genuinely confused. ''People? What people?''

''The people who lose. The Knickersons for starters.''

''You said it, Slade. Survival of the fittest.''

Marcus started toward him, his hands just itching to form fists. ''Or the slimiest.''

Eric started to back away. ''Now wait a minute. Nothing we've done is illegal. Standard business practice.''

Marcus was enjoying the faint sheen of fear on Ludington's face, so he kept moving toward him. ''And if your 'standard practice' just happens to make its way into the *Birch Bark*?''

Eric had reached the far wall, an *umpf* escaping his pale lips as his back bumped up against it. ''It'll mean nothing, Slade. The paper is a weekly. By the time the next edition comes out, the council will have voted the way we want them to. It'll be too late.''

Marcus let his hard gaze roam over Eric's face slowly, thoroughly, enjoying the man's swallow that was taking its time getting down his throat. ''But not too late for me to smash in that bland face of yours, Ludington.''

Eric swallowed again. ''Now see here!''

''Survival of the fittest, Ludington. In a contest between the two of us, who do you think is gonna win?''

Eric looked as uncomfortable as a man could without starting to shake. His pale blue gaze slid sideways, toward the stairs. ''Alice!'' he croaked.

Marcus started to laugh. ''Listen, Ludington, when I decide to smash your face in, even your Amazonian housekeeper isn't going to be able to protect you.''

With that, Marcus turned and stalked toward the front

door. "I'm going to stop you, Ludington," he said over his shoulder. "Count on it."

HE FOUND THEM out in the backyard under an apple tree. Rachel was sitting on the ground, her long yellow skirt spread on the grass around her, her soft laugh spreading over the yard like the moonlight. The light from a kerosene lamp hanging from a tree branch played in the streaks of her hair. Timmy skipped and frolicked like a young colt around her, blowing bubbles from the enormous bottle they'd picked out one afternoon at Knickerson's.

Quietly, he shut the back door behind him and went down the stairs to join them. Timmy saw him first. He stopped still as the dead for a second, then erupted with a whoop as he ran toward Marcus.

"Marcus! You came back!"

The boy launched himself at Marcus, and Marcus told himself there wasn't much else he could do but swoop Timmy up into his arms. But nothing was making him swing Timmy around—or hang on to him for seconds longer before putting him down on the grass.

"Yup, I came back, soldier."

"Cool!"

"But this is just a reprieve, you know, don't you, Timmy?"

The boys forehead crinkled. "What's a reprieve?"

"It means I'm back for a while. But I will be leaving again. I can't stay forever in Birch Beach."

"Why not, Marcus?" Timmy wanted to know. "You love Aunt Frannie's cooking and Crawford's doughnuts, and Knickerson's Five-and-Dime, and Grant and Rachel."

Yes, he loved all those things. And maybe especially the woman who was rising from the grass and starting toward them. "Yeah, soldier, I do. But my work isn't here."

"Grant'll give you a job, won't he, Rachel? Or you

could work with Stewie's dad. He needs someone to wash cars for him.''

Marcus laughed. ''Think I could handle a job like that, soldier?''

''Sure! I'd help!''

Marcus laughed again, but his eyes were on Rachel as she came up beside him. ''Did you have supper?'' she asked.

''Nope, been too busy to eat.''

''Timmy, go tell Aunt Frannie that Marcus is back. See if she's got some fried chicken left for him.''

Timmy hooted and started for the house.

''What are you doing here?'' Rachel asked as soon as the screen door slammed.

He stifled a grin. ''I sense, Rachel, that you're not as happy to see me as Timmy is.''

''Damn right, I'm not. How could you leave without a word for that child?''

Marcus could have said that he had wanted to get out of there before the house woke up or he never would have left. But he didn't say it. Too much was given away already in the way he couldn't take his eyes off her. ''I left him a note,'' was all he said.

''A note?''

''Yeah, on the table beside his bed.''

She shook her head impatiently. ''There was no note, Marcus.''

He let out a breath. ''Timmy never got it?''

''You know damn well he didn't—because there wasn't one.''

For some reason her anger amused him. ''You calling me a liar, sweetheart?'' he said softly, bringing up his hand to pull lightly on her braid.

She shrugged away from his hand. ''Don't call me sweetheart, you—you—''

He laughed softly. "Maybe Timmy isn't the only one who missed me, hmm?"

"You wish, Slade. What in the hell are you doing back here?"

"I had a little date with an old boyfriend of yours."

"You what?"

He slid his hand down her cheek and cupped her chin. "And you owe me one, sweetheart. Because I managed to keep from smashing his face in—this time. Time for my payoff."

He lowered his head and touched her lips with his own.

# Chapter Nine

His mouth felt good against hers. Firm, skillful, sweet. She thought she'd never feel it again. Thought she'd never touch him again. Her hand came up, her fingers reached toward his hair. She stopped herself just in time, formed the fingers into a fist and punched him in the chest.

"You arrogant, insufferable—"

His grin shot right to her toes. "So you did miss me."

"Oh, stop grinning at me like that and tell me what you're doing back here."

"Not until I get some of Frannie's fried chicken into me," he said, starting for the house.

"Marcus! You get back here!" She stalked after him, grabbing his arm just as he reached the steps.

"Can't get enough of me, can you, sweetheart?" He pulled her into his arms. "Tell me you missed me."

"In your dreams, Slade. Now tell me about Eric Ludington."

Timmy pushed open the screen door. "Aunt Frannie is heating up some mashed potatoes for you, Marcus! And gravy!"

He took Rachel's hand. "Come on, I haven't eaten all day. I'll tell you all about it over some of those mashed potatoes."

She waited until he'd started on his second helping and

Timmy had been sent to get ready for bed. "Now tell," she demanded.

And he did. He told her about spending the day in Milwaukee, unearthing information about Big Bill's, checking details by phone with sources he knew, piecing together the story about how Big Bill's operates.

"They saturate an area, grab the biggest customer base, forcing smaller businesses out. Then when they know they've made an impact, they start closing down the least lucrative stores, banking on the idea that the customers will be hooked enough to drive the distance."

"And since they always *lease* land and structure, they don't lose out that much," Rachel added.

Marcus nodded. "Exactly."

"It sounds like it should be illegal," Frannie said from the sink where she was doing dishes.

"It probably does violate plenty of regulations, but first someone would have to prove that Big Bill's was doing it on purpose. Hard to do."

"But surely the Ludingtons wouldn't want to get stuck with an empty building." Rachel said.

"Tax breaks, according to your old boyfriend. The building turns out to be just as valuable empty. You should have seen the slimy smile he gave me when he told me the facts. His skin is probably slipperier than the silk dressing gown he was wearing." He gave Rachel a look. "Honestly, sweetheart, I don't know how you could love a man who wears velvet slippers."

"I told you, Slade, that I never loved him!"

Frannie chuckled. "I been waiting for five years to hear you say that."

"You believe her, Frannie?" Marcus asked around a mouthful of chicken.

"Sure I do. Any daughter of mine would have better sense than to fall in love with a Ludington."

"But she was going to marry him."

''To my everlasting curiosity,'' Frannie said as she hung a damp kitchen towel over the rack. ''Don't know what she could have been thinking.''

Rachel looked from one to the other of them. ''Would you two please stop talking about me like I wasn't here?''

Marcus laughed and took a long swallow of cold milk. ''Maybe you wouldn't have minded after all if I had punched his lights out.''

''The only thing I would have minded was not being there to see it.''

She stuck her finger in his third pile of mashed potatoes, scooped up a hunk and put it in her mouth.

''Hey!''

She ignored him. ''He really said he didn't give a damn what happened to anybody else in this deal?''

''Yup. Thought it was funny that I didn't seem to know that. Nobody has ever called me naive before.''

Rachel smiled. ''I'll bet.''

She went for another scoop of mashed potatoes. Marcus batted her hand away. ''If you must eat off my plate, try for a little decorum, at least.''

He presented her with a forkful of mashed potatoes. She kept her eyes on his while he fed them to her.

''Mmm,'' he said. ''I like watching you do that.''

She swallowed. ''What?''

''Eat. I could sit here and feed you all night.''

''Oh no, you couldn't,'' Frannie said, making Rachel jump. In gazing into those green eyes and listening to that deep voice Rachel had completely forgotten that her mother was still in the room. ''You two promised to tuck Timmy in. Better get up there and do it before he comes down here looking for you. I'll never get him to bed if that happens. And he's got school tomorrow.''

MARCUS SAT in the chair next to the bed, listening to Rachel read from a book of children's stories. Snuggled on the bed next to Timmy, her skirt tucked around her knees, her braid over her shoulder, she looked like born mother material. Sounded like it, too. She could tell a story, using her voice just right, sounding exactly like a duck would sound if a duck talked.

"Another one, Rachel!" Timmy said when she'd closed the book.

"Uh-uh. It's getting late, little man. You've got to get some sleep."

She eased off the bed and bent to kiss his cheek, then smoothed the covers over him.

"What's this?" she said as she bent to pick up something that had fallen to the floor between the bed and the bedside table.

Marcus watched her open the folded paper before he realized what it was. He shot to his feet.

"Uh—that's the note I left for Timmy that I told you about. He can read it in the morning."

"No!" Timmy protested. "Now! Read it to me now!"

Rachel looked at Marcus and he shifted on his feet, feeling a hell of a lot more uncomfortable than he ever had dropping from a helicopter. When she started to read the note aloud, he turned away from the bed and paced over to the window, staring out into the darkened yard.

"Dear Timmy," she read.

"I have to go away but I want you to know that I'll miss you and I'll always remember the time we had together. It was more fun than I've ever had in my life. I'll be in touch again—I don't know where, when or how. But I'll never forget you or Frannie—or Rachel. If I had a son, I'd want him to be just like you. Love, Marcus."

Silence settled over the room after the last word was read. His eyes burned as he tried to concentrate on a calico cat slinking through the fence down in the yard. The words sounded so sweet, so real, coming from her tongue. He didn't hear her move up behind him. Didn't know she was there until she touched his arm.

"I think Timmy would like to give you a hug," she whispered.

He couldn't look at her, but moved past her to the bed and bent.

Timmy's arms came around him, and they felt like love.

"Thanks, Marcus," he said. "I knew you wouldn't leave without saying goodbye."

If he didn't get out of that room, he was going to start to cry. And he hadn't cried since he'd been six and his mother had walloped him for bringing home a friend without asking first.

"'Night, soldier," he said, giving Timmy a quick kiss on the forehead.

He'd reached the door when Timmy asked, "You gonna be here in the morning, Marcus?"

He didn't even hesitate. "Yeah, Timmy. I'll be here in the morning."

HE LAY ON HIS STOMACH, his head to the side, facing the door. It had been hours since he'd heard her go to bed, but still sleep eluded him. He wanted to go to her. Wanted to lie in her arms and listen to her talk, feel her hands smooth his hair. Hell, when he'd sat there and watched her read that bedtime story, he was wishing he was Timmy. But now, with the night sounds spilling into his window along with the smell of spring, he wanted more. He wanted it all.

And maybe if he hadn't been so shaken up by hearing her voice read the words he'd left for Timmy, he'd have her here with him now. But he'd needed to get away from that little boy's bedroom, from her sweet face, from the trust in Timmy's eyes.

Not only was he falling in love with Rachel, he was falling for Timmy, as well. He was keeping himself awake wondering if Knickerson's was really the reason he'd come back, when he heard the knob on his bedroom door start to turn.

He lay motionless, eyes nearly closed, as the door silently crept open and someone slipped in. It was Rachel. And his body was letting him know how glad he was to see her, how much he wanted her to tiptoe to his bed and crawl in beside him.

But the only thing tiptoeing toward the bed was her sweet perfume. Rachel herself was making her way, nearly soundlessly, across the floor in the opposite direction. He didn't turn his head to follow her, deciding that he would just as soon have her think he was sleeping, but he could hear her rummaging near the table he used for a desk. Then he heard a clicking noise and the rattle of papers being shuffled. She came back into his line of vision, and he couldn't help himself. He moaned and flipped over onto his back, letting the sheet drop away from his body.

Out of the slits of his eyes, he saw her stop, saw her hand go to chest and her mouth drop open. He had all he could do to keep from laughing. She'd obviously come into his room for something other than what he was so boldly displaying to her. But as he feigned sleep and watched her finally tear her eyes away and leave, he thought he knew what she really had come for. But he had absolutely no idea of what she planned to do with it.

"THE COUNCIL MAKES its final decision Monday, you know," Grant said as he read over Rachel's shoulder.

"I know," she murmured, intent on the computer keys and the screen.

"This should have gone in today's paper. Next Friday will be too late."

"I know that," she murmured again as she set the piece up to print.

"Then, why—"

She hit the print icon on the computer and stood up, turning to face her boss. "I don't know yet."

He tilted his head and gave her the same look he always did when he didn't believe a word she was saying. "Come on—you've got a plan in that head of yours, don't you?"

She shrugged and gave him the same enigmatic grin she always did when she was determined not to give out any information. The printer chugged along, and she collected the pages as they crawled out.

"We really need new equipment, Grant. This printer is so ancient it—"

"You're changing the subject, Rachel."

"Well, yes I am," she told him. "But that doesn't change the fact that we need new computers and printers around here."

She grabbed the last of the ten-page document, tapped the pages into a neat pile on her desk and grabbed a file folder, stuffing them inside.

Grant sighed. "Yeah, I know. We need a lot of changes around here. Something I need to talk to you about—and soon."

"Okay by me, Boss," she said as she grabbed her purse, slung it over her shoulder, and tucked the file under her arm. "But it'll have to wait for now. There's something I have to do."

"Spoken like a woman on a mission," Grant quipped.

"Yup," she agreed briskly as she headed for the door, "and definitely a woman in a mood."

"Tell me where you're going, Rachel," Grant called as she went out the door. "I'll call the poor sap and warn him he's got trouble comin'."

"Not a chance, Boss. I'm counting on the element of

surprise,'' she said just before she shut the door to the newspaper office behind her.

The smell of cinnamon rolls drifted from Crawford's Bakery across the street. It made Rachel's mouth water. Not only had she worked through lunch, but she'd skipped breakfast, wanting to get to work and get started on the scheme she'd lain awake half the night planning. Of course, not wanting to run into Marcus had served as further incentive. The note he'd left for Timmy had touched her deeply. But not as deeply as the rigid stance of his shoulders while he'd stared out the window as she'd read it aloud to the boy. He clearly hadn't wanted to hear his own words aloud. Was it because he didn't trust his own feelings? Or because he didn't trust other people with them?

From what Rachel had heard and seen, she'd bet on the latter. His feelings had been stepped on enough times, early enough in his life to have left some scar tissue. But the longer he stayed in Birch Beach, the more those feelings seemed to be digging to get through the scars of protection.

But Rachel knew that little four-year-old boy who'd taken that candy bar. She'd seen him often enough deep in those green eyes to recognize him standing at Timmy's bedroom window the night before, holding his breath while he listened to his own words of love for someone else's little boy. And she'd needed every ounce of her own protection to keep from taking him into her arms and giving him anything at all to make the hurt go away.

She reached her car parked down the block, opened the door, threw her purse and the file over onto the passenger seat and climbed in. She started the car and swung out into Main Street with a sigh of relief. She'd managed to avoid Marcus once again. She was afraid that he would show up at the *Bark* before she was through writing her piece. She didn't need him butting his nose into what she was planning to do—and she certainly didn't need to go through what she'd gone through last night in Timmy's room. That unbearable feeling that she wanted to take him in her arms and hold him. Just hold him. Offering comfort—not sex. But the kind of comfort she wanted to give him came with love. Sex would be a heck of a lot easier to control.

She was just about to make the turn into the road the Ludingtons lived on when she glanced at the rearview mirror.

"Oh, no," she groaned. She put on her brakes so fast that the rental car behind her had to screech to a lopsided stop to avoid hitting her car's rear bumper. Leaving the engine running, she flung open the door and slid out.

"What are you doing following me?" she demanded while Marcus eased the car to the side of the road.

"Are you out of your mind?" he yelled, getting out of the rental and thrusting his hands into his hair. "You trying to get us both killed?"

"Oh, I have no intention of dying alongside of you, Slade. But you apparently have a very real death wish or you wouldn't be following me."

His mouth quirked. "Think you're tough, don't you? A regular crusading reporter."

She put her hands on her hips. "I'm tough enough. Now get back into that fancy rental of yours and get out of here. I've got something to do, and I don't want company!"

She stormed back to the car and got inside. But before she could get it out of park, he slid in beside her.

"Well, that's too bad, Rachel, 'cause you've got company."

She gripped the wheel to keep her fists busy and out of his face. "Get out, Slade."

He made a show of settling himself into the passenger seat. "I'm comfortable here, thank you."

"Well, *I'm* not comfortable with you here—and it is my car. So, get out!"

"Make me," he said, shooting a grin at her that told her he was obviously hoping that she would.

She considered it for two seconds, then decided there would be no dignity at all in trying to drag the Helicopter Hunk out of her small car. He'd fight her every inch of the way—and probably win.

"Oh, for heaven's sake, okay. You win," she said grudgingly. "But you're staying in the car when we get—" She stopped suddenly.

"When we get where, Rachel?"

"Look, Slade, I don't want you along for this one. Couldn't you just be a good boy for once and get out of here? It's almost time for Timmy to get out of school. Go pick him up, take him to the Bee for some pie."

"Timmy is heading for Stewie's after school for a sleepover and why don't you want me to know that you're heading for the Ludingtons'?"

She couldn't look at him, because her eyes would surely reveal that he was right.

"There are other things on this road, Slade," she said evenly.

"Yeah, like the Yellow Dog Saloon a couple of miles away. If that's where you're headed, I'm definitely not waiting in the car. I've already checked it out, sweetheart." He ran two fingers lightly up her arm. "You and I could have all kinds of fun in a place like that."

His fingers were sending shivers to places that she didn't want to think about. Suddenly going to the Ludingtons' with him in tow looked like the safer choice over spending a long afternoon in a darkened, whisky-smelling roadhouse with blues wailing out of the jukebox. She brushed his hand aside and shot him a look. "Oh, all right! I *am* going to the Ludingtons'. But I prefer to go alone if you don't mind. What I need to do there doesn't concern you."

"Since when doesn't the main source for a newspaper story need to be concerned with the outcome?"

She couldn't hide her surprise on that one. "How did you know?" she gasped.

"Hey, you're a crusading reporter. You'd use all the information you could get your hands on." He grinned at her again, dangerously. "By the way," he said sweetly, "if you're going to sneak into a man's room in the middle of the night, leave the perfume behind. Unless, of course, you're looking to wake him up."

She shot him a look. "You were awake?"

His grin deepened. "The whole time, sweetheart."

"Just lying there, watching me?"

"Uh-huh," he drawled, running his fingers down her arm again.

"You rat!" she gasped. "How could you let me think you were sleeping while I—"

"While you were burglarizing my room?" he finished for her.

She pulled her arm away from him. "Well, I certainly wasn't after what you seemed to be offering."

He laughed. "A pity, but you did seem to be more interested in what was in my briefcase."

She gulped. "Your briefcase?"

"Yes, my briefcase. Several pages of handwritten notes seem to be missing—along with a few photocopies of pertinent information. You wouldn't know anything about that, would you?"

Rachel slumped in her seat. "Oh, all right. You've got me. So I cribbed a little. It's for a worthy cause."

He picked up the file from the floor where it had fallen. "This it?"

She nodded.

"Pull over to the side of the road while I have a look."

She glared at him, but did as he wanted.

She pulled to the side of the road and cut the engine, then just waited while he quickly read through the news story she'd worked on all morning. When he finished, he deliberately closed the file, leaned his head back against the headrest and closed his eyes.

After sixty long seconds, she could have ripped open his throat with her bare hands. "Well?" she demanded.

"Grant was right about you," he said before opening his eyes and turning his head to look at her. "You are one hell of a reporter."

She blinked. "Then you think it works?"

He nodded. "Oh, it works, sweetheart, and then some. It's a powerful piece, and if it runs in the paper it's gonna make people wake up and smell the roses."

"Coffee," she said.

"What?"

"It's wake up and smell the coffee. With the roses, it's stop and smell the roses. You're mixing your metaphors."

Before she had an inkling of what he was doing, he'd turned in his seat, put a hand behind her neck and brought her face close to his. "Don't press your luck. You *did* steal half the material that's in here."

"But—" she wasn't able to finish because he took advantage of her parted lips to steal a kiss that should have served as ransom for something far more serious than stealing a few pages of notes.

The kiss was hot, fast, thorough. When he pulled away, he merely settled back into his seat, looked front and center and said, "Okay, let's go."

She sighed heavily and started the car. "Okay, but you wait in the car. You don't come in."

"Like hell," he snapped.

"Look, Slade, I know what to do—I know what to say. I know these people. I can handle them without your help."

"Baby," he said in a passionate enough tone to get her attention off the road and onto the hand he'd placed on her knee. "I know you can handle yourself," he said, his hand snuggling its way beneath her waistband and heading toward her thigh. "I just want to be there," he said as he touched the edge of her silk panties, "when you knock the maroon velvet slippers off his feet." He looked into her eyes as his fingers found the heat between her legs, caressing her once, then twice, then just resting there, making her want to cry out in frustration, while he smiled at her.

Then, just as she was furiously planning to beg him for a thing or two, his hand pulled back, and he sat back in his seat again and said, "Let's go."

MARCUS TRIED not to laugh at the look on Eric Ludington's face.

"You wouldn't dare print this!"

Rachel gave him a sweet smile. "Want to bet?"

"Try it, Rachel, and I'll sue."

"On what grounds, Eric? Every word in that story can be corroborated."

Eric snorted. "A bartender? You think the people in this town who matter are going to take his word over mine?"

"There's another witness, Eric. Someone I intend to keep out of this unless I'm forced to use her."

Marcus had to turn away because Eric Ludington's face had gone deep pink, his eyes losing what little color they had, as he sputtered, "I...I have no idea who you're talking about."

"Your little redhead isn't going to be too happy to hear you've forgotten her already. But I'll be sure and let her know."

Rachel started for the door, but Marcus held his ground. Rachel was playing her old boyfriend like a pale-bellied fish and she was about to reel him in. Marcus had no intention of missing the spectacle.

The fish rose to the bait. "Rachel! Please...can't we work something out? I'm a married man!"

Hand on the doorknob, Rachel paused and turned. "Sure

we can, Eric—but you ought to remember that you're married more often.''

The fish started breathing easier. He even managed a nervous show of teeth that might have been a smile. ''I knew you wouldn't do this to me, Rachel. Not after all we've been to each other.''

''Oh, please—just save the trip down memory lane, Eric. Here's what I want, to keep the redhead out of it.''

Marcus leaned against the wall and watched her reel him in. She had it all worked out. Eric would withdraw his offer of the land to Big Bill's, then go to the council meeting on Monday and, using the notes she would give him, outline what he would say he felt was bad business practice on Big Bill's part and convince the council to vote down the rezoning and roadwork needed for Big Bill's to build anywhere in Birch Beach.

The fish tried to spit the hook out of its mouth. ''Are you insane?'' he said.

''No, but I am giving you a break here, Eric.''

''Just how do you figure that?''

''You're going to come out of this smelling like a rose in the gardens behind the library. You'll be a hero not only to the Knickersons but anyone who was going to lease space in your strip mall only to go out of business when Bill's pulled out. The whole damn town will know that you put people before profits.''

The fish started to think. And then he started to smile. ''You might have something here, Rachel.''

''Oh, I've got something all right, Eric. And when they find out what you're doing for the Knickersons, they'll probably throw you a parade.''

Eric's face had just been losing some of its rosy hue when it clouded over.

''What I'm doing for the Knickersons?'' he asked.

''Yeah, that fund-raising thing to get the building

painted and a new sign put up. You're leading it off with a thousand-dollar donation.''

"Now see here. If you think—''

"You're right, Eric," she cut in. "Make it two thousand.''

"Absolutely not! I won't be blackmailed this way!''

Rachel shrugged and turned to the door again. "Well then, I've got a phone call to make.''

And the fish flopped right into the bottom of the boat. "Oh, all right! You know I can't afford scandal. My father won't stand for it.''

Rachel smiled and turned toward him again. "Yes, I know," she said. "It's the reason we aren't married today. Remind me to thank him again for that sometime, would you?''

"YOU DON'T BY ANY CHANCE fly-fish, do you?" Marcus asked her on the way out to the car.

Rachel wrinkled her nose. "Fly-fish? No, why?''

"Because you reeled that one in like an expert, sweetheart. Couldn't have done it better myself.''

Rachel stopped dead. "Can I have that in writing, Slade?''

"Only if I can have your gratitude in writing for keeping my mouth shut.''

She grinned. "You've got a deal, Slade.''

She strolled over to the driver's side of her car, but when Marcus opened the door, he didn't step back and wait for her to slide in. Instead he got behind the wheel himself.

"Out, Slade," she said.

"Come on, sweetheart, let me drive.''

She narrowed her eyes. "Why?''

He shrugged. "Maybe I just need to do something manly after keeping out of it in there.''

She laughed and dropped the car keys into his hand.

''Oh, all right. Guess I do owe you one, and if driving will help restore your masculinity—''

She went around to the passenger side of the car and got in. Marcus started the engine and drove away from the Ludington house. But when he reached the main road, he turned in the opposite direction from town.

''Uh—you just made a wrong turn, Marcus.''

''Nope.''

''You did. Town is the other way.''

''We're not going back to town. Not yet, anyway.''

''Then where are we going?''

He gave her a look and a smile. ''My little secret.''

''Marcus, come on—''

''By the way,'' he said, ignoring her, ''you did good work getting the redhead's phone number.''

She gave him an innocent look. ''What phone number?''

He glanced at her, then back at the road, then at her again—a smile forming slowly on his face. ''Why, Rachel Gale, the little girl who kept Main Street from being desecrated by gum ball machines, did you tell a lie?''

She drew her chin in, pointing at herself and making her eyes go wide. ''Me?''

''Yeah, you.''

''Well, I believe that in the business we call it a bluff.''

Marcus threw back his head and laughed.

''Surprised?'' she asked him when he'd quieted down a little.

''Yeah—but I don't know why. You've been surprising me since I first blew into Birch Beach.''

He looked at her, more leisurely this time, his eyes taking a slow trip down her body then back up again. ''Wonder if the Yellow Dog Saloon will bring any more of your surprises out.''

''The Yellow Dog Saloon? Is that where we're

headed?'' But she took a look around her and saw that that was exactly where they were headed.

"Yup, that's where we're headed. My masculinity needs further confirmation, and you and the Yellow Dog are gonna help me get it.''

## Chapter Ten

Gravel spewed, kicking up dust, when Marcus pulled into the parking lot of the Yellow Dog Saloon. At four on a Friday afternoon, the parking lot was half-full. The front door, hanging slightly askew on its hinges, was propped open with a case of beer. The yellow paint on the clapboard was peeling.

A couple came tripping down the creaky wooden steps, laughing and seemingly holding each other up. The woman wore a dangerously short denim skirt and a body-hugging little black T-shirt. Rachel looked down at her yellow cotton, pleated trousers and her crisp, white shirt. The tail of her braid hung over her shoulder and she flipped it back, despairing at her small-town mode of dress, pulling at her collar as she remembered Molly Finch telling her mother when Rachel was fourteen that she wasn't like the other teenage girls in town, *Rachel always dressed so sweetly.*

The word made her cringe then and it made her cringe now. Yet she was still dressing the same way. She crossed her arms and scrunched down a little in her seat, watching the woman sway her hips and give Marcus a big-toothed smile while she tossed her blond hair. She refused to look at him, refused to find out what his reaction would be.

Oh, hell. She knew what his reaction would be. What any red-blooded American male's reaction would be. If she weren't sitting in the car next to him, he'd probably be stomping a foot and howling.

"Don't even think about it, Rachel," he said.

"Don't even think about what?" she mumbled, her eyes following the woman, who did her best to show more than leg when she slid into the sports car across from them.

"Don't even think about starting to dress like that."

She swung her head to look at him, wondering why she should be surprised. Those green eyes of his didn't miss much.

She thrust up her chin. "You don't think I could look sexy dressed like that?"

He switched off the motor, leaned back and slid his arm across the seat. "Not as sexy as you look in that pastel cotton you're always wearing."

She was stunned for just a moment, then she pulled her chin in, cocked her mouth and said, "Yeah, right."

He sat there contemplating her, his gaze running up and down her body, until she felt heat spreading over her skin.

"When I look at you in those soft, pretty skirts and pants you wear and those demure shirts, all I can think about is the fire I know is under that sweet, pastel cotton. You're like spun sugar with a lick of flame tucked inside."

Her lips parted in a soft gasp.

"And when you do that, with that wide, soft mouth of yours—" He leaned toward her, the hand on the back of the seat grasping her behind the neck and drawing her in close. "Then," he said, his gaze on her mouth, "you do something to me that all the bare leg in Wisconsin can't accomplish."

"I'm so sure," she threw out.

He drew her closer. "You can reach out and check for yourself what you do to me, Rachel," he said, his voice a rough, teasing whisper.

"Really?" she asked. And as soon as the word was out of her mouth she cringed at the eager naiveté of it.

He laughed softly. "Really. I even get turned on by that shy blush staining your cheeks."

He took her mouth, sweetly, softly, then traced her lips with his tongue. Her breath started to speed up, her eyes open and gazing into his.

"Maybe," he said, between licks, "we should find someplace more quiet and find out what else you can do to me."

She pulled back and grinned. "Suddenly the Yellow Dog seems like a pretty safe place to be."

He groaned. "I was afraid you were going to say that."

He opened the door and slid out, slamming the door shut, then coming over to her side of the car.

"Come on, then, sweetheart," he said, opening the door, grabbing her hand and pulling her out. "Let's get in there and play something sexy on the jukebox and drink something long and cool that has a kick that won't quit."

He held her hand all the way up the creaking steps and into the cool, dim interior of the Yellow Dog Saloon.

Heads turned when they entered, but only briefly. The crowd the Yellow Dog attracted didn't exactly care to get nosy, any more than they wanted anybody else to. An ancient yellow dog didn't take much more notice of them, padding over to sniff at them for a second with his grizzled white muzzle, then going back to lie down in a shaft of sunlight in the middle of the floor. The cocktail waitress stepped neatly over him with a tray of drinks. He was obviously a fixture there this time of day.

Rachel immediately started for a booth in the back.

"Uh-uh," Marcus said, pulling her toward the bar. "This is a sit-at-the-bar kind of day, sweetheart."

"But," she protested, "I think I'd feel more comfortable in a booth."

"Baby, you know it's not my aim to make you feel comfortable."

She was about to state huffily that if he refused to sit at

a booth, she was leaving, but his hand felt rough and good wrapped around her own. The blues wailing from the juke-box was already heating her blood, and it occurred to her that, yes, he had a way of slicing into her comfort. And she had a way of coming to enjoy it in the end.

So instead of getting huffy, she laughed. "Well, I can't argue with you there, Slade."

"Good," he stated, pulling out a stool for her and hitching himself onto one.

"Whiskey," he said to the bartender. "Rocks."

"Uh, that's one whiskey rocks, one with cola, plenty of cola."

The bartender, looking like a refugee from a biker gang, roared at that. "The little lady knows what she wants."

"Yup," Marcus said, grinning. "And you better give it to her 'cause she has a habit of throwing things."

"Then whiskey and cola she gets. We ain't had a brawl in here since '92. Nearly lost my license for it, too."

"Then keep my lady happy, 'cause she's been known to start a helluva brawl."

"You got it, man," the bartender said, sliding two drinks across the bar.

"Very funny, Slade," Rachel said when the bartender had gone to refill glasses at the other end of the bar. "You trying to completely blow my reputation around here?"

He took a gulp of his whiskey. "Now, you know I'm all for giving them something to talk about, Rachel. Always have been."

Rachel took a sip of her drink, then set the glass back down on the bar. "The original bad boy, huh?"

"Yup, that's me."

"Sure it is, Slade. Bad-boy Marcus Slade who misses planes to save dime stores. Who's careful not to break a little boy's heart. Who totes plants around for little old ladies."

Marcus laughed. "Who told you that?"

"Never do anything in front of a seven-year-old boy that you want to keep a secret."

"I'll keep that in mind," Marcus muttered, suddenly getting more interested in the ice cubes in his glass.

"Don't let the fact that you're a caring, sensitive man embarrass you, Marcus. It goes quite well with your rogue image."

"Does it?" he asked, raising the glass to his mouth again, looking straight ahead.

She reached out and took his chin in her hand, turning his head so she could see into his face. "Yes it does, Marcus," she told him quietly. "Don't be forever trying to fight it."

That green gaze looked into hers, searching, serious. So serious that she had all she could do not to look away. She'd started this. To run from it now would be cowardly.

"You see too much, Rachel," he finally said. "It makes you a dangerous woman."

She was sure she'd never been thought of as a dangerous woman before. But it was part of this man's power that he thought things about her that no one else ever had.

"It's sometimes safe to let your feelings out, Marcus."

He took her hand from his chin and held it. "And your secrets? Is it sometimes safe to let those out, too?"

There had been a shift somehow. He'd turned her words back on her, and she wasn't sure she liked it.

With her free hand she lifted her glass and took another swallow of her drink. It felt potent going down. But not as potent as the feel of his hand around hers or his waiting silence.

"Is it?" she asked him.

His hand tightened on hers. "Yes, it is. With me, it is."

She took a breath, put her drink down and looked at him again. "What do you want to know?"

"I want to know why you were going to marry him."

She laughed softly. "You surprise me, Marcus. Most people want to know why he didn't want to marry me."

His laugh was short, blunt. "I've met the guy, Rachel. I already know he's an idiot." He took another gulp of whiskey, draining the glass and replacing it carefully on the bar before looking at her once again. "But you're no idiot, Rachel," he said, his incredible green eyes roaming her face. "Tell me why you were going to marry him."

"You don't think the fact that he was the biggest catch in the county was enough to turn my head?"

"Nope," he said emphatically, "I don't."

She grimaced. "Well, maybe not. But I made myself believe it for a while."

"Why?"

She shrugged, looked away from him to fiddle with her drink. "My father had just died. He'd been sick a long time. My mother quit her job to care for him. He left a lot of bills and almost no insurance. My mother had put the house up for sale—the place that she'd come to as a bride. It was breaking my heart." She slowly shook her head. "It was so unfair. She'd loved my father so much. I hated the thought of her losing the house she loved, too."

"Eric had been after me to go out with him for a while." She laughed. "He'd already been through every available woman in town. Things moved fast," she shrugged, "and I let them. His father was after him to marry and settle down. I turned him down at first. Then he offered to help my mother keep her house."

"His kind is used to buying what they want," Marcus said.

"Yes. But maybe I was no better. I wanted a home and kids. The pickings in this town are slim at best, and I was never popular with boys—and later, men. I guess I saw him as a way to solve all my problems."

"But he didn't."

She let a breath out and grinned. "No, he didn't. To my everlasting gratitude, he didn't."

"Tell me why."

"I'd been thinking about breaking it off. My mother had come up with the plan for the guest house. It was summer and she was doing great business. I started to wonder how I would get through life as Eric's wife."

Marcus let go of her hand. "Did you love him?" he asked her.

She watched him for a moment before answering, "No, I didn't. I was telling the truth the other night when I told you that."

She thought she saw him visibly relax, then wondered if she'd imagined it because she wanted it to be true that it really mattered to him that she'd never been in love with Eric.

"But he was the one who broke it off?"

"Yes. His father had sent him to Chicago for the summer, to work in one of their many business holdings. When he came back, he had a girl with him. A girl who said she was pregnant."

Marcus shook his head, his brows lowering, a storm stirring in his eyes. "I knew I should have punched the guy's face in."

Rachel laughed. "It wouldn't be worth it, Marcus. The way I look at it, I narrowly escaped living in that mausoleum of a house of his father's trailing after poor, dear, vague Imogene for the rest of my days. I never should have underestimated my mother in the first place."

"Well," he said, raising his glass, "thank the lord for Eric Ludington's wild ways, then."

She laughed and raised her glass to his, enjoying the satisfying clink as they toasted.

Setting her glass back down on the bar, she looked around. "You know, when I was in high school, this is where the fast crowd came on Saturday nights with their fake IDs. It always seemed like such an untouchable, mysterious world to me.''

"Yup. Rachel Gale sitting right up at the bar like all those fast girls did back in 1982.''

"Yeah, with a big difference. I'm thirty-five and after this drink I'll be going back to my mother's house for supper.''

"Don't,'' he said.

She swung her head to look at him. "Don't what?''

"Don't go back after this drink.'' He leaned in close to her, his nose almost touching hers, the breath of his next words light on her own mouth. "Be one of those girls, Rachel. Just for tonight.''

Her answer was barely a whisper. "I wouldn't know how.''

He grinned, as lethally as he ever had, his green eyes going darker, glittering with amusement and fire. "Put yourself into my capable hands. I'll guide you every step of the way.''

She laughed softly while a shiver rippled down her belly. "Yeah, guide me straight to hell.''

"No. Straight to heaven,'' he said, his lips brushing hers. "All the way to heaven.''

Heaven. Yes, she wanted that with this man—even if she had to raise a little hell to do it.

"Then take me there,'' she whispered.

He smiled, brushed her lips again and trailed a finger down her cheek to her chin and lower, barely brushing her flesh on the way down to the first button of her shirt.

"First thing we need to do,'' he said, his gaze holding hers, "is loosen up your appearance a little.''

She heard her own breath catch and she sucked it in. "H-how do we do that?''

"Let's start,'' he answered, "by getting rid of some of these buttons.''

She followed his gaze as it moved down to her chest,

watching his fingers undo one button, then another, then a third. When he'd finished, he skimmed his fingers up the opening, parting it and on up to her collar which he turned up against her neck.

"Nice," he said.

She felt her breath quicken, her breasts swell a little under his gaze. In defense, she cocked her mouth. "Anything else?"

"Oh, yeah. I've wanted to see your hair down again since that first morning when I woke up to find you in my arms."

He picked up a knife from the bar, the one the bartender had used to cut up fruit, raised it to her braid and, with one swift movement, cut off the elastic band holding it together. She watched his fingers unraveling her braid, slowly, gently. When he was finished, he started to comb his fingers through the strands. She closed her eyes and the Yellow Dog vanished; the people left; the sounds receded. All that existed for her in that moment was the feel of his fingers brushing through her hair, his thumbs skimming the sides of her face.

"Beautiful," he breathed, and she opened her eyes. "You look so beautiful, so sexy, so sweet."

She tried for a laugh, felt it catch in her throat. "Sweet doesn't fit, does it?"

"Sweet is as sweet does. You look beautiful enough to be trouble, Rachel. Now you've got to act like you're trouble—and like you don't give a damn."

She picked up her drink and finished it in one long swallow, setting the glass back on the bar with a little click. "Bartender! Give us another round!" she called.

Marcus laughed. "You may just be a fast learner, after all, Rachel."

*Yeah,* she thought, *and I might learn to like it, too.* An old blues number was grinding out of the jukebox. Smoky voices, sexy rhythm, the beat of the drums like hot blood

in a broken heart. The bartender set their drinks down, and
Rachel took a big gulp. There was something else she was
sure those fast girls did. Something she wanted to do with
Marcus very much. She was sure they went out on that
dance floor, plastered themselves to their men and made
love to the music with their bodies.

She wanted that right now more than anything. She slid
off the bar stool, wiggled her way between Marcus's
parted knees and placed her hands on his thighs, something
else she was sure those girls did.

"Gonna dance with me, hotshot?" she asked.

He splayed his hands at her waist, letting his thumbs
brush the sides of her breasts. "Yeah, baby," he said, his
gaze moving with lazy insolence from her hair to her
mouth to the shadow of her cleavage in her open shirt,
"I'm gonna dance with you."

He slid off the stool, kept one hand at her waist and led
her to the area of floor over by the jukebox. The old yellow
dog raised his head for a look before settling back down
to his nap again. No one else seemed to take any notice
at all.

The record ended and another started. Marcus pulled her
up against him, parting her legs with one of his, and started
to move. They danced with their hips more than their feet,
a dueling of energy and desire, while they watched each
other's eyes.

She felt his thigh brush the hot, nervy juncture between
her thighs. Felt his hips moving with hers and the beat.
He bent her back slightly, and she let her eyes fall from
his, let her back and neck relax and dip, let her hair fling
back toward the floor. When he pulled her upright again,
he'd stopped moving, his face harsh with what she herself
felt inside.

"Let's get the hell out of here," he muttered roughly.

And then he was pulling her toward the door, not stopping until he'd reached the car, pushing her up against it

and taking her mouth, his hands in her hair, his body pressing into hers.

His mouth was open on hers, his tongue darting, dancing, capturing hers. His hands traveling over her, cupping her breasts, thrumming her nipples with his thumbs.

"Marcus," she gasped into his mouth.

"Rachel, nobody has to teach you a thing. You're as dangerous as they come."

She laughed and he pulled back to look into her face.

"Think it's funny, huh?"

"What?"

"What you do to me, baby," he whispered roughly.

He looked at her, his gaze going from her wide mouth, stained from their kisses, to her eyes, amused and lazy with passion, to her hair, free and wild in the last of the day's sunlight. Yeah, she was dangerous, all right. The most dangerous woman he'd ever come across in a life full of them.

"What do I do to you?" she asked. But the knowing in her eyes told him that he didn't have to tell her—or teach her—a thing.

He pressed his lower body into hers. "That answer your question?"

She gasped and he caught it with his mouth, moving lazily against her until he knew she was just as needy as he was.

Then he pulled away, opened the car door and shoved her inside.

By the time he'd let himself into the driver's seat, she was still looking dazed. He started the engine and pulled out of the Yellow Dog's parking lot, spewing enough gravel to kick up dust that didn't settle till they were well out of sight.

He fiddled with the radio until he was satisfied, turned up the volume, and slung his arm across the back of the seat.

"I think one of those girls I'm teaching you to be would be sitting over here, Rachel, not over there."

The sound of her laughter as she slid over went through his blood like a magic potion that sent him back—far back to a spring from his past where there'd been another, faster car, another faster girl. But not a girl like Rachel. Never.

The highway was theirs, and the tires spit it out behind them as the sky darkened and the music beat against the wind blowing through the open windows. His hand tightened on her shoulder and she put her hand on his thigh, running her fingers lightly back and forth, driving him crazier than he'd ever felt at eighteen. Crazy enough to find a spot somewhere in the trees to park and take her as far as she'd let him.

But not yet.

First he wanted to barrel down Main Street with her, music blasting, her hands on him, the whole damn town knowing that they were together. Hell, he felt like some brash kid who'd cornered the preacher's daughter and wanted everyone to know that she thought him worthy.

He glanced at Rachel. Her streaked hair blew around her head. Her shirt, teased by the wind, parted to show the first swell of her breasts. She turned her head, her gaze meeting his, her lips smiling like she knew what it was all about. And he thought, *Hell, yes—I do want the whole damn town to know we're together. For now, at least, for tonight, she's mine.*

"You're forgetting something, you know," she said as they drove back into town.

"No, I'm not. I fully intend to take you parking. Where's the best spot?"

Her laugh was that of a girl's. "Nice try—but what you're forgetting is your rental car. You left it back on the road somewhere."

He laughed. "Perfect. I'm an irresponsible kid tonight—

we'll pick it up tomorrow when we go back to being adults.''

They cruised past the library. Ariel Huffington was just closing up. He honked and waved, and Miss Huffington's mouth dropped open, a hand went to her considerable bosom as she followed their progress down the street with a scandalized look.

"Marcus! What are you thinking?"

"I'm thinking," he said, "that you're my girl for the night and the whole town is gonna know it."

"Well, I would much rather you didn't—"

He cut off her words with two more sharp honks of the car horn. Luke and Daisy Mae Watkins, just coming out of the *Bark* office, looked slightly startled, then smiled and waved.

Rachel hid her face behind her hand. "Marcus, really. Do you have to—"

"Yes, I do," he answered, honking again as they passed Molly Finch standing by her front gate talking to Mitzi Taylor from the Drug and Beauty Emporium.

Both women smiled and waved merrily. Rachel twisted to look back at them. They were still waving when Marcus pulled up in front of the Gale Guest House.

"Well, that was embarrassing," Rachel proclaimed when he'd cut the engine.

"Uh-uh, baby. Girls like you are tonight don't get embarrassed when they astound their elders. They love it."

"Do they?"

"Yup. Now kiss me and give the neighbors even more to talk about."

She shook her head. "You are outrageous."

"Yeah, I am. And you love it."

He covered her mouth with his own then, and to his surprise she kissed him back. Long and hard. His hand moved to her shirt, slipping inside the deep opening, surrounding her breast. She cried out and buried her mouth against his neck, and the sound flashed through his blood and hardened him until he thought he'd burst with need.

"Rachel, Rachel," he whispered, bending his head to kiss the shadow between her breasts, dragging his tongue lower, tracing the lacy edge of her bra, then suckling her through the cotton of her shirt.

He felt her hands thrust into his hair, holding him there, her gasps filling the cool night air, filling his head with magic, filling his body with more desire than he'd ever felt in his life.

Her words came to him as gasps between her sighs. "Take me into the house, Marcus. Make love to me."

THE HOUSE WAS DARK, fragrant with the night air from windows open to the quiet, safe town. Marcus started to lead her up the staircase.

"Wait," Rachel whispered. "Where is everybody?"

Marcus stood still and listened. "Wait a minute, Timmy is at Stewie's all night."

"That's right. And my mother is probably out with Grant."

Marcus smiled. "We have the house to ourselves, sweetheart. Your bed or mine?"

She thought her heart might have stopped. His teeth shone white in the shaft of moonlight streaming through the window on the landing. His hair was windblown and rakish, a light shadow of beard on his lean cheeks, the glitter of the rebel in his green eyes.

He'd mistaken her silence. Taking her face in his hands he said, "Rachel, be my woman tonight. Be the wild, wonderful woman I know is inside of you. Not the fast girl who wrapped her body around mine on the dance floor. Not the one who kissed me recklessly at the stoplight. Not the girl, Rachel, but the woman. I want that woman. I want her tonight. All night."

When she remembered to breathe, it came out in a rush between her lips as she smiled. "Then your bed. No one will bother us there."

## Chapter Eleven

They stood by the open window, the cool, gentle night air caressing them. Marcus stood behind her, his arms around her waist, his hands resting lightly on her belly. Her hair, still down, was glorious, shot with moonlight. Her subtle scent was sweeter than the scent of spring wafting through the window—and far more tantalizing.

"I like having you here with me," he said, knowing the words to be too simple to convey what he was feeling. Knowing that they were the only ones he had.

She stirred, the silk of her hair brushing the side of his face, and he buried his mouth in it. "Tell me you want me," he murmured, the longing of the words welling up into his chest.

She turned in his arms and looked up at him.

"I want you, Marcus. For tonight. For as long as I can have you. I want you."

The words filled his mind for a moment, and all he could do was cup her face in his hands and gaze into it, then brush her forehead, her cheeks, her eyes, with his lips. And then the words filled his body, and he needed far more than the feel of her soft, silken flesh on his lips.

He unbuttoned her shirt, his fingertips brushing her skin, pulled it from her trousers and slipped it off her shoulders. Her skimpy pale yellow bra cupped her breasts, pushing them up so they swelled above the lace. He moaned and bent his head to taste, to lick the plump flesh, to bite at the fabric with his teeth.

"Marcus!" she gasped when he found the front hook and ripped it apart, not even bothering to take the garment off all the way before swooping her breasts into his hands and burying his face in them, using his lips, his tongue, his teeth. He started to get to his knees, to rid her of the rest of her clothing, but she stopped him.

"No," she murmured, her voice quivering. "Let me—"

He stood still while she raised his arms and pulled his T-shirt over his head. When he went to reach for her, she shook her head, and it was all he could do to keep his hands from her. The picture of her in the moonlight, her streaked hair wild about her sweet face, the bra hanging open, the straps slipping down her shoulders, was more erotic than anything he'd known before.

When she sank to her knees before him, his body swelled even more. Enough to make him groan. She smiled up at him when she reached for the fastenings on his jeans. He held his breath while she worked them loose, slipped her hands inside and smoothed them off of his body, lifting his feet so he could step out of them.

And then she put her mouth on him. Right through the tight material of his black low-rise briefs, she put her mouth on him, and he thought he would lose his mind. He cried out, his hands threading into her hair, holding her head there against him. She moved her head and he thought for one sick moment that he'd gone too far, that he shouldn't have touched her, should have let her set the pace. Then he felt the cool night air on his swollen flesh as she lowered his briefs with her teeth.

"Rachel...Rachel," he gasped. And then her mouth was on his bare, hard flesh, her tongue circling him, her lips sucking him. He thought his knees would buckle, but she put her hands on his buttocks and eased him closer—and he no longer thought. The pleasure she gave him consumed his mind and his body. Wave after wave of need, desire, thrill, shot through him until he could stand no more.

He put his hands under her armpits and hauled her up to him, tearing the button off her trousers in his wild, rampant need, ripping at the zipper, shucking the fabric from her legs, then lifting her up against him. She wrapped her legs around his waist and he slipped into her slick, hot flesh.

"Rachel," he murmured, settling her against the wide window ledge and thrusting deeper into her.

"Marcus, Marcus," she cried, burying her soft mouth in the crook of his neck and taking his thrusts into her body, squeezing him with her muscles until he knew he had to slow this or it would all be over too soon.

He stopped thrusting and reached between them to touch her where she was slick and wet and needy. She threw her head back and cried out, and he took the sound with his mouth on hers, drinking it in while he stroked her.

She tore her mouth from his to cry out again and he bent and took her breast with his lips, pressing her nipple with his tongue while he sucked.

"Marcus," she cried. "Hurry, hurry. Please—"

He groaned and raised his head to look into her face. He'd never seen such open passion on a woman's face before. He stopped to savor it, to imprint it on his mind, but she gave a little cry of protest, moving her body greedily against his until he broke completely. His hands under her buttocks, he lifted her against him and, still inside of her, carried her to the bed, going down to the mattress with her and thrusting into her like there just might not be a tomorrow. Because, for all he knew, for them, there wouldn't be.

THE SUN was just coming up when Rachel opened her eyes. And there was that smooth, tanned expanse of male chest again. There was her hand cupping that muscled male breast, her fingers near the flat, dark nipple.

Slowly her gaze worked its way up that chest, over a tawny, corded neck, until she found a face. He was staring down at her, a rakish grin on his lips, a shimmering light in his cool green eyes.

"Good morning," he said, and she smiled and snuggled closer.

"Mmm," she murmured, sliding her hand lower to rest near his hip.

He laughed softly. "A little different from that first morning, huh?"

She moved her cheek on his chest to look up into his face again. "So you're remembering it, too?"

"Oh, yeah. Hard not to. But this morning is going to have a totally different outcome."

She raised a brow. "Oh? You mean you don't plan on removing me bodily from your bed?"

"Only if it's to carry you to the shower. You know how many mornings I lay here listening to you in there, wanting to join you?"

She shook her head and settled deeper against him. "Uh-uh. How many?"

He laughed again. "How many have I been here?" he asked, pulling her up and over his body, settling her onto him.

She squealed, then her eyes came open wide in surprise. "Marcus," she gasped, feeling his hard flesh pressing into her, "again?"

"Oh, yeah," he murmured, covering her breasts with his hands. "Again."

"But last night it was—how many?"

"If you're keeping score, this'll be four," he said, lifting her hips and lowering her body onto his hard flesh.

She closed her eyes and sighed. Yes, she wanted it again, too. Wanted it forever—or for as long as she could get him. With a smile on her face, she started to move on him, setting up a slow, sensuous rhythm. When he went to reach for her, to pull her down to him, she stopped him, taking his arms and pinning them to the sides of his body. "No," she said, "let me. It's my turn."

He groaned in protest, but let her have her way. She smoothed her hands up her own body into her hair and lifted it off her neck, all the while moving on him with a sensual rhythm she hadn't known she possessed. Slow, sinuous, she felt like a human cat, almost purring as she came close to sweet explosion again.

But she held back, held back until she knew he was at the edge. Until the sounds that came from his throat told her to move faster, to love him with her body, and then he cried out and the heat of him filling her made her explode along with him.

HE'D FALLEN ASLEEP again and she let him, creeping quietly out of bed and going to the bathroom to stand her sore, aching, happy body under the spray of hot water in the shower. She toweled dry, thrust on a robe and decided that she needed food. Now.

She opened the bathroom door, expecting to be greeted with the smell of bacon frying or biscuits baking. But there was nothing. She skipped down the stairs, wondering if her mother was making pancakes. But when she went into the kitchen, it was empty.

"That's funny," she muttered to herself. But Frannie was probably still sleeping. Rachel hadn't heard her come in last night. So maybe she and Grant had been having as good a time as Rachel and Marcus had.

She giggled and blushed at the thought. Not that long ago she'd felt uncomfortable when her boss even flirted with her mother. Now, after a night in the Helicopter Hunk's arms, she was actually hoping that Frannie had experienced a night like that herself.

She skipped back up the stairs and went to her mother's bedroom, rapping lightly on the door. When there was no answer, she turned the knob.

The room was empty. The bed hadn't been slept in.

"Marcus! Marcus!" she called as she ran back to his room.

She climbed onto the bed, kneeling next to him. "Marcus! My mother is missing!"

Marcus was sitting up almost before his eyes came open. On the job he had to be ready for anything, anytime of the day or night. But usually, what woke him wasn't nearly as pleasant as the sight of Rachel, her hair damp and still down, kneeling before him in a silk robe that just happened to be falling open enough to reveal the swell of her breasts.

He reached for her.

She batted his hand away. "Didn't you hear me? My mother is missing. Her bed hasn't been slept in!"

He ran a hand through his hair and flopped back down on the pillows. "Maybe she made the bed already, Rachel. You know how she likes things neat."

"It's seven in the morning, Marcus. She doesn't make the bed until after breakfast."

"Well," Marcus said, yawning and closing his eyes again, "maybe she has someplace to go right after breakfast so she got an early start."

"Then where is she? The kitchen is empty. Not so much as a slice of toast in the toaster."

Marcus's eyes opened again. Now that, he knew, wasn't at all like Frannie. He sat up, propping himself on an elbow. "Could she have run out of something? Gone to the store?"

Rachel scrambled off the bed. "I'll check. See if her car is in the garage."

She hurried from the room, and Marcus got out of bed, found his jeans where she'd shucked them off him over by the window and put them on. He was pulling on a clean T-shirt when Rachel came running back in.

"Her car's in the garage, Marcus. And the engine is stone cold. I'm worried."

He could see that she was, and he didn't like what the frown on her forehead was doing to him. Because it was making him feel worried, too.

He was in a rough business. Things happened to people, people you worked with, people you recruited as contacts. He didn't form attachments. Never allowed himself the luxury of worry or regret. The people in Birch Beach were chiseling away at that protective coating he'd built around himself. And he didn't like it. But there it was. If Frannie really was missing, then Marcus was going to be worried as hell.

He went to Rachel and put his arm around her. "Come on, don't worry yet. Let's make a few phone calls. See what we can find out."

"But who could we call?"

"Grant, for one."

"I thought of that. But if she was just spending the night with Grant, wouldn't she call?"

"I don't know." He grinned at her. "People have a way of getting carried away."

That, at least, got a smile out of her. "And if she isn't with Grant?"

"Then we'll check the hospital, call the sheriff."

Rachel groaned. "Marcus—no."

He pulled her up against him. "Listen, sweetheart. Let's not borrow trouble. If she isn't with Grant, maybe she's over at Molly Finch's. There are a million places she could be."

"You're right. Let's start making those calls."

Downstairs, on the phone in the front hall, they both listened as Grant's line rang and rang—and rang.

"I should have checked last night before we—before

we—'' She slammed the phone down, thrust her hands into the pockets of her robe. ''I can't believe that we were—that we were—all night! While something was happening to my mother!''

''Rachel, take it easy. You don't know something—''

Just then the front door opened.

Rachel stopped pacing. ''Mother! Grant! Where have you been all night? What have you been doing?''

Frannie looked like she'd been doing exactly what her daughter had been doing all night, Marcus observed. And looking mighty happy about it, too. She glowed. He looked at Grant standing behind her, looking tired but happy.

''Well?'' Rachel demanded. ''What have you been doing?''

''I've been getting engaged,'' Frannie said, holding out her hand.

''What?'' Rachel ran forward and grabbed her mother's hand. ''A diamond! Mother!''

Marcus came forward and grabbed Grant's hand. ''You did pretty well for yourself, old man. Congratulations.''

''Thanks, hotshot,'' Grant answered looking a little sheepish—and a whole lot proud.

Rachel and Frannie had their arms around each other, and Marcus heard soft sobbing, not sure which woman it was coming from. When they drew apart finally, he could see it was coming from both of them.

So there he stood in the vestibule of the Gale Guest House, his arms around and comforting the woman he'd spent the night with, while his old mentor, the man who'd been like a father to him, had the woman *he'd* spent the night with in his arms. It was enough to make him laugh. So he did.

And before he knew it, the rest of them were laughing with him.

''This is crazy,'' Frannie said. ''I need to get you men some breakfast and see when Timmy will be home.''

"Mom, I think I can make breakfast this morning. And Timmy will be home soon. You know he always comes home early. Now tell me, when? Where?"

"Soon," Grant answered. "And here. But then we'll be leaving almost right away."

"Leaving?" Rachel asked.

"For Arizona."

Rachel gasped. "Arizona? But why?"

"It's my ticker, Rachel. Doc says I gotta move to a warmer climate. So as soon as your mother and I get married, we're heading out West to find a place to live."

Behind them, the door slammed. Everyone turned to find Timmy standing there, a scowl on his face.

"See?" he yelled. "I told ya! Everybody leaves! Sooner or later, everybody leaves!" he cried, then ran past them and up the stairs.

Marcus felt Rachel jump as Timmy slammed his bedroom door.

"Oh, God, I wish he hadn't heard it that way," Frannie said.

"I'll go to him. Try to explain."

Rachel started to turn to the stairs, but her mother stopped her. "No, Rachel, I'll do it. I'm his foster mother—for now, anyway," she added ruefully.

"Guess I really screwed things up but good, huh?" Grant asked as he watched Frannie disappear up the stairs.

Rachel patted Grant on the arm. "Not your fault, Boss." She kept going, pushing open the screen door to the front porch.

"What's going on here?" Marcus asked.

"Ask Rachel," Grant muttered. "I'm gonna go heat some water for tea."

Marcus watched Grant head for the kitchen, then followed Rachel out onto the porch.

She was sitting on the swing, one foot up with her chin

on her knee, the other foot on the floor, pushing the swing back and forth in a short, tense pattern.

''What in the hell is going on here? Just minutes ago everybody was crying with joy, now the place feels like someone died.''

He looked at her, waiting for an answer, but all she did was turn her head away and rest her cheek on her knee.

''Rachel—for heaven's sake, tell me what's going on!''

He heard her sigh, but she didn't turn her head to look at him when she spoke.

''Timmy is a ward of the county. Milwaukee County. He's allowed to live out here with my mother as part of an exchange program to get inner-city kids out of the high crime areas. When my mother marries Grant and moves to Arizona, he'll automatically be sent right back to the city.''

He stood in stunned stillness for a moment, unable to absorb what he'd just heard. ''But…why? You'll still be here. Why can't you—''

She did finally look at him then, putting her other foot on the porch floor, her hands gripping the edge of the swing seat. ''I'll try to. Of course I'll try to. But it won't happen right away—if it happens at all.''

''What are you talking about?''

''I'll apply for foster parent status. But it'll take a while. Even if everything goes all right, he'll go back to those city streets for months at least.''

Marcus hated the thought of it. Yeah, he'd always hated the thought of small towns, too, but Birch Beach was home to Timmy. This house was home to him. These tree-lined streets, Molly Finch a few doors down, Hattie Crawford's doughnuts, Olive's scolding if you didn't finish your meat loaf. It all belonged to Timmy. Now, it even looked like he and the woman he'd made love to last night had given Knickerson's back to Timmy. And now, because two people loved each other, Timmy might lose it all anyway.

Marcus threaded his hand through his hair. "A few months," he muttered. "That means summer. Timmy will miss summer in Birch Beach."

"Yup. And that might not be all he misses."

"What do you mean?"

"I mean, that if Social Services doesn't approve me as a foster parent, he might lose Birch Beach forever."

"Not approve you?"

Rachel stood and paced the porch, stopping at the railing and leaning against it, gazing out to the water across the street. He knew what she was thinking, because he was thinking it, too. Timmy wouldn't be swimming there this summer—maybe not any summer.

He went to sit on the railing next to her. "Why wouldn't they approve you, Rachel?"

"I'm single, Marcus. Never been married, never raised a child. I have a career that keeps me away for sometimes long hours. I'd be living here alone. Put that on paper and it doesn't look so good."

Marcus swore. "That's crazy. You'd be a great mother to him." He thought back to the night he'd listened to her read Timmy to sleep. "You are already," he said, reaching out to touch Rachel's hair.

She leaned her head into his palm and gave him a wan smile. "Tell it to the judge."

THEY WERE SITTING at the kitchen table over steaming cups of tea when Frannie came down from Timmy's room.

"How is he?" Rachel asked.

"Upset. Worried. Says he wants to be alone."

"Leave him be for a while then," Grant said gruffly.

Marcus took a gulp of his herbal tea and grimaced. "How do you drink this stuff, old man?"

"You get used to it," Grant grumbled.

"Anybody want breakfast?" Frannie asked, sinking into a chair next to him and resting her chin in her hand.

"I don't think I could eat a thing," Rachel murmured.

"Nothing for me, either," Marcus added.

"Next time I get engaged," Grant muttered, "remind me to keep it to myself."

Frannie stood and bent down to place her head against Grant's. "Oh, honey, I'm sorry. This isn't much of a celebration, is it?"

Grant patted her hand on his shoulder. "It's okay, love. Timmy's situation is a problem. We're all worried about him."

Marcus wasn't used to sitting around worrying about anything. He was used to taking action. Besides, sitting in Frannie's bright yellow kitchen, the checked curtains ruffling in the breeze, the smell of orange and spice—herbal tea smelled a hell of a lot better than it tasted—was only reminding him that Timmy wasn't the only one who was going to lose this place. Lose these people.

He pushed his chair back with a screech and stood. "I'm going up to talk to him."

Rachel moved to rise. "I'll come, too."

"No." He pushed her back down into her chair and placed a swift kiss on her forehead. "You get someone to drive you out to pick up my car."

"I can do that," Grant said.

"Thanks." Marcus started for the door. Then turned. All three of them looked as morose as the child upstairs probably did. He shook his head. "And get those looks off your faces before I get him down here, will you? Start thinking of somewhere to take him. We're gonna have fun today—for Timmy's sake—if it kills us."

Upstairs, he rapped lightly on the boy's door.

"Awww—go away."

"Timmy? It's Marcus. I want to talk to you, soldier."

He heard bed springs creak, and a few moments later the door opened a crack.

"What ya want?"

You could have hung a coat on the boy's lower lip, it stuck out that far.

"I want to spend the day with you, Timmy."

Timmy refused to looked up. "What for?"

"'Cause we always have fun."

The boy sniffed and dragged the back of his hand across his nose. "So?"

"So...I'm all for having fun. Aren't you?"

Timmy shrugged. "I guess."

Finally the boy looked up at him. Through the crack in the door, Marcus could see one blue eye, suspiciously misted over. "They're gonna make me leave here, you know."

The statement was a heartbreaker. Marcus had to bite his lower lip before he could answer. "Listen, soldier, let me in. We need to talk."

Seconds passed before Timmy stepped back from the door so Marcus could push it open and enter.

Timmy scrambled up on the chest under the window where he kept his toys. Marcus crossed the room and joined him there. Below, the yard was green with spring, plenty of room for a little boy to play. Safe. Secure. Knowing he could run up those back porch steps anytime he liked and find someone there.

"You know they don't want you to have to leave, don't you?"

Timmy nodded. "Aunt Frannie told me. I know Grant has to go—or he could get sick. And I know Aunt Frannie wants to go with him so they can get married."

Marcus smiled and ruffled Timmy's hair. "You know a lot, then, soldier."

Timmy shook his head furiously. "Nope. 'Cause I don't know why I can't stay here with Rachel and you." He looked up into Marcus's face. "I don't know that."

And neither did Marcus. Rachel would be a wonderful

mother for Timmy, and he tried to hold on to the hope that that's what would happen.

"Rachel's going to try to keep you, soldier. You know that. But I can't stay here."

Timmy gave him a considering look for several seconds, then asked, "Why not, Marcus?"

The question was simple, loaded. And he didn't know how to answer it. Because at that moment he almost wished he was staying. Because he liked the idea that when he ran up those porch steps there would always be someone there for him. And that someone would be Rachel.

But his work wasn't in Birch Beach. His life wasn't here. And never could be.

"I don't belong here, Timmy," he finally answered. "That's why."

Timmy watched his face for a moment, then nodded, tucked his chin into his neck. "Neither do I," he muttered. When Marcus felt the small, strong body lean against his, he swallowed hard and put his arm around the small shoulders. Yes you do, he wanted to say. But he knew he couldn't.

THAT WAS HOW Rachel found them. She stood in Timmy's doorway for long seconds watching the man they called the Helicopter Hunk, the man she'd made love to the night before, the man who claimed no place as his home. She watched his dark, scruffy head bent to Timmy's bright red one, heard without comprehending the words they murmured to each other. The room was scattered with toy planes, trains, books, stuffed animals. The bed, with its blue plaid quilt, rumpled, a pair of red tennis shoes lying at an awkward angle at the foot of it. The trophy Marcus and Timmy had won at Fathers' Day sat on the dresser where Timmy polished it every day.

It all looked so real. So natural. Timmy belonged here, in this room that he'd made his own.

And maybe Marcus did, too.

She couldn't keep watching them, thinking these thoughts, or she'd start to blubber, and that would help no one. Least of all the little boy she wanted to cheer.

"Hey, you two—there's a big carnival over in Pine Village. Anybody want to go?"

She almost held her breath waiting for a reaction.

"Do they have a Ferris wheel?" Marcus asked.

"Of course," Rachel answered.

"And a Tilt-A-Whirl?"

"Uh-huh."

"And a house of mirrors where we can all see how we'd look if we ate too much of Frannie's fried chicken?"

Timmy giggled.

"Sure do," Rachel said.

"What about cotton candy?" Timmy chimed in.

"Yup."

"And snow cones?" the child asked again, getting into the spirit of Marcus's third degree.

"Snow cones, too," Rachel assured him.

Marcus and Timmy looked at each other, and it was as if some magic passed between them because they smiled at each other, then looked at Rachel, asking at the exact same time, "Corn dogs?"

Rachel burst out laughing, and Marcus and Timmy high-fived it.

"Of course they have corn dogs. Now are you two coming, or do I have to eat them all myself?"

"Well, soldier?" Marcus asked Timmy. "What do you think?"

Timmy hooted and jumped to his feet, throwing his arms up into the air. "I think yes!"

## Chapter Twelve

The parking lot of Holy Redeemer Church in Pine Village had been transformed into a throbbing sea of machinery and neon, so Marcus parked on the street, managing to find a place only two blocks away. Timmy linked Marcus and Rachel, all three of them holding hands, as they followed Grant and Frannie, who gave no sign at all that this might be an odd way to be celebrating an engagement.

"There's the Tilt-A-Whirl!" Timmy yelled. "Let's go on that first, Rachel!"

"Uh-uh. Count me out of that one, Timmy."

"Aw, come on, Rachel. You promised."

"No, I promised the Ferris wheel. The Tilt-A-Whirl is Marcus's domain. My stomach would never handle it." As she said the words, she became aware that her stomach was totally empty. No one had had breakfast, and it was already time for lunch. The scent of popcorn and sizzling sausages filled the air, revving her previously forgotten appetite.

"I wonder if they have those elephant ears," she murmured, pressing a hand on her protesting stomach.

Timmy hooted. "Elephant ears? This isn't a circus, Rachel, it's a carnival!"

"Don't tell me you never had an elephant ear, Timmy?"

"Nope."

"I haven't, either," Marcus added.

"Then you've got to try them."

Timmy leaped into the air and landed back on the blacktop with a thud. "I'm not eatin' anything off an elephant."

"Trust me on this one, Timmy. This is a part of the elephant you're going to want to eat."

As soon as she said the words she wished she could swallow them back. Hadn't they expected Timmy to trust them all along? And weren't they about to let him down? She looked ahead at her mother and Grant, arm in arm, their heads together, laughing about something. She certainly didn't want to take happiness away from her mother. She'd been alone for too long. She deserved to be happy with Grant. And Grant—well, Rachel loved him, too. And if going to Arizona was the only way for him to live the long life he was entitled to, then she didn't want to take that away from him, either.

She looked down at Timmy's bright head, his wide blue eyes, his small freckled hand holding tightly to hers. She wanted to keep him. Wanted to give him a childhood like she had had in her mother's house, on the streets of Birch Beach. If the powers that be had any sense, they'd let her. All she could do was wait—and hope.

"Come on, Marcus!" Timmy yelled when they hit the midway. "The Tilt-A-Whirl! The Tilt-A-Whirl first!"

"Okay, soldier, let's go!"

Timmy hauled Marcus away while Rachel, Grant and Frannie followed more slowly, taking up a stand near the ride, watching as Timmy and Marcus bought their tickets and waited their turn to get on the ride.

"I've got to have some of that corn they're roasting over there," Grant said. "You girls want some?"

Rachel shook her head. "I'm holding out for a corn dog."

"Frannie?" he asked.

"I'll pass, honey. You go ahead."

Grant ambled off and Frannie turned to her daughter. "Do you think I'm being selfish?"

"Oh, Mom, no. You love him, don't you?"

"As much as I loved your father."

"Then you've got to go for it."

"But I worry about what will happen to Timmy. I'd adopt if I could, you know that. But at my age—" Frannie stopped, gazing at the boy as Marcus and he inched up toward the front of the line "—and with Grant's health problems…"

Rachel listened to her mother's voice trail off, knowing the pain she was feeling along with her happiness, wanting to spare her it. "I'll apply for foster parent status," she said.

"And if you don't get accepted?"

"I don't know, Mom. We'll figure something out."

"Any chance he'll stay?"

Rachel didn't pretend to not know what her mother was talking about. "No," she answered. "No chance at all."

"But you'd like him to, wouldn't you?"

Rachel nodded. "Yes, Mom. I'd like him to."

"So would Grant. That's why he asked him here, you know. He felt it was time Marcus settled down. Grant hoped he'd take over the *Bark.*"

"That would never happen, Mom. Marcus hates small towns."

"Well, for a man who hates small towns, he sure seems to have taken to this one. Grant told me how he worked to save Knickerson's."

"Yes, he did. But I think he just can't turn his back on a crusade. He's been talking about leaving since he got here."

"Yes. But he's still here, isn't he?" Frannie asked.

Grant came back with his corn on the cob, and Frannie became busy scolding him about the butter that was dripping off it, insisting on wiping half of it off with the wad of napkins Grant was clutching in his hand.

Laughing, Rachel turned away from them and watched as Marcus checked Timmy's safety strap on the ride. She waved when Timmy looked up and saw her just as the ride started. And then the boy was lost in laughter, his mouth wide, his eyes gleaming. Every time the ride made a full circle and they swirled past her, she heard Marcus's deep laughter mixed with Timmy's chuckles and her heart swelled. She wanted to keep Timmy. That she'd always been certain of. But as she watched Marcus, his thick hair blowing back from his face, his white teeth flashing, the glow of the sun on his tanned cheeks, she knew she wanted to keep him, too. She wanted them both.

AFTER TIMMY and Marcus returned, they hunted down the elephant ears. Rachel licked honey off her fingers then took another bite of warm elephant ear. "Mmm."

"Rachel! You were right!" Timmy cried. "There is a part of an elephant I'll eat!"

"Good, huh?" she asked Timmy.

"Mmm-hmm," he murmured around a mouthful of warm dough laden with cinnamon sugar and honey.

"Even Frannie's nagging can't keep me from eating these," Grant said.

"Nagging?" Frannie cried indignantly.

"Now, honey, you know you've been getting the jump on being a wife all day."

Frannie's mouth dropped open, but before she could say anything, Grant kissed her hard enough to render her speechless.

"Aw, honey, I'm just teasing. Besides, I've kept my little problem to myself so long it's kind of nice to have someone worry over me."

"Why did you keep it to yourself?" Marcus asked.

Grant shrugged. "Guess I needed to come to terms with

my own mortality before I let people know just how broken down I really was.''

Frannie put her arms around Grant's ample waist. "If you were any less broken down, Grant, I wouldn't be woman enough to handle you.''

Grant laughed and hugged her back. "You're woman enough to handle any man, Frannie, girl.''

Timmy was looking from one to the other of them, his head moving so fast his straight red hair swung out to catch the wind. He opened his mouth, and Rachel knew a question was coming. And she had a feeling it was going to be an embarrassing one.

"What's mort...mortali—that word Grant said?''

Marcus burst out laughing and Rachel glanced at him, knowing that he'd been thinking the same thing, probably as relieved as she was that Timmy's question wasn't of the birds and bees variety.

"I'll take this one," he said, putting his arm around Timmy and leading him off.

Rachel watched as Timmy looked up into Marcus's face as they walked away toward the churchyard.

"He'd make a hell of a father, Rachel," Grant said beside her.

"I know he would," she answered. "But we both know that Marcus Slade isn't going to latch on to anything permanently. He's too afraid that he'll just lose it in the end.''

"The right woman could make him see he's got nothing to be afraid of.''

"No, Grant. You can't hold what doesn't want to be held.''

"Hell, honey, the man just doesn't know he wants to be held.''

"Spoken like a man who just became engaged.''

"I know him, honey. Known him for years. He needs to light someplace.''

"He's allergic to small towns, Grant.''

"Naw. What he's allergic to is feelings. Help him get over it, Rachel. Bring him in from the cold."

MARCUS LISTENED to Rachel's voice as it grew softer, slower. Timmy had already fallen asleep, but Rachel didn't seem to notice. She was too close to nodding off herself. He sat on Timmy's toy chest, leaning back, his elbows propped on the windowsill behind him. The window was open, the crickets making a racket out in the dark yard.

Rachel's voice trailed off, the book she'd been reading to Timmy dropping to the floor with a soft thud. Her head lolled to her shoulder, the soft light of the bedside lamp burnishing the champagne streaks in her braid to dark gold. She sighed suddenly, and scrunched farther down on the bed, curling up next to Timmy, one hand under her head, the other thrown around Timmy's middle.

What a sight they made. His heart was weary, worn inside, a thick hide covering the outside. Or at least, he thought there was. But the sight of Rachel turning to Timmy like that in her sleep, the sight of the little boy's face, peaceful, knowing he was safe, was piercing that hide around his heart. But the thought of the two of them being pulled apart just might break it.

He stood up to draw the blue quilt up over them. Then he bent to kiss Timmy on the forehead. But when he went to do the same for Rachel, he found that all he could do was gaze at her.

In sleep she looked young and sweet and innocent. But he knew if he carried her to his bed right now that volcano inside of her would erupt and carry him away in its heat.

And he wanted that. Yeah—he wanted it. But if he had her once more, if he sank into her hot innocence, could he ever leave this place?

He brushed the hair back from her forehead and straightened, switched off the lamp, moved quietly to the door and slipped out. He let himself into his own room down the hall, undressed without turning on the light, pulled back the covers and threw himself onto the bed.

The springs creaked—a lonely sound.

It had taken him years to push aside the hurt another small town had given him. He was feeling too much already. And feeling led to only one thing. Pain. He needed to get out of there—before leaving brought more pain than staying would.

HE THREW THINGS in his duffel bag, thinking to sneak out while they were still at church, or the store—or wherever small-town America spent its Sunday morning. The damn birds outside his window were a hell of a lot happier than he was. He stalked over to his dresser to make sure he had everything. And that's when he saw it. The trophy. Timmy must have put it there yesterday. He picked it up. Rachel had had it inscribed at the jewelry store on Main. "Timmy and Marcus" it said, linked together forever in metal glued to plastic.

"Jeez," he muttered. How could he leave without seeing Timmy first? Without trying to explain? Without saying goodbye?

Well, damn it, he couldn't.

One more breakfast under the roof of the Gale Guest House wouldn't kill him. One more morning, one more walk with Timmy. One more chance to try to tell him something that no longer made much sense—even to Marcus.

He left his bag on the bed and went downstairs to find Timmy.

What he found instead was enough hustle and bustle to put the birds to shame.

"What's going on?" he asked Rachel, who was struggling with a pile of blankets she was trying to get down from a shelf in the front hall coat closet.

"Help me with these, would you?"

"Sure." He easily grabbed the stack just as they were about to slide to the floor.

"Put them out on the porch swing. Oh, and there's a card table out there, you might as well haul that right across the street."

Marcus paused on his way out to the front door. "Across the street? What's going on across the street?"

"Oh, that's right—you don't know yet. Half the town is turning out to give Mom and Grant an engagement party."

"A party? Already? They just got engaged yesterday."

"Well, it seems Molly Finch mentioned it to Mabel Harper after church this morning and—"

"And the rest is history," grumbled Marcus. "I'm sure Mabel Harper went at spreading the news like it was a holy crusade and she was the handmaiden of the god of gossip."

"Well, you're in a foul mood this morning, Slade. Get up on the wrong side of the bed?"

"Maybe it was getting up alone," he muttered before pushing through the front screen door and letting it slam behind him. But he knew that wasn't really it at all. He was grateful when he'd woken that he hadn't taken Rachel to his bed the night before. Because then he would have to feel even worse about leaving today.

He put the stack of blankets on the porch swing, grabbed the card table leaning against the porch railing and headed down the steps and toward the street.

"Yoo-hoo, Mr. Hunk!"

Marcus groaned. He was in no mood for Molly Finch this morning.

"If you're heading over to the park, I'll come with you!" she called, and he turned to find her bustling toward him, a huge basket of grapes dangling from one hand and an angel food cake perched on the other.

He shook his head at himself for the smile that wouldn't be held back. Miss Finch, in one of her wide straw hats, this one festooned with sunflowers and ribbons in deference to Sunday, he supposed, white gloves on her tiny hands and a flowered dress floating about her, looked like she'd been caught in a time machine around about 1952.

"That's where I'm headed, Miss Finch. Hear there's going to be a party."

"My, yes! It's about time that young rascal, Grant Phillips, put a ring on Frannie Gale's finger."

Marcus laughed. Only Molly Finch would think to refer to Grant as a young rascal.

Traffic was nonexistent as they crossed the street and started across the grass toward a group of people already milling around a long table covered in a white cloth.

Sam Cheevers drew away from the pack to meet him. "Marcus," he said, taking Marcus's free hand and pumping it, "I want to thank you again for your help that day Adelaide was in the accident. Don't know what I would have done if you hadn't happened along."

"Listen, Sam, I'm just glad she's okay."

"Oh, she's fit as a fiddle. Had me up at the crack of dawn to raid the store for food and paper plates and such. Ain't it great about Frannie and Grant? Here, let me help you set that table up—and Miss Finch, let me take that cake from you. Gosh, I haven't seen an angel food cake that high since I ate a piece of yours at the church bazaar last year."

Molly tittered and smiled and proudly handed over her angel food cake. Marcus decided that now, while she was occupied elsewhere, was a good time to sneak off. He needed to find Timmy and say goodbye, kiss Rachel one last time and get the hell out of this town.

He jogged across the street and sprinted up the steps,

almost running into Frannie as she struggled out the door with a pail full of ice and a huge jug of lemonade.

"Oh, Marcus, can you take these over? I've got to grab the croquet set and get Timmy to put on a clean shirt. He already spilled strawberry jam on his best white one."

She thrust the pail and jug at him, and he had no choice but to take them. "Where is Timmy? Because I need to talk to him. I need to—"

"Oh, he's in the kitchen. You'll have plenty of time to talk to him at the picnic this afternoon."

Frannie disappeared back into the house, leaving Marcus holding the pail, so to speak. And just a little mad about it, too.

"These people are starting to take you for granted, man," he muttered to himself as he started back across the street. "They just assume you're gonna stick around for this bash. They just assume you're going to be here tomorrow—and the day after—and maybe the day after that."

Well, they were wrong. Hadn't he said he was leaving right from the beginning?

"Marcus! Wait up!" Timmy called from behind him. "The Knickersons are coming to the party, and they're bringing a surprise from the store for everyone! What do you think it'll be, Marcus?" Timmy asked when he'd caught up to him on the curb.

"I don't know, Timmy. And I don't think I'm going to be around for—"

"Could you help me with this, Marcus?"

Marcus finally looked down at Timmy. The kid was still struggling to get into his clean shirt, an arm sticking out of the hole for his head, an elbow sticking out of an arm hole, his tummy bare as he struggled with the striped T-shirt.

Marcus laughed. "Soldier, you've got trouble." But as

he put the pail and the jug down on the curb and knelt to help the boy into his shirt, he knew that Timmy wasn't the only one who had trouble. Because Marcus knew, suddenly, that he wasn't leaving. Not until after this damn party, anyway.

"DON'T THE TWO LOVEBIRDS look wonderful together?" Molly Finch punctuated the question with a dramatic sigh and a coquettish tilt to her head, her pink straw hat shifting a little precariously to the right.

Agnes Summers made a scoffing sound in her throat, grabbed one of Hattie Crawford's brownies off a plate and made a show of a sweeping exit—even if it was just to the picnic table on the other side of the old oak tree.

"Yes, Miss Finch," Rachel answered, trying to stifle a laugh. "Both my mother and Grant look very happy."

"I saw it coming, you know," Molly Finch confided.

Rachel grinned. "Did you?"

"My, yes. Grant has been smitten for years."

Rachel knew it was true. She'd watched the whole thing unfold, with mixed emotions, right before her eyes. Her emotions were no longer mixed. She was all for the union, even if it was going to take her mother away. She sought Timmy out where he played at the shoreline with Olive's youngest. That was the one bleak spot on the whole day, as far as Rachel was concerned. The fact that she was going to lose not only her mother, but Timmy, too.

"What's with those two?" Marcus murmured beside her.

"What two?" she answered, her mind already adding another name to the list of dark clouds marring this beautiful day. She was going to lose her mother and Timmy…and Marcus.

"Molly Finch and Agnes Summers. If looks could kill,

poor Miss Finch would be headed for the funeral home at the end of Main.''

"Oh," Rachel flapped her hand, "those two. They haven't spoken in years."

Marcus raised his brows. "You're kidding? Molly Finch is the sweetest little thing. And Agnes Summers almost single-handedly made me fall in love with a five-and-dime store. What could possibly have come between those two?"

Rachel glanced at Molly Finch to make sure she was occupied elsewhere. "Bingo," she whispered when she saw that Molly had turned her attention to Adelaide Cheevers and the subject of the food at the hospital.

Marcus frowned. "Bingo?"

"Shh, she'll hear you."

"How the heck could bingo come between two women?" Marcus whispered back.

Rachel bit into one of Sam Cheevers's prized sour pickles, then thought that maybe it wasn't exactly what she should be eating if she was going to tell the tale of Molly Finch and Agnes Summers's falling out.

She put the pickle back on her paper plate and led Marcus down toward the lake.

"They were over at Holy Redeemer in Pine Village at the usual Monday night bingo session. Agnes and Molly always went together, always sat next to each other. It'd been that way for years."

"So what happened?" Marcus asked.

"Well, one night, just as Molly had covered *O*-5 to give her a winning card, Agnes got up to get a cup of coffee. Well, you've seen Agnes, her behind, is a little, well—"

Marcus grinned. "Generous?"

Rachel laughed. "Nicely put. Well, Agnes Summers's generous behind brushed Molly Finch's bingo cards and sent them scattering to the four corners of the earth to hear Molly tell it.''

Marcus whistled under his breath. ''And no winning card for Miss Finch.''

''Right.''

He shook his head. ''Still seems a little drastic—them not speaking for years over it.''

''Oh, there's more,'' Rachel said as they walked out on the short pier that was home to a couple of fishing boats and a rowboat or two. ''Molly Finch accused Agnes Summers of doing it on purpose. Said she was just like her mother before her, who was an inveterate cheat and could never stand to see anyone else win.''

''Sweet little Miss Finch accused Agnes of cheating? Said it ran in the family?''

''Yup. And to make matters worse, the whole argument was witnessed by almost the entire Ladies' Club of the Holy Redeemer Parish and the members of the Birch Beach Garden Club. And that was it, the end of their friendship.''

Marcus didn't say anything for a time, so Rachel looked at him. His brows were down in a scowl as he gazed broodingly into the water. She touched his arm lightly. ''Marcus, what is it?''

He didn't look at her, just continued to stare into the gently lapping water. ''And was Molly right? Was Agnes's mother a cheater?''

''Well, she had been caught with her hand in the Garden Club treasury once, and there was a rumor that she'd rigged the veterans' raffle one year because she just had to have that twenty-five-pound turkey.''

Rachel thought the whole thing was pretty funny. But when Marcus finally looked at her, she knew without a doubt that he wasn't finding any humor in it anywhere.

''Marcus? What is it?''

"Small towns, Rachel. The poison of little minds that won't let you live down the mistakes of your forebears no matter how hard you try."

"Marcus, this is just two old ladies who are holding a grudge—"

"No, it's not. It's a woman who can't live down what her mother before her did—and a woman who won't let her forget it."

"Come on, Marcus. This isn't like your situation at all."

"Isn't it?"

His words were clipped and carried enough anger to make her physically draw back from them.

"Maybe Timmy is better off leaving this town."

"You don't mean that?"

But she could see by the bitterness in his face that he did. That little boy who'd been forever labeled a thief when he'd childishly taken that candy bar had never lived down the legacy of a father who really was a thief. But this was different. Agnes and Molly were two old maids with nothing better to do than keep up a feud to spice up their lives. Surely she could make him see that?

She moved to touch him, to put her arm around him. But he shrugged her off, his green eyes deep and glowering. "I told you small towns are poison. Timmy will be better off out of it—and so will I."

He started to stalk off, and she went after him. "Marcus, you're being stubborn, as narrow-minded as you accuse everyone else of being. Don't you see that?"

He stopped suddenly, so suddenly she ran right into him. He put his hands on her arms to steady her. They were hard—as hard as the look on his face.

"What I see, Rachel, is that it's time for me to move on."

"This is crazy! You're leaving because two old ladies had a fight years ago over bingo?"

He stared down at her, the lines of his face harsh, his mouth grim. She almost wanted to laugh, the whole thing seemed so absurd. Didn't he see that if he left because of that bingo game, it was even more ridiculous than two old friends not speaking for years because of it?

"Marcus," she began.

But she didn't get to finish. Her mother was running toward them, calling their names.

"Marcus! Rachel! The Knickersons just drove up and Agnes says they want to meet the man who is helping you save the store!"

## Chapter Thirteen

Rachel hadn't seen Bernie and Elsie Knickerson in years. They'd been keeping to themselves out at a winterized cottage on the other side of the lake and left the running of the store to their niece, Agnes Summers. When they climbed out of their old maroon Buick, Rachel noticed that Bernie seemed to have shrunk several inches. His wizened face was still creased with the same smile she remembered from the days she'd gone into the five-and-dime to spend her daily nickel. But if Bernie had shrunk, Elsie, always an imposing woman, seemed to have grown in stature. Her back still ramrod straight, she towered over her husband, who was still so crazy about her that his face glowed every time he looked at her.

Frannie had linked her arm into Marcus's, almost like she knew he was ready to leave both the party and the town. Rachel trailed behind as her mother led him to the couple.

"Bernie, Elsie," Frannie said, "I'd like you to meet Marcus Slade."

"Ahh," Bernie Knickerson said, "the young man who is helping to save our little store."

Rachel watched Marcus take the man's offered hand. "I think Rachel is the one to thank, Mr. Knickerson."

"Oh," Bernie said, still pumping Marcus's hands with

more energy than it looked like he had, "don't be modest. I'm not real clear on what you and Rachel did, but I hear it's likely the council is going to vote in our favor tomorrow."

Elsie pushed her husband aside. "Oh, let go of the man's hand, Bernie, before you pump it off. Don't know why he insists on doing that," she said to Marcus. "Man's been a hand pumper since the day I first met him. We're pleased to meet ya...and beholden to ya. Agnes," she added, "tells me you're fond of them burned peanuts."

"Yes, ma'am, I am," answered Marcus, and Rachel had to hide her smile behind her hand. Elsie Knickerson was the kind of woman who inspired the title of ma'am—but it was still funny to hear rough, rugged and arrogant Marcus Slade pick up on it.

"Well, you just go into the store and get yourself some anytime you've got a hankerin' for 'em—on the house."

"Generous of you, ma'am," Marcus said.

"Hey, it's the least we can do for the Helicopter Hunk," Elsie said with a wink. "Now, Frances, where is that handsome man of yours? I want to tell him how lucky he is, just in case he hasn't figured it out yet for himself."

"Quite a woman, isn't she?" Rachel asked as she watched them walk off.

"Yeah—this town is full of characters," Marcus answered roughly. "Another reason I'm getting out."

He started for the street.

"Hey, you're not leaving right now, are you?" Her heart thudded as she asked. One more night, she thought, give me one more night with him.

"No. I'll wait till morning just to make sure Ludington follows through at the town council meeting."

She grabbed onto his arm to halt him. "Then come back to the party, Marcus. Grant will be so disappointed if you don't stay longer," she said. *And so will I,* she added to herself.

He looked into her face for a moment before the hardness started to leave. "Look, Rachel, I need to pack. To make a few calls. The network isn't expecting me for a while yet, but I need to get back to work."

She hated the sound of his words, but she hid behind a teasing smile. "Come on, Marcus, you've hardly got anything to pack. And the call can wait until tomorrow, can't it? Who's going to be around on a Sunday, anyway?"

He looked around the park, then back at her. Finally he gave her a grin, small enough for her to know that it was reluctant. "Okay, you win. The packing can wait until morning—so can the phone call."

It wasn't relief she felt, but elation—elation that lifted and expanded her heart, setting it free once more. Taking his hand, she started to head toward the others. But he was immovable. Suddenly he tugged hard on her hand and pulled her into his arms. Her body came up against his with a thud. "On one condition," he murmured, his eyes scanning her face.

Her heart had started to pound, her skin grew hot and she laughed at the sheer joy of the sensation being next to this man gave her. He might be leaving tomorrow—but that was tomorrow.

"Oh?" she asked. "And what condition would that be?"

He brought his finger up to trace her lips, softly, gently. "That you cross the hall tonight—spend it with me."

"Yes," she said breathlessly.

"Then come on. Let's go find Timmy."

HALFWAY THROUGH the afternoon, Elsie and Bernie Knickerson revealed their surprise. They asked Marcus to do the honors, handing him the key to the trunk of their old Buick. Timmy at his side, Marcus unlocked the trunk and threw it open.

"Wow!" Timmy said.

"Hey, soldier, one of our favorite things, huh?"

"I'll say!"

The trunk was packed full of kites in all shapes, sizes and colors.

"We've been stockpiling kites out at the cottage for years," Elsie said. "Anything that doesn't sell in one season. Bernie and I stayed up half the night putting them together. So, come on, gang!" she called. "Everybody grab a kite and get them up into the air. I can't think of a better way to salute Grant and Frannie on their engagement!"

"Elsie," Frannie said, "I don't know what to say."

"Good. Then don't say anything. One thing I can't stand is a speech."

"Elsie," Grant said, "you only pretend at being gruff and you know it. You're as soft as they come."

"Of course she is," Bernie said, beaming at his wife. "Why do you think she wanted kites today?"

"Why?" Rachel asked.

"Because it's how we spent our first date together. A Sunday afternoon in this very park, chaperoned, of course. When I saw this handsome woman here running up the beach with that kite, well, I knew I'd love her forever."

He reached up to kiss his wife on the cheek. She allowed it for a moment, then she shoved him away with the palm of her hand. "You're making a damn fool of yourself!"

Bernie chuckled. "Always have where you're concerned."

"Fool!" Elsie growled as she bustled away toward the table of refreshments.

Bernie winked and trotted after her.

"Aren't they something?" Rachel asked.

"Yeah," Grant agreed. "Something, all right. Just don't know what."

"Like I said, this town is full of characters," Marcus added.

"Come on, you guys! Let's fly some kites!" Timmy yelled, and half the town lined up at the trunk of the Buick.

It was nearly dark before the party broke up. Timmy was dirty, tired and happy, having played ball with Olive's brood and Marcus all afternoon.

"You need a bath," Rachel told him as they mounted the front stairs.

"Awww, do not! Do I, Marcus?"

"Soldier, the only one in town who needs a bath more than you do is me," Marcus answered.

"Think so?" Timmy piped up.

"Yup."

"I bet I'm dirtier 'en you!"

"How much you want to lay on that bet, soldier? A bag of burned peanuts?"

"Aww, that ain't fair! I heard Mrs. Knickerson say you could have 'em for free!"

Rachel laughed. "I'll settle this bet before it even takes place. You're the dirtiest, Timmy. Now get upstairs and into the tub."

Timmy's lower lip came out. "Marcus never takes baths. He always takes showers."

Marcus looked at her. "How about it, Rachel? Why don't we let him go with a shower tonight?"

Rachel, who was in the mood to give in to anything with these two tonight, made a show of thinking it over. "Oh, all right. A shower it is."

"Cool!" Timmy yelled, thumping all the way up the stairs.

"Do a good job," Rachel called after him. "I plan on checking your ears!"

Marcus came up behind her and slipped his arms around her waist. "You gonna check my ears, too?"

"Behave yourself, or I'll make you stand in the corner."

"Sorry, sweetheart," he said, nuzzling her neck. "I can't resist you when you go into your mother routine."

She laughed and he loved the sound. But what he'd said was the truth. As sexy as he found her in those silky underthings she wore beneath her simple clothing, she also stirred his senses when she did things like boss Timmy or bake brownies. He found her exciting on so many levels. Her passion for her work, her passion in bed—and her passion for those womanly things that his mother had never had a predilection for.

"Where is your mother?" he murmured while he explored the whorls of her ear with his tongue.

"Sh-she and, uh, Grant went for a walk."

"Mmm," he bit lightly on her earlobe.

"Uh, I—uh, think they wanted some time alone."

"Great. Then we've got the house to ourselves."

"Well, Timmy—"

"Is in the shower," he said, taking a bite out of her neck. "And you're coming upstairs with me."

She let him lead her by the hand up the staircase and into his room. When he went to shut the door, she stopped him.

"Don't. It wouldn't look good with Timmy."

"Okay, sweetheart," he said, pulling her into his arms. "But, later, after he's in bed—"

"Yes," she whispered, then he felt her silky arms go around his neck as she drew him down for a kiss.

He tried not to think that tomorrow he'd be gone. Tried not to spoil this night by remembering that it would be their last.

Instead, he inched her backward, toward the bed, while his tongue swept her mouth to find hers, and his hands moved from her waist to her bottom. By the time he'd backed her to the bed, she was moaning into his mouth.

He gently lowered her to the cornflower blue quilt.

"Umpf! Marcus, what—"

She pulled out what she'd landed on.

His duffel bag. Packed and ready to go.

She looked from it to him and back again, knowledge rising in her eyes.

"You're already packed!" she finally said.

"Well, I—"

"You intended to leave tomorrow all along didn't you?"

When he didn't answer, she tossed the duffel at his middle. He grabbed it just as she got to her feet.

"All that stuff about Agnes and Molly was just an excuse, wasn't it? You were already packed to go."

He shook his head. "It wasn't an excuse, Rachel. What happened between those two women only made me see that—"

"Bull! What happened between those two women only offered an excuse for you to run! So you don't have to face the fact that you might have fallen for this town and these people. That you might have fallen for Timmy. That you might have fallen for—" She stopped, and he wished he could take her into his arms. Not only because her eyes were glaring at him and her cheeks were infused with the color of her anger, making her look beautiful and passionate, but because he wanted to stop the next word from coming out of her mouth.

"Rachel!"

Timmy's voice sped along the hallway like a reprieve that Marcus wasn't sure he wanted.

"You gonna check my ears, Rachel?"

"Yes, Timmy," she called to him in answer. "I'm coming."

She stared at him for one hard moment more, then she turned and left him standing there, his bulging duffel bag in his hands.

"RACHEL?" he whispered, rapping lightly on her door. "Let me in."

"Go away," she insisted.

It was crazy—Marcus Slade begging to be let in to some woman's bedroom. Wasn't he the man who had trouble keeping women out of his? Wasn't this the very room where he'd had to pick Rachel up bodily and toss her out in the hall to get her out of his bed?

"Yeah, hotshot," he muttered to himself. "But that was all a mistake, remember? And you've been trying to get her back into bed with you ever since.

"Rachel," he said more loudly. "For heaven's sake, at least talk to me."

He heard the springs creak as she got off the bed. A moment later the door opened, but only a few inches.

"What do you want?"

"You. You promised me tonight, remember?"

She gave him a look. "So I lied," she said, and slammed the door in his face.

Swearing under his breath, he started down the stairs, thinking to hit Grant's apartment and appropriate his last bottle of Jim Beam. Then he remembered that Frannie and Grant were together over there.

"Damn!" he said again, slamming out of the screen door and onto the front porch. The whole damn house to themselves except for a little boy who slept like a baby bear in hibernation, and he couldn't get near her!

He threw himself onto the porch swing, setting it rocking furiously from side to side. Hell of a way to spend his last night in Birch Beach—alone with the crickets while the woman he was probably in love with refused to even talk to him.

WHEN HE CAME DOWN the next morning, she was already gone.

"You and my daughter have another fight?" Frannie asked him, the faintest of twinkles in her eyes as she sipped coffee at the kitchen table.

"Your daughter can be unreasonable," he muttered, going to the stove to pour himself a cup.

"And you can be pretty stubborn yourself, from what I hear."

Holding the cup in his hands, he turned and leaned against the counter. The kitchen, as always, was bright with the morning sun, fragrant with the smell of biscuits and eggs, warm with the breeze blowing through the windows—and the special warmth of the woman who sat at the table.

"She tell you all about it?"

Frannie gave a little grin. "I've been her mother for thirty-five years, I'm pretty good at worming things out of her."

Marcus snorted and took a swallow of his coffee. "I bet."

"She doesn't want you to go, you know. And neither does Timmy."

"I know." He couldn't look at her when he added, "But I have to."

"Do you?" she asked him gently.

He didn't want to look at that question too closely. He poured the rest of his coffee into the sink. "I'm heading over to the paper to say goodbye to Grant—and to her. Then I'll go over to Timmy's school."

Finally he looked at her, not knowing whether to crave the look of concern on her face or to hate it. "Think the school will let me take him over to the Bee for lunch?"

She nodded. "I'll call, tell them you have my permission."

"Thanks, Frannie," he said as he pushed himself away from the counter and headed out of the room.

Frannie caught up with him in the front hall, just as he was slinging his duffel bag over his shoulder.

"You don't think you're getting out of here without a hug, do you?"

He threw his bag back down and went into her arms.

"I'm sorry, Frannie. I never meant to hurt anyone," he whispered against her hair.

"I know, Marcus. But you hurt yourself most of all. Don't you know that?"

Another question he couldn't look at. "Good luck with Grant, Frannie. Keep him in line."

"Stay in touch, Marcus. He might not ask you himself, but he'd like that."

Not trusting his voice, Marcus nodded, picked up his duffel bag again, and let the screen door bang behind him.

He threw his bag in the back seat of the rental car, then got behind the wheel to drive the few blocks to the *Birch Bark* office. In the morning sun, Main Street looked like a spring morning in the American dream. He pushed aside the thought. He had to, he told himself, as he got out of the car in front of the newspaper office. He was leaving this time—for real. In a few weeks the place would be only a memory. And Rachel would be merely another woman he'd made love to along the way.

At the glass door to the newspaper office, he paused to watch her. Her head was bent over her computer, the sun turning her hair into something his hands itched to get into. She had it down today, swept back from her face with two combs, and he wondered if she'd done it on purpose, just to torment him. It spilled over the shoulders of her simple white shirt, and he thought of how it felt against his skin, against his lips, brushing his eyes.

He might be able to kid himself that the town meant nothing to him, but Rachel would never be just a woman he'd made love to along the way.

When he thought back to this time, and he would—he knew that as sure as he knew he was standing there wanting her—he would remember her as the only woman he'd ever fallen in love with.

He pushed open the door and went inside for what he knew would be the last time.

She looked up. Something leaped into her face, but she tamped it down before he could get a handle on what it was. "I thought you'd be long gone by now, Slade," she said dryly, "the dust already settled behind you."

"Did you think I'd leave without saying goodbye?"

Her eyes on his were steady, unyielding. "You did once before, as I recall."

"And I promised Timmy I'd never do it again. As soon as I say goodbye to you and Grant, I'm heading over to the school to spring him for one last piece of pie at the Bee." He tore his gaze from hers and looked around the office.

"Think you'll really get out of here this time, hotshot?"

Marcus didn't take his eyes off Rachel when he answered Grant. "Yeah, old man. Time for me to get back to work."

"Can't get you to stay for the wedding, huh hotshot?"

Marcus shook his head, finally breaking eye contact with Rachel. "No, old man. Time I moved on."

"It's what he does best, apparently," Rachel said. "Move on."

He couldn't resist. He never would be able to resist playing the bad boy when he was around her. So one last time he walked over to her desk and leaned down over it, not stopping till his face was only inches from hers.

"Now you know, sweetheart, that there are other things I do even better," he drawled.

The blush that shot up her cheeks belied the hardness in her eyes. He savored it, putting out a finger to touch her hot cheek.

Behind him a phone rang.

"Don't mind me, you two," Grant said, amusement lacing the words. "I'll just get this fax coming in and maybe get lost in a closet or something."

Marcus smiled. "How about it, Rachel? Why don't you and I get lost in that closet?"

"You haven't got time, Slade. Your getaway car is waiting."

"Oh, jeez," Grant said behind them.

The reporter in them made them both turn.

"What?" they both said at the same time.

Grant ripped the fax off the machine. "It's for you, hotshot. You got trouble—big-time."

Marcus took the fax and started to read.

"Looks like the newsman is gonna make a few headlines of his own," Grant said.

"What's going on?" Rachel asked.

"It's from my network," Marcus answered. "A warning."

Rachel stood. "A warning?"

"Yeah. About a story that's about to break. A story that says I falsified a report I radioed in during a news blackout in the Middle East during the Gulf War. That I wasn't anywhere near there."

"But...but who would claim such a thing?"

"Kyle Cooper, that's who."

Rachel recognized the name immediately, the image of that tall, rangy, blond correspondent for another network springing into her mind.

"He's been trailing just behind me for years—always a little late to break a scoop for his own network. Now he's written a book. It's coming out this summer."

Grant snorted. "Digging up dirt on you will give him more publicity than anything else he could do."

"But...where does he say you were?" Rachel asked.

Marcus had dreaded that question. As soon as he'd read the fax, he hated the idea of Rachel knowing what was in it. Hated the idea that she was probably going to believe it—along with everyone else in Birch Beach.

When he didn't answer her, she made to grab for the fax. "Let me see it."

Quickly he crumpled the thing in his hand and tossed it toward the trash.

"Will someone please tell me what's going on?"

When Marcus stayed silent, Grant said, "Cooper is alleging that Marcus was holed up with a woman—miles away, safe and sound."

"But why—after all this time—"

"That's the report that won hotshot here his reputation, Rachel. He was the only newsman left in the city with any equipment that worked."

"I remember," Rachel said.

"The whole damn world remembers," muttered Marcus. "This damn story will be picked up by the services. By the time I get to any damage control, it'll be too late."

"Too late?" Rachel asked.

For the first time since he'd read the fax, he looked at her. "Well who's going to believe me, Rachel? Who isn't going to be ready and willing to think the worst of me?"

"Me," she said.

He stared at her. Shouldn't she be one of the first to want to think the worst of him? But here she was, in her baby blue skirt down to her ankles, her prim white shirt tucked into it, her hair soft on her shoulders—here she was with her hands on her hips declaring, without so much as a question, that she believed him.

If he hadn't already been in love with her, he would have fallen in love with her on the strength of that alone.

What the hell was he doing leaving her?

"Rachel…"

The door from the street burst open and Molly Finch and Sam Cheevers bustled in.

"Grant! Grant! Is something going on we don't know about?"

"Yeah," Sam added. "There was a stranger in the store just now, asking questions."

Molly was nodding her head so quickly that her hat was sliding off her hair. "And there are people with a van and camera equipment out near the highway. I saw them myself when my sister was driving me back from visiting in Pine Village."

"We figured you'd know what's going on, Grant, having the newspaper and all."

Grant looked at Marcus, and Marcus knew what he was thinking.

"The tabloids," the old man said.

"Ohhh," Molly Finch exclaimed. "You mean like that perfectly awful show that I watch every afternoon? The one that is forever shoving a microphone in someone's face asking embarrassing questions?"

"Nah," Sam Cheevers said with a flap of his hand. "He's talkin' about those newspapers I sell at the checkout down at the store."

"Actually," Grant said, "Marcus is a big enough name to attract both."

Both Sam and Molly looked at him.

"Is Mr. Hunk in trouble?" Molly asked.

As Grant started to explain, Marcus walked away from them all, not wanting to see the reactions on their faces, certain that he knew what that reaction would be. The same reaction people were going to have all across the country. No matter how much they liked you when you were on top, they just loved to see you go down. He had no doubt that some enterprising up-and-coming reporter was digging in his past this very minute, probably grinning with glee when he unearthed the Hershey bar scandal to tie in with the fact that his father was a thief.

He stopped at the huge front window to gaze over at Crawford's bakery. Hattie was out on the sidewalk, talking to a man and a woman Marcus had never seen before.

He heard the voices behind him, but refused to listen to the words. And it came to him, as he watched Hattie Crawford shake her head, that he didn't give a good damn what the *rest* of the world believed of him, but he did care what this town thought of him. He cared that the next time he craved one of Hattie's doughnuts, she might not look at him the same way when he went in to buy one. He cared that Molly Finch might not give him lemonade and ask him to sit a spell on her shaded front porch. And, most of all, he cared what Timmy would see when next he looked at him.

"Oh…oh!" Molly Finch exclaimed behind him. "There they are! The people from the van. They're asking Hattie Crawford questions now. What are we going to do?"

"He can hide out in the store for a spell," Sam said. "They've already been there."

"Hide out?" Marcus asked, surprise breaking his silence. "What are you talking about?"

"Why, you, Mr. Hunk!" Molly Finch cried. "You can't possibly talk to those people now. You can't possibly be ready to defend yourself—not if, as Grant just told us, you only just found out what's going on." She came over to Marcus, poking a gloved finger into the air. "I've seen what they do to people, shoving cameras and microphones into their poor shocked faces, asking all sorts of embarrassing questions. You just steer clear of them, Mr. Hunk," she said, pointing the gloved finger at him now, "until you've got proof to show them that they're wrong."

"She's right, Marcus," Rachel said. "They'll never stop hounding you if they know you're here. We've got work to do before you make any kind of statement."

"Come along, Marcus," Sam said. "We'll take you through the back door and down the alley to the store. Let Grant and Rachel here figure out what to do. The main thing is to get you out of sight."

"Oh, my," Molly exclaimed, "they're headed this way. Go! I'll go out and waylay them."

She pushed open the door, calling, "Yoo-hoo! Haven't I seen you two on the television?"

"She'll keep 'em at bay," Sam said knowingly. "I'll check the alley, make sure the coast is clear."

"This is unbelievable," Marcus muttered as he watched Sam leave.

"No," Grant said. "I think they're right. You need some thinking time before you face the media."

"I don't think that's what he means," Rachel said, watching him carefully. "What did you think, Slade, that they'd throw you to the wolves the minute they had the chance?"

Marcus grinned at her, suddenly feeling a whole lot better. "Is this the start of your I-told-you-so speech?"

She grinned back at him and shook her head. "Speech to follow. I've got to get down to the town council meeting and make sure Eric behaves himself. You go with Sam. As soon as the meeting's done, I'll come over to the store and we'll plan what to do."

"Here they come," Grant said from his station by the window.

"Go," Rachel said, jerking her chin toward the back door.

He turned to find Sam beckoning to him from the doorway. The next thing he knew he was out in the alley, following an old man who insisted they keep close to the buildings. If his reputation hadn't been on the line, he might have taken the time to stop and laugh at the whole thing. As it was, he found he was damn glad when Adelaide Cheevers opened the back door to Cheevers' Market and let them in.

# Chapter Fourteen

Marcus couldn't seem to stay away from the deli in the back of Cheevers' Market. He was on his third sandwich—pastrami this time—and he'd moved on from Adelaide's potato salad to her three-bean salad. He'd already devoured two of Sam's sour dills, Adelaide scolding him every time he came out of the back room to snatch one.

"You get out of sight, Marcus Slade, or I'm not fixing you another thing to eat!" she'd hissed at him.

He had his eye on some of her fruit salad, so he'd obeyed and hustled back out of sight.

He'd hidden out before, of course. But never in a slice of the American dream like Birch Beach. In the past he'd hidden from danger of possible capture, torture or death in some third-world country or a reemerging Eastern Block country. But never from an enemy as dubiously dangerous as a couple of tabloid reporters.

He swallowed the last of his sandwich, took another bite of pickle and settled on a case of canned peaches with a glossy magazine Adelaide had given him. He was trying to decide between an article on sponge painting woodwork and one on how to keep an Easter lily in bloom, when he heard the back door open. His mind went on fast alert while his body went still as he wondered if he'd underestimated the resources of the members of the media milling about the town. Whoever had let themselves in the door off the alley wasn't in any hurry to show themselves. He waited long seconds before he heard another sound.

"Pssst!"

Suddenly a watery blue eye and part of the brim of a hat peered out from behind a stack of cartons containing paper towels.

"Pssst" came the hiss again. "Mr. Hunk!"

He slid off the carton of peaches and walked with exaggerated stealthiness over to Molly Finch.

"What?" he asked in a stage whisper.

"We're going to move you," Molly whispered.

"Move me? Where?"

"Over to Knickerson's. Luther Ross says that during the war they moved members of the resistance around frequently. So we thought—"

"Luther Ross? Is the whole town in on this?"

Molly Finch's hand fluttered near her breast. "My, yes. Word got around fast after the town council meeting."

"What happened at the council meeting? Did Ludington—"

"Oh!" Her hands flew to her cheeks. "That's right! Rachel said to tell you, um, let me see." She tapped her lower lip with a finger. "Oh, yes—mission accomplished. That's what she said," Miss Finch emphasized by nodding her head. "Mission accomplished."

"So Knickerson's is safe, even if I'm not," Marcus said wryly.

"My, yes. And that's where I'm taking you next. To Knickerson's. Agnes and I discussed it, and she's expecting us."

Molly Finch started tiptoeing toward the back door, beckoning him to follow.

"Wait a minute..."

She turned. "Yes?"

"I thought you and Agnes weren't speaking?"

The tiny woman gave a peal of laughter and flapped her hand. "Oh, that! My, yes. Silly of us, wasn't it? Everybody knows that Agnes isn't anything like her mother. Why Sally Summers would cheat the Pope himself at a game of fish!"

Marcus laughed. "Miss Finch?"

She turned. "Yes, Mr. Hunk?"

"Just this," Marcus said, then pulled her into his arms for a gentle hug.

"Oh, my," Molly said, fanning her hand in front of her face. "What was that for, Mr. Hunk?"

"That was for speaking once again to Agnes Summers."

"Oh…that! My, I should have done that years ago," she answered. "Now, come along, Mr. Hunk. Stay right behind me and as close to the wall as you can get."

"I doubt it's necessary to be so careful any longer, Miss Finch."

"Oh, you're wrong, Mr. Hunk. Another television crew showed up. Of course, no one is talking to them. No one but Eric Ludington, that is."

Marcus groaned as he started to follow Molly down the alley. "I can imagine what he had to say."

"Well, I'm not sure," she whispered over her shoulder. "But he did tell them that you're a friend of Grant's and that you were in town to visit him." She paused and checked to make sure the coast was clear. "We—that is Agnes and I—feel he did it just to get his face on the television. The Ludingtons are like that, you know," she whispered, pursing her lips and nodding her head emphatically enough for her hat to slip another inch or two. "Now, come along before Agnes gets worried."

AGNES AND MOLLY were up front giggling like a couple of schoolgirls, while Marcus sat in the back room of Knickerson's Five-and-Dime, munching burned peanuts from a bag. It was all very entertaining, listening to the two women reminisce and catch up on all they'd missed. But Marcus was getting itchy to do something about the situation. Ludington had talked. The media knew he was in Birch Beach. He couldn't hide out forever, no matter how entertaining half the town was finding this little episode of espionage.

He yawned and shook himself. The rest of the town might be having a ball with this, but he was getting damned tired of it—and bored with waiting. He needed to get to a computer and a telephone. Try to get hold of someone who could verify his whereabouts on that day in Iraq when the world seemed to have exploded with him in the middle of it.

For another thing, he needed to talk to Rachel. Tell her that maybe he'd been wrong about small towns. Or Birch Beach, anyway. Tell her that—

He yawned again and leaned back in the old-fashioned, wood desk chair, put his feet up on old man Knickerson's desk and closed his eyes, wondering just what he was planning on telling Rachel.

WHEN HE WOKE UP, it was nearly dark. He straightened with some difficulty, the old chair creaking just slightly louder than the bones in his neck and knees.

"Agnes?" he called. "Molly?"

There was no answer from either of his freedom fighters. He stood and made his way to the front of the store.

The place was closed, locked up tight, and he was alone.

Well, what now? Did they expect him to cool his heels in here all night? Well, he wouldn't. He hadn't folded to the authorities in a hostile Middle-Eastern country and he wouldn't fold to them in Birch Beach. He was heading over to the *Bark* office to find out what the heck was going on.

"TWO OF THEM checked into the Birch Beach Inn, and two more of them were seen going into the Bee and ordering the special," Rachel said as she hung up the phone.

Grant snorted. "Gettin' late. Looks like they're not giving up yet."

"Thanks to our friend, Eric Ludington," Rachel muttered.

"Well, at least he withdrew from his deal with Bill's Bargain Palace and managed to convince the town council that any deal with Bill's wouldn't be in the town's interests."

Grant looked at Rachel for a moment, his eyes narrowed in speculation. "Now what do you suppose would make Eric Ludington decide he didn't need the money that deal would have made him?"

Rachel grinned. "I have no idea, Boss."

Grant tapped a pencil on his desk. "Something tells me you're not as innocent as you look."

She laughed at that. "I never have been. Now, I'm getting over to Knickerson's. Marcus must be going stir crazy."

"Bring him back here. We'll put our heads together and come up with something to clear up this mess."

"Okay. Better lock up then, in case our visitors come snooping around again."

She took the keys to the back door of the five-and-dime that Agnes had given her from her desk drawer and slipped them into the pocket of her skirt. "I'm heading out the back way," she told Grant.

"Rachel?"

She stopped and turned. "Yes?"

"You didn't for one second believe he filed a false report, did you?"

"No," she answered simply. "I didn't."

"You in love with him?"

The smile on her lips felt sad even to her, but it neve

occurred to her to lie to him. He was, after all, going to be her stepfather. "Yes, Grant. I'm in love with him."

Grant studied her for a moment. "You'd be the best thing that ever happened to him, you know that?"

"Yes," she answered simply again. "But he doesn't. Now get those shades down on the front window and the door while I go get him."

The alley was dark and deserted, the night air almost balmy, holding a touch of summer. School would be out soon, which put her in mind of Timmy and where he'd be spending his summer. The day had been too hectic and full to contact Social Services about him, but it would be the first thing she'd do come morning. No matter what happened tonight. If Marcus decided to clear out—well, she knew he would eventually, anyway.

But right now he must be going seven kinds of crazy, waiting to be let out of Knickerson's back room. She reached the five-and-dime's alley entrance and struggled for a moment with the ancient skeleton key before getting the door open.

The back room was empty.

Quietly she brushed through the curtains to the front of the store.

At first she didn't see him. Then she heard a whirring sound followed by a masculine laugh. Her gaze followed the laugh.

He was perched on top of the ladder Agnes used to get to stock on high shelves that went to the ceiling. In his hand he held a remote control.

"And here I thought you'd be going stir crazy in your confinement," she said, her hands on her hips, shaking her head.

He laughed again. "Baby—come on up here. Take a look."

Because she was relieved he hadn't bolted, relieved at his mood, she did as he wanted and started up the ladder.

When she came to the top she put her hands on his shoulders and leaned lightly against his back.

"Take a look," he said, thrusting his chin toward the front of the store.

Rachel looked. What she saw was a radio-controlled toy tank, all done up in camouflage paint, and Marcus was doing his best to make it navigate a pile of building blocks he'd stacked up like a pyramid.

"This is just like the ones they used in the Gulf War. Agnes must have just got them in. Timmy will go crazy!"

"If you ever let him play with it," Rachel said dryly.

Marcus laughed. "Maybe I better buy two of them, huh? Can you imagine the time we'll have over at the beach? We can build sand hills to navigate, use stones for obstacles—"

Rachel rested her chin on his shoulder and ran her hands up and down his arms. Everything he said conjured up the word *stay* for her, the word *home*. But she knew better than to ask him anything now. They had work to do. And if she was wrong, she didn't think she wanted to know the answer. Not yet.

"Listen, G. I. Joe, Grant told me to fetch you back to the *Bark* office. We've got some work to do. Playtime is over."

"YOU HUNGRY?" she asked him on the way over to the newspaper office.

"Are you kidding? I've been hiding out all day, first behind a deli counter, then behind a candy counter. I must have put on five pounds."

Rachel laughed. "Little different from being holed up in a bombed-out hotel with no electricity, no water and no food, huh?"

"Did have something in common, though," he said.

"What could that possibly have been?" she asked him.

"Neither place had you."

Before she could react, he'd spun her into his arms and pressed her back into the shadow of the building that housed the *Bark*.

"I missed you, sweetheart," he said, and then he took her mouth in a kiss that was so sweet, so deep, so long and lingering that when it was over she could barely think.

When she managed to focus her mind and her eyes, she grinned up at him. "Remind me to put you in hiding more often."

He kissed her nose. "Remind me to take you along next time."

Again, words that meant tomorrow. And again, she wouldn't allow herself to ask the question.

"Come on. Let's see what Grant has up his sleeve to clear your name."

"I'M TELLING YOU, GRANT, the only people who saw me in that bombed-out hotel were Iraqis. None of them spoke English or gave a damn who I was. Even if they did know why I was there, how would we ever find them? And what would be their incentive to help us?"

"He's right, Grant," Rachel said. "There must be some other way."

"What about the girl? The one who claims she was with me?"

"I've been on the phone half the afternoon, tracking her down," Grant answered. "Finally found her holed up in a very expensive hotel in Washington."

"And?"

"And no comment."

Marcus thrust his hands into his hair. "Why should that surprise me? As I recall, she always did go to the highest bidder."

The fax machine started to ring. Grant was first to reach it. "This might be worth looking into," he said.

Marcus took the fax from Grant's hand and scanned it. "Ian Hunter," he said. "With the BBC in London."

Rachel waited while Marcus read the fax.

"Damn!" he said.

"What?" she asked.

Marcus thrust a hand into his hair. "Ian was the first one I saw when that long night was over. His crew was stationed just over the border. The Iraqis left me with them when they marched me out of the country."

"Well?" Rachel asked impatiently. "What does he say?"

"He says he remembers me talking about an American who'd been staying at the hotel. A writer, who, like me, was trying to avoid getting expelled from Iraq. I'd forgotten all about him."

"And he was there with you that night?"

"No—which is why I didn't remember him. After the hotel was bombed and everyone had cleared out, I was exploring what was left of the place, looking for any equipment that might have survived, anything I could to get back to transmitting a picture. He was hiding out in one of the upper rooms—scared out of his wits. I gave him some chocolate I had on me, helped him get oriented and, after I'd convinced him that the Iraqis had nothing to gain by shooting him, pointed him toward the authorities. I knew they were still escorting news crews over the border. I figured he'd get out safely."

"You think he did?"

"God, I hope so. For his sake—and for mine."

Marcus only remembered the man's first name, but he did remember the publication he said he often sold his stuff to. Rachel got on the phone immediately.

As she'd hoped, someone was burning the midnight oil. And that someone knew immediately who she was talking about.

"It seems our man has been going out to lunch and

romancing the ladies at the water cooler for years on this little story. The editor I talked to said he heard the guy was in the midst of writing an account of it at this very moment.''

''Who the hell isn't writing a book?'' Marcus muttered. ''You get his name?'' he asked.

Rachel handed him a yellow legal pad. ''Even better,'' she said. ''I got his home phone number.''

THE GUY DIDN'T ANSWER his phone until nearly dawn. The three of them paced, drank Grant's overbrewed coffee and ate sandwiches that Frannie smuggled in to them through the back door.

Grant was snoring softly in his desk chair while Rachel kneaded Marcus's shoulders as he talked to the man who was going to save his reputation.

When Marcus finally hung up the phone, Rachel asked, ''Well?''

''The man is more than happy for a little free publicity. He'll fly to Washington as soon as I can set up a news conference.''

Her arms went around his neck from behind, and she kissed his ear. ''And another long night is over.''

He spun in his chair and pulled her into his lap. ''Yup. And the crusading reporter has saved the day again.''

''With a little help from the Helicopter Hunk.''

''Baby,'' Marcus murmured, nuzzling her neck with his lips, ''I'd love to take the time to demonstrate all my special powers to you, but there are more phone calls to be made. Call the airport for me, would you? Get me on the first available flight to Washington? I've got to get through to my network. See if they can set up a press conference as soon as possible.''

She left his lap and used the phone in Daisy's office to call the airline. All the while she was on hold, she watched Marcus through the window to the outer office. After the long night, he looked more rakish than ever, a dark stubble covering his chin and lower cheeks, his hair rumpled, his clothes a mess. But he also looked in his element, a man meant for bigger things than a weekly newspaper in a small town in Wisconsin. So, she would make his reservation and watch him fly out of her life.

But she'd never forget him—and she would never love anyone else.


THEY WOKE GRANT and sent him upstairs to bed. Then Rachel went out to the front walk and checked to make sure Main Street was deserted of anyone who looked out of place.

"Coast is clear," she told Marcus.

"Okay, let's get out of here. I need to get home, shower and change before I catch that nine a.m. plane."

She heard the word *home* and her heart jerked a little. But she knew it was only a slip of the tongue, something said off the top of his head because he was exhausted but wired.

She locked the door to the *Birch Bark* behind her and took a deep breath of the sweet morning air. The sun had just come up, the glow of it casting something magic over the town. Marcus took her hand.

"Let's go over and see if Hattie has any doughnuts for us," he said.

"Good idea. I could use a little sugar high right now."

They crossed the street at an angle and peered through the glass door of Crawford's Bakery.

"I see lights on back there," Marcus said.

"Oh, Hattie'll be in already. Her husband bakes all night, then she comes in at dawn with breakfast for him."

Marcus grinned and rapped on the glass door. "Come on, Hattie, love," he murmured, "I need one last doughnut to get me to Washington."

Oh, hell, she thought, gulping down something that felt

like tears in her throat. One last doughnut. Well, at least she'd be sharing that last doughnut with him.

Marcus rapped again, louder this time, and Hattie's head poked around the corner.

You could see her mouthing the words "Land sakes" as she wiped her hands on her apron and came bustling toward the door to let them in.

"Goodness, you two gave me a fright! Is everything okay?"

"Couldn't be better, Hattie," Marcus said. "I'm off to Washington to meet with the man who'll clear my name. And I need one of your doughnuts to keep me going."

"Land sakes! Well then, come on in. Got some still warm and freshly sugared the way you like them."

"Great. Give me five dozen."

Hattie stopped bustling toward the back of the shop and turned. "Five dozen?"

"Yup, gonna serve 'em at my press conference. The cream of the Washington press corps will be eating your doughnuts, Hattie, and cursing the fact that they'll never taste them again."

And so will you, Rachel had on the tip of her tongue to say. But she swallowed it down with everything else. She wasn't about to spoil these last precious minutes with him.

"Well, won't that be somthin'? Five dozen, coming up."

"And a couple to eat right now, Hattie, if you don't mind."

Hattie, grinning broadly certainly didn't mind, and soon they were out the door with a shopping bag loaded with white bakery boxes and a small sack of them to eat on the way.

"The town is just waking up," Marcus said, his mouth full of doughnut.

"I love it like this. Kitchen lights coming on, cats heading for home, the sun starting to glitter on the lake."

"Hmm. And one of Hattie Crawford's doughnuts to make it all the more sweet."

"Better watch it, Marcus. You're starting to sound as though you like it here."

"Maybe," he said. "Just maybe."

Then he took her hand and held it all the way back home.

AND AN HOUR LATER he was gone. And it was the shortest hour Rachel had ever experienced. Part of it he spent in the shower. Part of it he spent on the phone. And part of it he spent in Timmy's room, sitting on the bed, talking to a little boy who was barely awake. She stood in the doorway for a moment, but his voice was so low, so intimate, that not only could she not hear a word he said, she felt like an intruder, witnessing something that should only be between the boy and the man.

So she went downstairs and waited. By the time he came down it was time for him to go. She walked him out to his rental car and he swept her up against him.

"Gonna miss me?" he asked.

"Get out of here, you rat," she answered, because she knew that he already knew that she would.

"Just as soon as you kiss me goodbye."

She grinned and shook her head, more to stop the tears from falling than anything. Then she threw her arms around his neck and kissed him like it would be for the last time. Because it was.

"Don't forget—six tonight," he said when he broke loose and headed around to the driver's side of the car.

"I'll be there. And so will half the town."

"See you," he said.

And then he got in the car, started the engine and roared up the street.

She stood there until she couldn't hear his car anymore.

AT SIX O'CLOCK they were assembled in front of the television in the living room of the Gale Guest House. Molly Finch, Agnes Summers, Sam and Adelaide Cheevers, Hattie Crawford, Olive from the diner, Grant and Frannie and Timmy and Rachel.

"When's he gonna be on?" Timmy kept asking.

"Soon, Timmy. Just listen."

And then all of a sudden he was there, behind a bank of microphones, looking impossibly handsome—far too handsome to have been her lover, if only for a few days. Beside him was a pale, scared-looking young man—trying his best to hide it.

"There he is!" Timmy yelled, jumping up and down. "There he is!"

"Shhh," Rachel whispered. "Listen."

So Timmy settled down next to her, snuggling under her arm, and listened with the rest of them as Marcus talked about that day long ago when he'd been the last newsman to be ejected from the country they had declared war on. When he was finished with his statement, reporters shot questions. Marcus handled them deftly, then introduced the man at his side, who stumbled over his statement at first, then picked up confidence from somewhere. Probably from just sitting next to someone as dynamic and compelling as Marcus Slade, thought Rachel. By the time the reporters started firing questions at the young man, he was able to handle them almost as well as Marcus had.

Rachel stared at that face on the screen hard enough to burn the image forever in her mind. Timmy was quiet and still at her side. She suspected that he was doing the same.

When it was over, and he'd thanked the reporters, he stood and said he had one last thing to say.

Everyone went quiet.

Marcus looked directly into the camera and said, "Hi, Timmy, how you doing, soldier?"

Timmy squealed and jumped to his feet. "All right! He

said he was gonna do it! And he did it! Marcus said hi to me on TV!''

And the tears that had been threatening all day started to slip through her lashes. She jumped to her feet. ''That's great, Timmy. I'll bet everyone would like some coffee. I'll go make some.''

She hurried to the kitchen, letting the door swing shut behind her.

''Get a grip, girl,'' she told herself. ''He's gone. You knew he would be.''

Yeah, but she had no idea it would hurt quite so much.

''You okay, honey?'' her mother asked as she came into the kitchen.

Rachel nodded. ''Just a little sorry to see him go, that's all.''

''I think we all are, honey. But he took part of your heart with him, didn't he?''

''Yes, he did. And he's welcome to it, because it'll never go to anyone else.''

''Oh, honey,'' Frannie crooned, rubbing Rachel's back with the palm of her hand. ''Maybe he'll be back.''

''No. He's gone, and I'll survive,'' she said with the practicality she'd always been known for. But inside, she wondered if she would. She was going to lose her mother, Grant, quite possibly Timmy, too. Ahh, Marcus, she thought, if only—

Timmy came running into the kitchen. ''Rachel! Did you hear him? He said my name!''

''I heard him, Timmy. And it was great. Why don't you call Stewie and tell him all about it?''

''Hey, yeah!''

And then he was gone again, charging out of the kitchen, his sneakers slapping on the floor as he ran into the front hall to use the phone.

AN HOUR LATER everyone was gone. Even her mother had left to go for a late supper at the Buzzing Bee with Grant.

Rachel wasn't hungry, but she fixed a grilled cheese sandwich for Timmy and managed to get him into the bathtub, then into his pajamas without having to say much at all. Timmy was full of chatter about Marcus, and Rachel was more than content to let him go on and on.

When she'd finally tucked him in and sat at his bedside, he said, "Rachel, you better put our trophy back in Marcus's room. I want it to be waiting there for him when he gets here."

The statement almost knocked the breath out of her. Didn't Timmy understand? Marcus was gone—for good. "Marcus isn't coming back," she told him softly.

"Yes he is. He told me so."

"When was that, Timmy? When did he tell you?"

"This morning, when he came in to say goodbye. He brought the trophy with him and told me to keep it until he got back."

"Oh, Timmy, maybe he'll be back someday to visit you. But not tonight—or tomorrow. And I'm sure he'd want you to have the trophy here with you."

Timmy shook his head. "No, Rachel, he's coming back, and I want him to have it on his dresser waiting for him."

He looked as certain of the impossible as only a child can. She saw no point in trying to convince him. Let him have his dream for the night.

"All right, Timmy. I'll put the trophy in Marcus's room. Now you go to sleep. You've got school in the morning."

She bent to kiss his forehead, swallowing hard when she felt his thin arms go round her neck.

"Remember the day you and Marcus pretended to be my mommy and daddy?"

How could she forget? It was the first night Marcus had made love to her. "Yes," she whispered.

"That was fun, wasn't it?"

She nodded. "Yes, Timmy, it was fun. But only pretend."

"I wish it was real. I wish that you were my mommy and Marcus was my daddy and I could live in this house with you guys forever."

She took in a deep breath. "So do I, Timmy," she whispered, stroking his hair. "So do I."

# Chapter Fifteen

She walked down the hall and put the trophy on the dresser in Marcus's room—or what Timmy still wanted to believe was Marcus's room. His heart was going to be as broken as hers when he found out the truth.

She wandered around the room for a few minutes, touching things, smoothing the comforter on the bed with her palm. There were ghosts in this room now, and there always would be.

Finally she went across the hall, shutting her bedroom door behind her.

She started to undress, then realized that she was wearing the same ivory teddy she'd worn that first morning she'd woken in his arms. It was little comfort, but she left it on anyway and crawled between the sheets. She lay awake for a long time, listening to crickets. She finally fell asleep, remembering the feel of his mouth on hers.

RACHEL SLEPT HEAVILY. Birdsong finally woke her. But she wasn't ready to open her eyes—not yet. She burrowed deeper into the mattress, breathing in the scent of spring in full bloom wafting through the windows and another spicier scent—a scent she would remember for the rest of her life.

She felt surprisingly peaceful and rested, considering

what she knew she'd be facing as soon as she got out of bed—the rest of her life without Marcus Slade.

"Mmm," she moaned, stretching and arching her back, running her hand languidly over the smooth, warm bed.

And then the bed sighed and moved!

Her eyes flew open and she found herself staring at a smooth, tanned expanse of male chest. Slowly her gaze worked its way up that chest until she found his face. He was smiling down at her, a look of love shimmering in his cool green eyes.

"Good morning," he said.

She smiled. "Now I know I must be dreaming," she whispered.

"Why is that?"

"Because you're supposed to be in Washington."

He shook his head. "No—I'm supposed to be right here. It just took me a while to figure that out."

The kiss he gave her was tender enough to bring tears to her eyes. When his mouth left hers, he kissed her nose then just gazed into her eyes for a long time.

"I love you, Rachel. You know that, don't you?"

She nodded and smiled. "And I love you."

He traced her lips with his finger. "You gonna marry me?"

She nodded again. "Yes."

He closed his eyes for a moment, and she knew he'd been just as scared of losing her as she was of losing him.

When he opened his eyes again, he said, "I talked to a lawyer friend of mine in Washington. He says there's no reason why we shouldn't be able to adopt Timmy."

Now it was her turn to squeeze her eyes shut. "You mean it, Marcus?"

He put his hands at her waist and pulled her up and over so she was lying on his chest. "I mean to take over the newspaper, marry you, adopt Timmy."

"But will you be satisfied with that? Will you be content?"

"I already told you I love you. You must know I love Timmy."

"No, I mean the paper. It's a lot tamer than what you're used to."

He laughed. "Yes, it is. But I've got a few projects up my sleeve."

"Oh, do you, Mr. Hunk?" she asked him playfully.

His eyes glittered with laughter. "Yes, I do. Everyone else is writing a book. Why not me? And if I get restless, I can always leave the running of the paper in your capable hands to take a freelance assignment for a newspaper or magazine."

"You'd give up television?"

"Yes. And gladly. Being the Helicopter Hunk isn't all it's cracked up to be. Besides, it's about time I got back to my roots in journalism."

She grinned down at him. "He was so sure you were coming back."

He threaded his hand into her hair and pushed it back from her face. "Timmy? That's because I told him I was. I also told him that I wanted to spend the rest of my life with you and him and the people in Birch Beach."

She could hardly believe what she was hearing. "Truly?" she asked.

He kissed her nose. "Truly."

She sighed for the pure joy of it. "You always said this was the town for miracles."

"So I did."

Her smile trembled on her lips. "Have you come home, Marcus?"

She felt him take in a shaky breath and let it out before answering, "Yes, Rachel," he said, "I've come home."